SWEPT UP *by the* SEA

SWEPT UP *by the* SEA

A Romantic Fairy Tale

TRACY & LAURA
HICKMAN

SHADOW
MOUNTAIN

Library of Congress Cataloging-in-Publication Data

Hickman, Tracy, author.
    Swept up by the sea : a romantic fairy tale / Tracy & Laura Hickman.
       pages cm
    ISBN 978-1-60907-661-0 (hardbound : alk. paper) 1. Dragons—Fiction.
2. Storytellers—Fiction. 3. Sailing ships—Fiction. I. Hickman, Laura, 1956– author.
II. Title.
    PS3558.I2297B57 2013
    813'.54—dc23   2013001723

Printed in the United States of America
Publishers Printing, Salt Lake City, UT

10   9   8   7   6   5   4   3   2   1

To Matthew Lampros

Who taught us that the book is the souvenir
we keep from the journey of our story

Contents

CONTENTS

Madame Zoltana's Fortunes

C ome in! Come in! So you have come to Madame Zoltana, have you? The fates have led you here to me at this most auspicious conjunction! Step inside, for here in the darkness the past and the future merge as one.

You say that you are only passing by, but this is not so . . . it merely *appears* that way because one cannot see one's own future. Only the Gifted of the Third Eye can divine such ends. Surely a learned youth such as yourself . . . and with such a handsome cape . . . and a scholar, I see, by that book which you carry . . . can learn wisdom from a woman who sees beyond learning and written words to the spirits and powers that govern our lives.

Come closer! Do not fear Madame Zoltana or the powers that I possess. I see you are a seeker of knowledge and adventure—troubled, perhaps, and longing to know what is to

1

come. You have chosen wisely, for my talents are connected to the roots of the world and extend upward to the stars! All the powers are in alignment and destiny opens up before you . . . all for the very low price of twenty Imperial coins . . .

Wait! Do not leave . . . for the fates have chosen you above all others. You are indeed unique among the travelers in this world, and for you there is a special price of ten Imperial coins . . .

No? Then at least rest a while within the shade of my tent and tell me of your travels . . . of what you have seen and where you have been and those of your acquaintance whom I might meet along the way. Madame Zoltana wants to hear all about your friends. Tell me of their families and their loves . . . perhaps of some recently departed relatives? No detail is too trivial. Who might have given you that book, perhaps, or . . .

Will you repeat that? No . . . not about the dead uncle . . . who gave you the book?

The Dragon's Bard? Do I *know* him?

Whatever makes you ask such a ridiculous question?

Oh, *that*! No that twitch is just a manifestation of my powers. No, I do not know the Dragon's Bard—not really, I mean, it was such a very long time ago and I've forgotten all about it. I'm sure he wouldn't remember *me* at all . . . not after all I've done for him, the ungrateful thief! Tell me, is he still wandering about the countryside as the pet story-dog of that old dragon Khrag, or has the monster gotten tired of his sorry tales and eaten him at last? No? Pity.

Your fortune? Oh, so *now* you want your fortune read, do you? Well, that is why Madame Zoltana is here on your behalf. Now, set your fine-looking satchel down here next to me and stare at the deck of mystic cards! Place your hands palm down on the table, the thumbs touching each other. Now close your eyes and think hard. No, harder! And close *both* eyes! Keep them closed until I tell you—for the spirits are here and will be angered if you open them while they make a little noise about your bag.

I am sensing something . . . it is coming through . . . something about a tailor . . . your name? Yes, I see it now . . . Percival Taylor. And you are worried about money . . . no . . . a woman . . . yes! A woman! A woman you want very much . . . no, wait, it is coming clearer to me . . . a woman you want to leave you alone . . . no, that's not it . . . er, the spirits are still a little obscure . . .

Wait. Does this have something to do with the Dragon's Bard?

Ah, of course it does . . . that lousy son-of-a- . . . good friend of mine! And it *would* involve a woman in a small town . . .

Is her name . . . Vestia? The spirits have divined it! I take it that this Dragon's Bard has seduced this poor village girl and . . . oh, you say he is arranging a marriage between you? Ah, the spirits are clearing now above the cards! I have divined it all!

Yes, you may open your eyes now.

Your satchel? Ah, the spirits were most agitated by the power of your destiny and kicked all your possessions out of your bag and across the floor! Do not concern yourself with that right now . . . watch closely as I reveal your destiny in my cards! This is the fabled Mystic Deck of Zoltana. We shall see your future as we play Zoltanair: the game of fates! I deal your fates in turn to the four winds! Now you take the Fate-dragon—that small carving on the table—and place it before one of the five Towers of Destiny—those stacks of tiles in the middle of the table! Do not think about it . . . just let the spirits of fortune be your guide!

Now, pick up the cards in front of you and we shall each play a card! Well played, Percival! The first fortune is yours . . . now move the dragon again and play another . . . drat! Are you certain you've never done this before?

Never mind, the cards are speaking to me anyway.

I see a long journey . . . a very, very, *very* long journey . . . far away from Vestia and the Dragon's Bard. A terrible fate awaits you if you remain at home. Something with plague and disease and maybe some poison. You must flee at once to the sea . . . prove yourself strong and courageous, wealthy and successful . . . only then can you fulfill your destiny and become great in story and song! Your future is at sea, young man! There on the vast ocean you will prove yourself heroic and great . . . a hero worthy of any woman's love and the envy of all other men.

No, I do not jest! Look for yourself. The cards do not lie! You will find your destiny at sea. You must go . . . now . . . right away.

No! Don't tell the Dragon's Bard! Don't tell anyone! Just leave now! Remember? Plague . . . disease . . . poison . . . bad things if you stay and wonderful things if you run away to sea.

Where? Well, the fates don't particularly give an ogre's toenail where you . . . how about Blackshore? I feel like the fates want me to leave town as well, and Blackshore would be just the kind of place where I would not be seen.

What? No, you heard me wrong. I said . . . Blackshore is just the place for a boy to go to sea!

Bad Impressions

CHAPTER 1

The Mistral's Mistress

S heets of rain fell hard against the windows. The downpour sounded as though sand was being tossed against the thick glass. Beyond, the wind moaned mournfully in the darkness, interrupted from time to time by the spectacular, resonant growl of thunder rolling up the channel of Mistral Sound and across the waters of Blackshore Bay. Lightning occasionally ripped the air, replacing the distant rumble with an explosive crack and boom, each instance occasioning a renewed vigor to the waterfall outside that put to shame all gentler precipitation.

Yet within the low-ceiling confines of the Mistral's Mistress tavern's common room, the air was leaden, warm and stifling. The windows, normally open to admit the evening breeze, were now latched shut. The biting wind had robbed the town of its afternoon sunlit warmth, which now was being compensated for by a roaring fire in the great hearth at the side of the room. The gray-cloaked seamen who had found harbor in the tavern had settled in the room along an arc of accommodating anchorages among the heavy tables and chairs, far enough away from the cold windows braced against the wailing bluster and not too close to the entirely too enthusiastic fire waging its own war against nature beyond. All along this temperate band the conversations were low and drowsy—a burbling sound of the well-fed and the sheltered that ran like an undertow beneath the muted fury outside.

And, as was common in the evenings, the weather was of complete indifference as every man's attention was fixed on the bar.

Far from the door, the wide bar ran almost three quarters of the width of the room, its finely cared-for surface gleaming from the crackling light of the fire and the brightly trimmed lamps mounted at either end. The lamps had originally been part of a ship, taken from the quarterdeck of a galley that had foundered on the rocky entrance to the harbor on a night not unlike this one some years back. They were, therefore, oversized for the room, let alone the elegant bar.

It was just past eight bells of the Last Dog Watch.

Rhenna MacKraegen was, as usual, polishing the lamps.

Rhenna was acknowledged by every man who stepped ashore and entered the Mistral's Mistress as "a woman and a half." She was tall for a human female—nearly six feet—and carried her curvy, voluptuous build in a statuesque, straight-backed manner that was entirely unapologetic about her height. Her dresses were always perfectly fitted to her beauteous frame, gathered at her narrow waist in a way that accentuated the curve of her hips. Her long, red hair was always perfect—combed to a shine each night and yet still maintaining a bounce in the damp air next to the harbor. Those curls framed a face of unparalleled beauty: high cheekbones and creamy skin without blemish, full lips drawn into a slight bow at the corners, and large, sleepy eyes of a shocking emerald hue that defied description. The graceful slope of her shoulders and her ample breasts were the model for every figurehead of every ship that came to port in Blackshore, though none had yet adequately duplicated them.

So it was that at eight bells—coincidentally eight o'clock to any of the landlubbers who might mistakenly venture into the sacred precincts of the seamen's tavern—there was always considerable interest generated among the storm-tossed patrons as Rhenna moved around the bar, reaching up and polishing the great lamps.

Rhenna did not care a fig. She was perfectly aware of the interest her presence created in men—keenly, in fact, among those who had been too long at sea. But as much a woman as she was outside, it was also generally acknowledged by all who frequented the regions of the Mistral's Mistress that she was every bit as much a lady on the *inside* as well.

And that meant she was utterly in love with and completely devoted to her husband.

So as the seamen just watched and dreamed, it was perfectly natural, in the midst of her routine, that she was the only one who heard the insistent sound.

"Stoney! There's a banging at the door!" Rhenna bellowed. Her voice-and-a-half was recognized to be both beautiful and capable of cutting through ten miles of fog when necessary.

"Coming, my darlin' . . . coming!" Sturvant MacKraegen burst through the swinging door behind the bar. He was about three fingers shorter than his wife and with shoulders that barely fit through the door frame. He had a wide face with a broad nose, a perpetual boyish grin despite his middling years, and cheeks that were quickly and easily flushed. Mischief played constantly at the corners of his eyes, and some swore that Stoney's hands had the mischief in them as well. His occasional pranks were most often directly followed by the innkeeper's belly laugh. It was admittedly a larger belly than Stoney would have preferred, but the years in the tavern had dictated the change. His hair was still a dark brown with a tempest of waves, although the tide of its shoreline was most definitely receding. He sported a great beard and mustache— all carefully trimmed—because, he would loudly proclaim to anyone who mentioned it, his wife insisted that she preferred to know she was kissing a man in the dark.

"What is it now?" Stoney beamed, his face red from the steaming stew in the kitchen beyond.

"The door, man! Can ya not hear it?" Rhenna said, planting her fists on her hips.

Stoney squinted in an attempt to improve his hearing. "There's naught but the storm, love. Perhaps it's that wee bit of a bark tied up at the wharf that you're hearing."

"I know the sound of a hull in the breakers, Sturvant MacKraegen!" There was a storm brewing inside the tavern now as well. Rhenna had used his name. The sailors in the room battened down over their drinks, hoping this new threat would blow over quickly. "That's the door and it needs answering!"

"Aye, love, I'll answer!" Stoney had never been at sea, but he knew enough about his wife to understand that you had to tack if you were going to make any headway into the prevailing wind. He stepped quickly across the room. The unfortunate sailors whose anchorage was nearest the door prepared for the worst.

Stoney took in a deep breath, leaned his weight against the door, grasped the crossbar with his large hands, and pulled it free.

The raging storm pressed him back with the door. The gale whipped through the opening, mists careening around the shadowy figure standing with both hands planted against the door frame. Lightning tore across the sky behind him, etching the silhouette in stark outline. The cape flew about the shoulders of the greatcoat in the wind, the face held high and proud against the storm, a rapier glistening at his side.

All eyes in the room were fixed on the striking figure framed against the fury of the storm.

Then the youth fell into the tavern, creating a wet and confused pool of cloth, boots, and jutting rapier on the floor.

A disappointed sigh went unheard above the storm as the innkeeper once again secured the door and the sailors turned back to their ale flagons and preoccupation with lamp polishing.

"Who is it, Stoney?" Rhenna called out from the bar as she reached for the highest part of the lantern.

"Better I find out *what* before we worry about the *who,*" the innkeeper replied. "Looking more like a drowned rat than anything at the moment." He gazed down at the mess that had fallen on his floor. The coat and cape were splayed out about the figure, but after some consideration of the position of the boots, the innkeeper made a stab at the presumed collar with his right hand and was gratified to discover he was right. He lifted the entire soaked bundle up off the floor, holding it out at arm's length. No head immediately presented itself at this angle, so he spun the wet coat about.

The narrow, young face with the cleft chin might have been handsome were its wet, flaxen hair not hanging down over it.

"Are you ashore there yet, lad?" Stoney poked the limp form with the thick forefinger of his left hand.

The youth's gray eyes fluttered open. "Did I make it?"

"Aye, you made it," Stoney replied. "Assuming that this is where you were trying to make it to. If you were looking for some other harbor in this storm, then obviously you've missed the mark."

"Where am I?"

"You're enjoying the hospitality of the famed Mistral's Mistress tavern and inn, lad!" Stoney gestured with his free hand to encompass the limited grandeur about them. "This here establishment has been operating continuously since the coronation of Queen Elibert at the beginning of the Fourth Kingdom. That's long before any of our father's fathers were even born. My name is Stoney MacKraegen and this is my tavern. Now, who be you?"

"Well, I'm . . . I'm . . ."

"Speak up, lad! I've not got all night, you know."

"Sir, I'll tell you, but could you please set me down first?"

"Oh! Right, then!"

Stoney lowered the boy until his high, leather boots rested on the soaked floor beneath him.

The young man drew back his shoulders into his sodden greatcoat, lifted his chin, and proudly proclaimed: "I am Percival Taylor, gentleman adventurer!"

Snorts erupted about the common room.

Percival glared at the seamen with a look as threatening as possible, given his soggy state.

Stoney coughed through his own chuckle. "Well, then, welcome . . . er . . . adventurer. And what brought such an honor to my humble tavern?"

"Destiny!" Percival said with earnest. "I have come to find my fortune on the high seas!"

The laughter around Percival apparently confused the boy.

"Well, if it's adventure you seek, then you've found it, lad!" Stoney said, stripping the wet greatcoat off of the boy and dropping it unceremoniously on the floor behind him. "You're in the Mistral's Mistress, home of pirates, rogues, and privateers!"

"I am?" Percival squeaked.

"Let me introduce you to your new mates, boy!" Stoney said, wrapping his enormous arm around the thin shoulders of the youth. "Most of these scalawags are just off the *Revenge*. That there is Dead-Eye Darrel. Yonder is William Volnak— some call him Butcher Bill but best not to do so to his face. That goblin in the corner is known as Cutthroat Karka. The minotaur sitting in the other corner—don't look directly at him, boy!—well, his name is Mad Morkie. Hook-Hand Horvath left earlier, but if you wait long enough he'll be glad to shake your hand. They all answer to the Captain and the Captain alone . . . best you understand that right now, eh? Remember that, and you'll get by just fine."

Percival swallowed hard, shrinking deeper under Stoney's arm with every step they took toward the bar. "I . . . I got lost in the storm. This was the only place with light that I could see."

"Always good to heed the light when you're lost in a storm, lad," Stoney said with a smile.

"Is this . . ." Percival swallowed hard again, failing to appear confident. "Is this a *pirate* tavern?"

"No, lad," Stoney said, giving the boy's frame a jocular shake. "This isn't *a* pirate tavern . . . this be *the* pirate tavern! It says so right on the sign coming into town." Stoney gestured with his right hand while still pinning Percival under his left arm. "It reads 'Blackshore: Pirate Lair, home of the Mistral's Mistress. Visitors welcome.' Did you not see the sign, boy?"

"Well, it *was* getting late . . . and the storm was breaking."

"Well, some other time then," Stoney said with disappointment.

Percival's eyes flicked from face to grim face among the pirate crew as Stoney dragged him between their tables toward the bar. "I've heard of pirate taverns, of course. They're supposed to be dens of all kinds of vice, satisfying the adventurous spirit of sailors who have conquered distant shores. I, of course, am myself an adventurer and no stranger to such houses as your own, worthy master Stoney."

"Indeed," Stoney replied as seriously as the smile playing

about his lips would allow. "I am relieved that you are such a hardened man of the world."

"Well, when one has been an adventurer as long as I have—"

Percival stopped cold. He had been so preoccupied with the threatening men in the tavern that he had completely missed where Stoney was taking him.

The towering figure of Rhenna MacKraegen suddenly filled his vision not a foot in front of him. He gazed up into her emerald green eyes, her perfect face, and the nimbus of red hair.

"Will you be wanting a bed for the night?" she asked.

Percival gaped; his jaw was working, but no words came out.

"Let's put him in with Silva, love," Stoney said with a smile.

Percival blinked furiously.

Rhenna nodded as she reached down into the pocket of her apron and pulled out a key. She pressed it into Percival's quivering hand. She said, "Top of the stairs and second door on the right."

"No!" Percival blurted out. "I mean, thank you, but . . . I really want my own room . . . just me!"

"Are you sure?" Rhenna asked with a pout. "It's extra if you sleep alone."

"Extra?" Percival squeaked. "What kind of place is this? I'll pay it! Just . . . give me my own room!"

Rhenna shrugged, took back the key, and found him another. "End of the hall at the top of the stairs. Are you sure? Silva's very nice and—"

"I'm *sure*," Percival said loudly, pulling free of Stoney's grip. He rushed across the floor to the pool where his wet coat and cape lay, swept them all up in his arms, and ran up the stairs, taking them two steps at a time, trailing rainwater the entire way.

He slammed the door closed behind him.

Everyone in the common room erupted in laughter.

"You *might* have told the boy," Rhenna said, shaking her head and curls.

"Told him what?" Stoney grinned. "That Silva is a pleasant old man or that it's common for sailors to share rooms when they are in port so as to split the expense?"

"You know what he was thinking," Rhenna said, flicking her polishing rag at her husband.

"Well, looking at you, I know what *I'm* thinking," Stoney said. "Besides, why disillusion the boy on his first day out as an adventurer?"

CHAPTER 2

The Governor's Daughter

Tuppence Magrathia-Paddock knelt on the curved stone bench fitted into the balcony wall of her private suite in the Governor's House and gazed down the hillside that sloped from the confines of her sweet prison to the harbor below. She laid her perfectly dimpled chin on her crossed alabaster arms resting on the balustrade and emitted a long, heartfelt sigh worthy, she knew, of the most ardent heroines from any of Eunice Wurtz's secret books. Her large, dark eyes were a mirror of longing and boredom in turns, framed by her jet-black, perfectly arranged curls.

Eunice sat on a chair placed inside the doorway to the balcony just far enough so as to be out of the direct sunlight peeking around Mount Molly to the east. She was a thin woman with a drawn face and a soft chin that always faced the world with disapproval. She was lady's companion to Tuppence

Magrathia-Paddock, imported from Mordale expressly for the purpose. It had seemed a perfectly profitable arrangement for all parties—certainly for her father, who was a courtier to King Reinard and was most enthusiastic at the prospect of his eldest daughter finding some employment outside his home. Yet in everyone's mutual haste to seal the bargain, a few problematic issues were somehow missed. It was true that Eunice was nearly fifteen years older than her charge—who was perfectly seventeen and therefore in her own eyes entirely ready for the world, with the occasional advice of her newly purchased friend. Yet somehow everyone had missed the fact that Eunice had been just as sheltered in her upbringing as her charge and was entirely lacking in the seasoning of wisdom that such a difference in their ages should have accomplished. Thus, Eunice was every bit as ignorant as the esteemed Tuppence Magrathia-Paddock in regards to anything real in the world.

Both of them, however, were well versed in all other aspects of the human condition.

Tuppence Magrathia-Paddock was the first lady of Blackshore. She hosted social gatherings for the old ladies, sailor's wives, and widows of Highstreet, who never once openly despised her. Her dinner parties were attended by everyone who received her summons. She had first pick of the new gowns when they came into Morjak's Emporium on Hangman's Square, and none of the other women in the town ever complained within earshot. Every young man in the town was appropriately impressed with her, and they all said so whenever their mothers were too far away to hear their words. She was the undisputed mistress of the manor, which possessed no fewer than twenty-seven rooms, one of which was devoted entirely to her faithful guard dog, Triton. The manor, Governor's House, was the largest structure in the town, and Tuppence Magrathia-Paddock knew it as a crushing responsibility that stood between her and her destiny.

Her father, Governor Alphonsis Paddock, also lived there.

Tuppence was a stunning beauty with full lips set in a perpetual pout. Her large, liquid eyes were perfect, she knew, both for adoration and for being adored. She had read in one of Eunice's books—the ones her father had forbidden her to read—about "languid pools in which the soul of a man could drown with longing and desire." She knew at once that this passage had been written about her and not the tarty woman named Marquetta who had been carried off in the tale by the dashing Rodrigan. The book was a terrible story titled *Marquetta of the Tempest* that she had read only six times before Eunice took the book back.

Privately, she had rather fancied the book title would have been much better as *Tuppence of the Tempest.*

Fortunately for Tuppence Magrathia-Paddock, Eunice had brought with her an extensive collection of books that her own father had forbidden *her* to read. While Eunice was supposed to be teaching her younger companion about the histories of the Epic Wars, the proper manners of presentation at court, and the foundations of natural order and magic, neither Eunice nor Tuppence found these subjects nearly as interesting as the secret collection, nor did they seem as relevant to the women's condition here in the manor. So reality was too often relegated to a position of lesser importance. How could it compete in the face of a rapscallion in colorful costume sweeping in on a rope to trespass on the moonlit balcony of a trembling young maiden?

True, what happened after the daring scoundrel appeared on the balcony was often skipped in Eunice's books, but Tuppence knew that it had something to do with getting married and living an adventurous life thereafter.

So Tuppence Magrathia-Paddock gazed across the balustrade of her balcony toward the town below. The unchanging line of roofs continued down to the curving shore of Blackshore Bay. The masts of a ship rose above the roofline from where it lay tied up against one of the wharfs at the water's edge.

Tuppence's gaze shifted to the book lying open in her hand atop the low wall.

Swept up by the Sea, the title read.

Tuppence frowned despite the unsightly lines she knew it would make on her face. This book, too, featured a scoundrel by the name of Rodrigan, and, despite her initial hopes, this one seemed to be an entirely different Rodrigan from the rogue in the terrible book she had previously read. She raised the book again and read the frontispiece with a critical eye.

"Eunice?"

The Lady Wurtz looked up from her book. "Yes, milady!"

"This Edvard the Just . . . the author of this dreadful book," Tuppence said, raising her chin with disapproval. "He writes a great many of these, doesn't he?"

"Oh, my, yes, milady!" Eunice responded, rolling her eyes. "He's called the 'Dragon's Bard.' They say that Khrag, the king of dragonkind, once put him under a tragic curse. He's compelled to wander all the realms and collect tales of romance and adventure for the dragon's amusement, or his life will be forfeit! He's rather popular among the ladies of Mordale— none of whom share your finer sensibilities."

"It is a fine autumn day, and we shall go into town," Tuppence announced abruptly.

"Oh, no, milady!" Eunice was instantly appalled.

"No?" Tuppence was very familiar with the word *no* in her own usage but unaccustomed to hearing it from others.

"Your father is out of town, milady!" Eunice replied in some distress. It was her most common response to anything unexpected. "He left specific instructions that you were to stay close to the house until he returned."

"We govern Blackshore, do we not?" Tuppence always resorted to the "royal we" when she was about to assert her authority. She also believed that her father's patents of position, granted him by King Reinard, had excluded mentioning the extension of his authority to her only through clerical omission. "And, after all, Blackshore itself is close to the house, is it not?"

"But, milady," Eunice stammered, "it is a town of ruffians and . . . and *sailors!* We shall be without protection! I fear my nerves cannot—"

"Oh, bother your nerves, Eunice!" Tuppence stood up at once, stomping her foot. "The town watch is set and I've never read of anything happening to women abroad during the morning. Nefarious deeds always happen at sundown, near breaking dawn, or in the dark of night. They *never* occur just after breakfast!"

"But, milady . . . your father . . ."

"Has my father ever denied me anything?" Tuppence demanded. She could speak with authority on this subject. Her father, the governor, had occasionally blustered against her willful desires or whims, but he always gave in to her in the end. It was a constant of the universe for Tuppence—like seasons. "Besides, we shall have Triton to protect us. Come, Triton! Come!"

"But I've never been to town before!" yelped Eunice.

A rapid scampering on stone approached from within the house. The noble Triton, guardian of Tuppence Magrathia-Paddock, padded across the walk, a blur of bouncing hair that so obscured his six-inch-long legs that the position of his paws had to be inferred rather than observed. Normally the juxtaposition of the head and rump was also largely a matter of conjecture based on the direction of the creature's travel. However, it was a measure of Tuppence's concern for the devoted creature that she had tied back the hair over his eyes with pink and yellow ribbons so he could actually see. With a yap, Triton leaped from the stone, nearly reaching Tuppence's lap . . . while she graciously caught him, making up the difference between the dog's ability and imagined ability by drawing him up in her arms. He gratefully responded by licking her face with his tiny pink tongue.

"There! You see?" Tuppence replied with a smile. "Triton here will defend our honor with his life! Won't you, Triton?"

"Arf!" Triton responded, demonstrating the magnitude of his ferocity.

"Come, Eunice," Tuppence commanded as she strode back into her private rooms, Triton's hair waving back and forth as they moved. "Put on your hat. We are going to town at once!"

Tuppence Magrathia-Paddock set her guardian dog down to scuttle about her feet as she reached for her own wide-brimmed hat on a brass rack. She was a determined woman of seventeen, convinced that she was practically in charge while her father was away, and a woman who had practically everything necessary to ensure a proper romantic life.

All she needed, she knew, was the right rogue to sweep her off her feet and into a life of romance and adventure.

Percival stood before the metal plate, tried one more time to polish its scratched and cloudy surface, and then stood back to admire himself. The tight breeches were carefully tucked into his high-strapped boots and cinched at his waist with a wide leather belt and an enormous buckle fashioned with a crossed-wands relief. His silk-collared shirt was untied at the throat and open to nearly halfway down his torso, rakishly exposing the center of his hairless chest. The sleeves were after the puffed fashion, in the best tradition of sea rogues. Percival had taken great care in tying his hair into a tight tail at the back of his neck, vowing to grow it longer at every opportunity. He completed the effect by buckling on the scabbard containing a rapier that his father had brought him from Mordale on his last cloth-buying trip. It was the perfect accent to his costume—completing the effect in his mind—especially with its ornate swept hilt that still shone new.

Was anyone ever more ready for the sea? he thought with a deep and abiding appreciation for himself.

Percival Taylor gazed at the poor reflection in the mirror and managed, with practiced ease, to imagine what was not clear in that obviously imperfect reflection of himself. His strong, cleft chin was cleanly shaven whether his scarce beard demanded it or not. His flaxen hair had been carefully combed. He again practiced his "smoldering" look in the mirror and was satisfied with its effectiveness. He had carefully cultivated the image of a heroic adventurer, firmly believing with youthful exuberance that appearance and determination would magically make up for a complete lack of ability, experience, or substance.

"Away!" Percival cried as he flung open the door of his room with a loud bang. Old Silva awoke with a loud snort in the next room, but otherwise his exit was unappreciated.

Percival tripped down the stairs of the Mistral's Mistress, his left hand resting on the hilt of the sword at his side. The night's sleep had revitalized his spirits. The spring had returned to his step and he was prepared to begin his life of adventure at once.

"Ahoy, there, Master Percival," Stoney called out from behind the bar where he was cleaning the ale mugs. "Off to see the sights, are you, now?"

"I'm off to see the world," Percival crowed, "*and* make it mine!"

"In a hurry, then, are you?"

"My destiny will not wait, friend innkeeper!" Percival nodded with a gleam in his eye and his jaw set.

"Well, then, I'll not be waiting breakfast on you," Stoney said, turning back to cleaning the ale mugs in front of him. "I'll be holding your room for your return."

"There will be no need, innkeeper," Percival exclaimed with a confident sigh. "I'll be on the high seas by ten bells."

"Ten bells, is it?" Stoney glanced up with a chuckle. "Well, if it's ten bells, then I think I'll hold your room for you all the same. Good luck to you, Master Percival."

"Thank you, innkeeper," Percival replied with his sincerest expression of polite condescension. "I shall look you up on my return!"

"Which," Stoney muttered under his breath, "will not be long indeed."

Hand still on the hilt of his rapier, Percival pushed through the door of the tavern and into the brilliant morning sunlight beyond.

"Oh, Mistress Tuppence," keened Eunice again, "please let us go back to the house before anything terrible happens!"

Tuppence continued to flounce down the wet road with her long skirt lifted delicately just above the mud with her right hand and her trusty Triton firmly cradled in the grasp of her left. This left Eunice acting as Her Ladyship's third hand, holding the parasol so as to shield her delicate complexion from the bright and climbing sun. Eunice was finding it difficult to simultaneously keep the parasol properly in place and not trip all over Her Ladyship's hem.

"Oh, tish-tosh!" Tuppence exclaimed in her strongest language. She was out of the proper confines of the manor house and, being on her way into the rowdy seaport, considered the use of coarse words entirely in keeping with the customs of the region. "Such nonsense! Really, Lady Eunice, you need more experience with life."

"I've experience enough," Eunice countered. "At least enough to know that we'll likely get in trouble with your father and that I'll be the one to suffer for it!"

Tuppence pursed her lips and wrinkled her nose, a gesture of disapproval and highest disdain. She rarely resorted to it, since the expression required making her face less attractive, but the situation was dire and called for extreme measures. "Say what you will, Eunice, but I will be walking through the town whether you accompany me or not!"

Eunice's mouth clamped shut. She might survive the displeasure of Alphonsis Paddock over their leaving the house, but she would be turned out at once if she allowed Mistress Tuppence in public without a chaperone.

"Now, Eunice, you must relax," Tuppence said, allowing her face to relax into a more appropriate sweet smile. "I know this town very well indeed! Attend me now: this is Reinard Road—named after King Reinard, as I'm sure you suspect."

Eunice glanced furtively about them. There was nothing about the street that lived up to the pretentions of its name. The wooden walls of the surrounding buildings sagged somewhat, the paint on their trim occasionally well kept but for the most part weathered and fading, peeling away to leave the wood exposed in most places.

"Now, down there—where the road splits off to the right—that's Gentlemen's Way."

Eunice swallowed hard. Gentlemen's Way was, if anything, more tawdry than the area she had just passed. The road ran almost straight down the slope between townhouses that all seemed to have faded to the same gray color. The street itself was a churned-up mess, with a number of freight wagons stuck behind several teams of oxen struggling to get up the slippery thoroughfare.

"You didn't want to go that way, did you, miss?" Eunice asked, dreading the possible answer.

"Oh, no," Tuppence beamed. "There's nothing down that way but sailors' homes, guilds, and warehouses. Come along!"

They followed the road as it turned southward. Here Eunice began to breathe with greater ease. The shops were better kept here, some of them reaching up to a second story. It was more civilized and reminded Eunice a bit of the home she had too recently left in Mordale. "These are lovely shops here, miss! I like that shingle there—'Freider and Violet Gaines: First and Last.' Isn't that a romantic family crest?"

"Oh, Eunice, you are so funny!" Tuppence laughed sunshine.

"What do you mean, miss?"

"That's not their crest—it's their professions."

"I don't understand . . ."

"Violet Gaines is the midwife in town," Tuppence said,

continuing to pick her delicate way between the puddles in the road. "There's not a baby born in Blackshore that she has not assisted into the world . . . and collected her fee for it, too."

"I see, miss," Eunice replied. "But what of her husband?"

"Freider?"

"Yes, miss."

"Oh, he's the town grave digger."

Eunice could find no reply and so continued to follow Tuppence in silence. Triton looked about him with little concern from his perch on his mistress's arm. They came to the end of Reinard Road, where the dirt gave way, gratefully, to cobblestones.

"Oh, what a lovely square!" Eunice exclaimed. "And that statue before the Guild Hall is so very . . ."

Eunice could not finish the sentence.

It was not a great square like those in Mordale, but of good size for the town. A lovely fountain bubbled in the center of the square, the cobblestones all still shiny from the rain of the evening before. Bright shops lined the square on all sides and the impressive Guild Hall—where the duties and tariffs were collected and the governor held his offices and court—dominated the northeast side. It was the statue before the Guild Hall that had caught her attention.

It was a marble rendering of a large hooded man holding a noose.

Eunice found her voice. "I suspect you'll be telling me this is . . ."

"Yes, the famous Hangman's Square," Tuppence nodded with a prideful smile. "Of course, its actual name is Bartholemew Square—or some such nonsense—but everyone calls it Hangman's Square. You've no doubt heard—even in Mordale—the story about Captain Black Phillips and how he met his end right here?"

"No, Mistress, I fear I have not," Eunice confessed.

Tuppence's face fell in disappointment. "A pity . . . well, perhaps some other time. Come along!"

Tuppence wheeled, her skirts flaring as she turned down the street where a lamp sign proclaimed Queen Nance's Lane. The smell wafting up the street, however, was making Eunice's eyes water.

"Where are we going now, milady?" Eunice managed to blurt out.

"Down to the quays, of course!" Tuppence proclaimed. "Where all the ships are docked. It's just down this way past the fishmonger's! Keep up, Eunice! Keep up!"

Percival was surrounded by angry pirates, his rapier drawn against their cutlasses.

Things had not gone as he had expected that morning.

It had seemed a straightforward proposition to him from the beginning. He would walk down to the place where they kept the boats, get on one of them, and tell the crew he wanted to join them. He had thus presented himself aboard the *Demeter,* the *Albatross,* the *Jasmine,* and a number of smaller fishing vessels but had been tossed back off the ship by each of the crews and in each case with a hearty laugh at his expense. One of the captains asked him if Captain Dorsey had put him up to it as a lark. So anxious had Percival been to fulfill his destiny at sea—as Madame Zoltana had proclaimed—that he had even approached Butcher Bill Volnak, whom he had seen at the tavern the night before, and paid him to let him aboard his vessel on the off chance that Percival could find the infamous Captain Swash and thereby present himself as a candidate for temporary piracy until something better came along. Butcher Bill was happy to oblige, showing the boy about the ship, thinking that all the lad wanted was a tour, but when Percival refused to go ashore, things became heated and a bit confused.

The pirates had managed to chase him off their ship twice, but the determined youth continued to clamber back aboard. At last, Butcher Bill enlisted the minotaur Mad Morkie to join in their side of the game, and together with Dead-Eye Darrel, Hook-Hand Horvath, and the goblin Cutthroat Karka, they had chased Percival back down to the end of the quay, determined to keep the boy safe from a life of piracy.

Percival Taylor made up in courage and determination

what he lacked in understanding and experience. He leaped up atop a stack of cargo crates and kegs, drew his rapier, and, striking a stance, brandished the blade before him.

The pirates, shrugging at the sudden escalation in the game, drew their cutlasses in response.

Percival looked to his own thin, light blade, then at the multiple thick, heavy blades drawn against him. He swallowed hard, suddenly desperately aware of the value of discretion over his own pride. He was surrounded on three sides by pirates, with his back to a ten-foot drop ending in water. He had never learned to swim . . .

"AYEEE!"

The woman's scream cut through the noise of the quay and the ships docked next to it.

Percival turned toward the horrified sound.

The pirates turned toward it as well.

Two women stood before the doorway to the Laird's Lair shop. One of the women was still screaming despite holding a parasol.

The other, who stood immediately beside the screeching woman, was to Percival's eyes a perfect vision of shocked beauty holding a yapping little dog.

Percival, his heart pounding, realized at once that the pirates too had been distracted by the appearance of this vision of loveliness. Propelled by fear, the young man in the puffy shirt leaped over the backs of the pirates, running toward the women.

The parasol woman screamed again, but it was the wide-eyed, incomparable splendor, frozen except for the barking dog, that Percival addressed.

"Flee, milady!" Percival said to her. Even as he said it, he could hear the pirates approaching behind him.

In a panic, Percival wheeled around, the tip of his sword catching on the vision's dress and tearing it slightly. The two women were now behind him, blocking his escape. The pirates smirked as they approached.

"Who . . . give me your name, rogue!" the younger woman's words were filled with breath behind him.

The pirates were positioning themselves around the trio.

"This is hardly a time for introductions," Percival said. "Get out of the way, lady!"

The young beauty's arms suddenly wrapped around him from behind, her soft cheek brushing against his ear. Tuppence's warm lips gently kissed his cheek.

"Thank you . . . my Rodrigan!" she whispered.

The screaming woman vanished.

The dog stopped yapping.

And she was gone.

Percival stood there for a moment blinking. He barely noticed the pirates' rough hands lifting him off of the ground and dragging him over to the edge of the quay. Even as the chill of the water closed over him, his mind repeated again and again . . .

"Thank you . . . my Rodrigan!"

CHAPTER 3

Swept Up by the Sea

Percival lay once again in a pool of water on the floor of the Mistral's Mistress tavern, gasping like a guppy just hauled out of the water.

"You'll be carrying a bucket and mop with you from now on!" Percival was vaguely aware that Stoney MacKraegen was standing over him although all he could manage to see were the squared, scuffed toes of the innkeeper's boots. "Can you not manage to enter my inn one . . . single . . . time without sopping in half the Lycandric Ocean with you? This is a *floor*, boy, not a bath!"

Percival tried to say something in his own defense. It came out as a burst of spray from his lungs over the boots before him.

"Oh, the boy's hopeless!" Stoney snapped above him.

"Now, that is not entirely correct," answered a fluting voice.

Percival seemed to think he knew the speaker but could not yet manage to move his head far enough to investigate. The floor was solid beneath him, and he found that very comforting.

"He is a most noble young man who is only now come to appreciate the wild world beyond the quaint boundaries of his ancestral home," the voice continued, rising and falling like a melody, "and, no doubt, barely comprehending the dangers that lurk just beyond the horizons of his understanding."

Percival rolled over onto his back with a squishing sound.

"Oh . . . it's you again."

The narrow jaw was jutting down toward his face, accentuated by the carefully groomed beard and dark mustache. He had acquired another hat from the Eventide milliner, Merinda Oakman, who had taken as much interest in the man as anyone else back in Percival's hometown of Eventide. The hat was made of leather this time and fitted with his telltale—if the expression could be applied with a straight face—roc feather fixed to the brim and falling down over his left shoulder. His angular features and bright eyes had peered at Percival before, although the young man had never experienced their gaze from the floor.

"Ah, yes, 'tis I," the Dragon's Bard replied, straightening into a dramatic pose, his left fingers splayed against his chest, his right hand reaching skyward as though to accept the blessing of the Lady of the Sky. "I have returned to the rustic and

intriguing locality of this adventurers' den with but one purpose, lad! I have come to fetch you away from this iniquitous,
scurrilous locale and out of the clutches of ne'er-do-wells, cutthroats, and thieves!"

Abel, the Bard's scribe, was sitting wearily atop his master's
entirely overpacked trunk. He wore a traveling cloak across his
wide shoulders and an embroidered doublet over a linen shirt.
His face was wide and his eyes keen, if somewhat careworn.
He was shorter than the Bard by nearly a hand's width—and,
truth be told, the far more gifted of the two when it came to
the written word. Still, the differences in their professions separated them, as did the technical division between the master
and the apprentice. Abel gave a great sigh and pulled out his
parchment and pencil as he felt the anticipated exchange worthy of careful chronicle.

"Here, now!" Stoney bellowed. "I run a respectable establishment! At least it always *were* a respectable establishment
until you kept showing up!"

"He's been here before?" Percival sputtered.

"Aye, curse the dawns that bring him," Stoney scowled.
"Every time a ship makes port, I check to see if this peacock
gets off of it; when he *doesn't* . . . then I buy a round of drinks
for everyone in the room."

"Such a jest, of course, friend Stoney!" the Dragon's Bard
replied with a bright grin. "But I fear that our stay with you
shall not be prolonged. My good friend here has seen the sea,

and it would appear most obvious that the sea has seen *him!* Thus having satisfied his thirst for adventure in every reasonable way, we shall be returning to his home and his destiny early tomorrow morning—"

"My destiny!" Percival squeaked, his voice breaking in his excitement. The young man stood up suddenly. "I have found my destiny, Edvard! I came in search of it and did not know that it would find me first!"

"And so I have found you, lad!" Edvard the Dragon's Bard nodded, although his smile was dimmed somewhat by his vague comprehension of what the youth meant. "Now that I have, we can return in the morning to the welcoming arms of your mother. It was she herself who compelled me to come hither and—"

"No! Not *that* destiny!" Percival's face turned upward, the picture of rapture. "Fate has spoken and led me here, called me to a new life and a better destiny. Fortune came to me framed in coal-black, shimmering curls. Fortune is a pair of large, liquid eyes of green-flecked brown that looked through my soul to my valiant heart and dreams. Fortune is the perfect pout of plump lips whispering 'Rodrigan! . . . Rodrigan!'"

Edvard looked puzzled. "Who? What did you say?"

The scribe, still seated on the bulging trunk, looked askance at the innkeeper.

Stoney drew in a breath. "I'm thinking the poor boy hit something when they tossed him over the side. Best keep him awake for a bit to make sure he's just shaken his skull rather than cracked it altogether."

"You don't understand!" Percival said in frustration. "She was *real!* She was in a dress on the . . . the . . . the . . . boat-holding place out in front of the tavern and a brimmed hat. She had some furry thing in her arms and . . . no, there were *two* of them!"

"Two furry things?" Stoney scratched his head.

"No . . . women," Percival said.

"Furry women?" Edvard said through a squint.

"I've got to find her!" Percival said. "She's my destiny! She's the one that we saw in the cards . . ."

"Wait!" Edvard said, grasping the soggy youth by both shoulders and staring into his eyes. "*What* cards?"

"The Cards of Fate," Percival replied. "Madame Zoltana said that—"

"ZOLTANA!" Edvard shouted. "I might have known she was behind this! What *is* it with that woman? It's not enough that I'm trying my best to get away from her . . . no, she had to *follow* me like a plague . . . worse than plague . . . like some foul spirit that stalks me like a cursed shadow on a cloudy day. Three years with that carnival troupe . . . three years and you'd think she would get over it, but *no,* she has to change the winds just to make sure we're blown together."

"You know Madame Zoltana?" Percival asked.

Edvard suddenly stopped speaking. He straightened up at

once and smiled graciously. "Oh, no, not really. I mean, our paths have crossed a time or two, but I . . . well, I hardly know the woman."

Abel had anticipated Edvard launching into a long harangue about Madame Zoltana, their escalating hatred for each other, and how both of them desired nothing so much in the world as to exact their revenge on the other. He had begun composing a long passage detailing their mutual animosity, but, given the Bard's denials, it now seemed pointless. He struck out several paragraphs that he had just composed and resumed his duties.

The entrance door to the Mistral's Mistress creaked ominously as it slowly traversed its hinges. Percival, Edvard, Stoney, and the scribe all turned toward the sound. A widening square shaft of light entered the room.

A thin head with quivering curls stuck through the light.

"H-h-hello?" The woman could barely speak for fear. "I . . . oh, um . . . h-h-hello?" Her voice then collapsed from words into a series of unintelligible, keening groans.

The woman was as out of place as a daffodil in an open rum jug. She gingerly held the handle of the door by her handkerchief as though in fear that the stench of the waterfront was emanating from that single object alone. Her other hand, knuckles white, gripped a bound book to her breast with such fervor that one might think it were armor. So ardent was her intent that she was bending its cover. Her steps were so tightly shuffling that they hobbled her progress across the stoop. Her thin face and receding chin emphasized her large eyes, which were bulging so wide that the whites could be seen all around their brown irises. Her mouse-brown hair was streaked with gray and threatening to go white at any moment out of sheer terror. The patch of doily that passed for a hat tied to her head was quivering uncontrollably.

"Aye, madam?" Stoney said, his thick eyebrows knitted over the odd, nervous bird that appeared to have landed at his door. "Can I help ye?"

"Oh!" The woman jumped at the sound of the innkeeper's voice. Her book, suddenly released from its bowed tension, sprang from her hand, clattering on the floor in front of her. This somehow dislodged the words that had piled up in her throat, which now exploded in a rush. *"Please, sires, take pity on this poor woman who is unaccustomed to these rough surroundings and do not impose your will upon me for I am the companion of a gentlewoman and have come only to deliver her message!"*

It was all delivered in a single breath, the last words of which required a considerable effort as the thin woman was nearly out of air.

"But, my dear woman," the Dragon's Bard said, sweeping his arms wide in welcome. "Fear not, for we are at your service. We shall gladly vouchsafe your honor while you deliver your message . . . but here, I see you have dropped your book. Allow me!"

Edvard scooped up the tome from off the floor and held it out toward the woman as he offered the most gallant of extravagant bows.

"Oh, thank you, good sir," the woman offered, taking the book from him with some hesitation.

"And in whose name do I have the privilege of serving?" Edvard asked.

The thin woman gave a curtsy of the briefest duration possible. "You may know me as the Lady Eunice of Mordale . . . and may I ask the name of the gentleman to whom I am indebted?"

"It is my pleasure to be of service!" Edvard flashed his most winning smile. "You see, I am in the trade myself, a writer of books, collector of tales, and purveyor of stories from beyond the horizons of all possible knowledge or refutation . . . I am . . . *the Dragon's Bard!*"

The woman's eyes suddenly widened once again. Her jaw dropped open and she stood gaping in astonishment.

"You?" she sputtered. "*You* are the Dragon's Bard?"

"Why, yes," Edvard replied; then his brows knotted in concern. "Have we met before?"

To the astonishment of everyone in the tavern, Eunice suddenly giggled. "Oh, no, sir! Why, I should certainly have remembered if we *had* met!"

Abel began furiously scribbling on his parchment, wishing to miss no detail of the encounter.

Eunice thrust the book in her hands out toward the Bard at once. "But this is one of your very own titles!"

"It is?" Edvard blinked.

"'Tis your name right here on the cover, is it not?" Eunice exclaimed, bouncing slightly up and down on the balls of her feet and completely having forgotten the dire circumstances of her surroundings.

"Is it? I mean . . . why, so it is!" Edvard recovered his smile at once.

"Oh, Edvard . . . may I call you Edvard?"

"Of course you may!"

"Edvard . . . *I am your most . . . very, very MOST ardent admirer!*" Eunice exclaimed, giggling once again as she held the book out toward him.

"Ah, and of course you are." Edvard's smile appeared slightly less enthusiastic than before. His eyes glanced at the open door behind the woman and then back toward the door behind the bar. "What a treat for me to happen upon so ardent and enthusiastic an admirer."

"You simply *must* inscribe my book for me," Eunice whined. "I should die without a memento of this occasion!"

"But of course." Edvard took the book from her, motioning for Abel to join him. The scribe gave a great sigh and stood up from where he had previously settled onto the trunk, handing his pencil over to the Bard. Edvard opened the book to the back and began scribbling with a flourish.

"Oh, I've read *all* of your writings," Eunice cooed in front of the Bard. "My first was *Rodrigan and the Crier's Daughter* . . . but then my father found it and sadly burned it . . . but I still have all the others. Let's see, there was *Swept Up by the Sea* and *Ethel, the Pirate's Bounty* and *Dragon Sacrifice* and *Satyr's Rampage* and *Mistress of the Darkened Shore . . .*"

At the mention of this last book, Stoney MacKraegen flashed a deep scowl at the Dragon's Bard.

"That last was *entirely* a work of fiction, I assure you," Edvard interjected at once, glancing with some discomfort at the innkeeper as he handed the book back to the chirping woman.

"Oh, but it moved me nearly to swoon!" Eunice said, her large eyes flashing. "That passage where the innkeeper's wife tries to seduce the young, dashing rogue in an effort to save her husband from the clutches of the pirate Captain Swash was so compelling . . ."

The Dragon's Bard removed his cap and wiped his brow. "Fiction often is far more interesting than the truth."

Eunice looked at the mad scribbling on the page, somewhat confused. "I can't quite make out what you've written here."

"That's just the typical signature of a creative genius," Edvard said with an uncomfortable cough. "You mentioned that you came with a message or something . . ."

"Oh, pardon my manners, indeed I did," Eunice giggled

again, her high-pitched cackle grating on everyone else's nerves. "I've come with a message for the young rogue who but a short time ago defended the honor of my mistress before this very establishment."

Percival stepped forward, water still squishing in his elegant high boots as he moved. "I believe I am the rogue that you seek!"

Eunice took a step back, the fingers of her right hand rising to her lips after the fashion practiced by young ladies in storybooks who imagine themselves threatened. "You are indeed, sir! Here is what my lady wishes be conveyed to you."

Eunice removed a flattened scroll of parchment from where she had tucked it inside her bodice. A ribbon—pink and most likely taken in her haste from off Tuppence's guard dog—was fixed around it.

Percival stared at it.

"My lady asks that you read this at once," Eunice said.

Percival glanced around and then shrugged. "Oh, I'm sorry . . . I'm so wet from defending your lady's honor . . . I wouldn't want to get it all smudged by dripping on it. Maybe the Dragon's Bard could read it . . ."

"I would gladly do so at once," the Dragon's Bard quickly interjected, "were it not for the fact that I took a vow just this morning not to read again today until after the sun set . . . a strictly religious observance of my guild . . . and one which I dare not break. Abel, however, is but an apprentice to the craft and not under the strict rules that govern my behavior, so perhaps—"

"Oh, give me that!" Stoney MacKraegen demanded, snatching the scroll from the woman and stripping the ribbon from around its flattened girth.

Stoney MacKraegen then read the note aloud.

My Rodrigan:

I know not your name nor what dire and terrible past has led you to a life of piracy, plunder, and adventure. Perhaps you were kidnapped as a child from your royal family, or sold by your nursemaid into slavery aboard a ship of cutthroats and cads. Or you may have innocently fallen in with bad company. I can only imagine the privations you have suffered in your life—a noble soul who has been forced into questionable deeds despite your better nature.

I know we must never meet again . . . although, if we were to meet (and I assure you that I respectfully and reservedly swoon at the thought of such an impossible occurrence taking place) I should be moved to thank you with all my heart for defending my honor against the rough buccaneers who threatened our lives or worse earlier this morning.

I know that this must never be, and so I would caution you not to be in the vicinity of Gentlemen's

Way on Memory Lane or especially the Port Anghel Road near Prow Rock any time between midafternoon and tea nineteen days from now—when my father is scheduled for his trip to Mordale—lest by some chance of fate we would meet, as surely we must not do.

Know that I will forever carry you in my heart as the tragic, romantic buccaneer of my dreams—and I shall look longingly over the seas wondering as to your tragic fate.

Respectfully,
Lady Tuppence Magrathia-Paddock
The Governor's Daughter

"Tuppence," Percival whispered in awe. "Her name is Tuppence!"

"Wait, now," Stoney said, holding up his hand. "There be more here. '*P.S. I forgive you . . . and now you must forget me and my ardent heart.*'"

Only the distant creaking of the ships on the quay filtered across the silence.

Percival uttered a heartfelt sigh.

"Milady would beg the name of the dashing rogue," Eunice urged.

Percival was lost in his own dreams as he spoke. "Rodrigan . . . tell her that I am her Rodrigan . . . er, Percival 'Rodrigan' Taylor, that is."

"And does Rodrigan have an answer for milady?" Eunice asked.

Before Percival could answer, the Dragon's Bard interjected, sweeping his arm about the shoulders of the suddenly awestruck Eunice. "Of course, but we must make a proper reply of it. Something . . . considered and appropriate. I assure you, Lady Edna . . ."

"Eunice," the woman corrected.

"Lady Eunice, I personally shall assist this dashing rogue in his reply," Edvard smiled as he propelled the woman out the door. "Tell your lady her answer shall be forthcoming!"

With that he slammed the door shut.

"I see that our sojourn in this place may be longer than anticipated," the Dragon's Bard said. "Master MacKraegen, are my usual accommodations available?"

"Aye," the innkeeper answered, "and at the usual rate."

"Then my good friend Percival and I shall be staying here for a time . . . a *short* time, if at all possible."

CHAPTER 4

The Bard's Commission

The Bard's "usual accommodations" consisted of a corner of the wine cellar behind the potato sacks—a slight improvement on his scribe's lodgings, which were *on* the potato sacks. The room was damp, cold, and without hope of any natural light, but Edvard accepted it with unaccustomed grace and his most radiant charm.

"And what do you think of it, lad?" the Bard said, sweeping his arm gracefully as he bowed. It was a position forced upon him on account of the unusually low ceiling.

"It's a big hole dug in the dirt," Percival exclaimed, trying to keep the shoulders of his tunic from touching either side of the steep and narrow stair that they had descended from the kitchen floor above.

"Indeed it is!" the Bard smiled. "But on the positive side of the ledger, it maintains the virtues of a refreshing chill year round. One is seldom disturbed during the night, thus promoting unusually sound rest—so long as the sound of rats does not bother you. One is not forced to bunk with strangers here, for only those whom I deem worthy of entry are allowed within its confines, save only our good friend Master MacKraegen, who must occasionally enter our realms to procure his stores for the running of his business."

"But his wife is the cook," Percival said, trying to pull his head down lower than his collar for fear of what might drop down his neck. "Doesn't she have to come down for—"

"No! She above all is barred from coming into the wine cellar," Edvard said with quick emphasis. "It has to do with . . . local customs. Indeed, our accommodation here is most secure, as the door is barred from above each night."

"So," Percival sniffed, the damp air and an odd smell making his nose itch. "You live in a storeroom underground where there's no heat or light so that you may sleep on a hammock or sack of potatoes and you're locked in each night. Does this room have any additional charms?"

"Two additional and most attractive charms," the Dragon's Bard noted with a warm grin.

"And those might be?"

"First, the accommodation comes free of any encumbrance," the Bard said with a wink of his right eye. "I may have use of these accommodations without making my meager purse any lighter."

"And, no doubt, worth every silver piece charged for it," Percival observed as he glanced warily about him. "And this second charm?"

The Dragon's Bard flicked his eyebrows up twice above his radiant smile and stepped toward the back of the cellar. A large set of shelves holding a variety of small casks lay inside a rectangular frame half buried at an angle in the dirt wall. Edvard put out his hand to the latch on one of them and flicked it open. He then reached to three more, flicking each of them open in turn.

A sudden "thunk" resounded behind the shelves, and the frame shifted forward with a creaking sound. The Dragon's Bard reached out and swung the frame into the room, a groaning noise scraping on its old iron hinges.

Beyond lay a dark tunnel from which came a dreadful smell.

"A secret passage?" Percival whispered in awe, his eyes stinging from the vapors drifting out of the passage.

"That is it," Edvard said in triumph. "This was once the lair of the pirate Gentleman John Brennan. This secret passage was used by him personally to move about the town unseen, appearing at will as though he were an apparition out of the fog!"

"But, that's *good!*" Percival said, blinking as his eyes began to water from the fumes. "Did he command his pirate crew to dig this elaborate network secretly beneath the foundations of Blackshore?"

"Well, no," Edvard confessed. "Actually, he only had to dig about five feet of this passage and see to this elaborate portal being installed. Most of the tunneling was done by the Imperial Sappers under the direction of King Reinard almost thirty years ago now when he—"

"The sewer?" Percival gaped. "The secret tunnel leads to the sewer?"

"The most discrete way to travel, young lad, I assure you," the Bard said with a curt nod. Edvard reached for one of the torches stacked in a corner of the room. He ignited it with some effort on the single oil lamp that illuminated the cellar. "Besides, no one looks in sewers."

"Or goes into them," Percival affirmed.

"Come, Abel, there is little time to waste. Percival, stay here, my good friend!" Edvard called back through the door, his smile glorious in its exaggeration as Abel scurried beneath the Bard's arm into the rank, black passage beyond. "I've a quick call to make, and when I return, you and I shall address the question of this woman who has so tempestuously secured your heart! Be assured, my friend, that soon the Dragon's Bard will mend all!"

With that, Edvard slipped through the opening with his torch in hand, the door slamming shut behind him with a precipitous bang.

The Dragon's Bard's smile fell with the sound of the closing concealed door, as though his face were a cake in the oven jarred at the most inopportune moment.

Edvard turned, his expression drooping into a scowl that threatened to pull the upturned edges of his broad-brimmed hat down with it. He stalked off down the tunnel and into the brick-lined sewer, being careful of his step in the torchlight. It was true, he supposed, that the pirates had once traveled this sewer for their own concealment, and he had availed himself of it from time to time as circumstances in the town occasionally warranted a hasty act of discretion over valor. However, the truth was, he had a loathing of the sewers in any town. He followed this one quickly to its nearest opening, climbed up, and, as he had remembered, gratefully found himself and Abel standing in an actual alleyway just off of Centaur Alley. He followed the curving path northward and turned right up Master's Street, climbing the still mud-slick road with his high boots slipping from time to time beneath his stride. This angered him further as he made his way, and he began to mutter to his scribe, who was dutifully writing down every word for posterity to review. Abel knew from experience that the Dragon's Bard was at his most entertaining when he was not thinking about what he was saying.

"How could this happen to me . . . to *me!*" he snarled. He

spoke under his breath for the moment, but Edvard had no sense of the volume of his voice except when it came to hitting the furthermost seats in the largest of the guild halls or courts. True to form, his voice was rising with every uncertain step. "Have I failed to pay homage to the gods whenever they occur to me? No! Have I failed to give them offerings whenever I had more coins than I could spend? Never! Whenever I recognize that they have wrought a miracle in my behalf, have I not thanked them? Not once!"

Edvard wheeled around on his scribe, poking his boney finger into the shorter man's chest. The move dangerously threatened to bump Abel's pencil and mar the page on which he wrote. "So perhaps you can tell me *why* the gods themselves seem to have conspired against me with this Taylor whelp!"

Abel paused for a moment and opened his mouth to offer a thoughtful and carefully considered opinion . . . but the moment was lost as the Bard turned and continued his rhetorical conversation with the afternoon air.

"It does not matter why the gods have thus thrown these challenges before us in our course," Edvard declaimed, gesturing upward toward the sky. "We shall be magnanimous in our acceptance of these tests whereby we may *prove* ourselves more wise, more cunning, more determined, and more humble than a thousand priests of the Lady of the Sky put together! Yes, Abel, the gods themselves shall see that there will be none more humble than we . . . and it shall be through our undaunted efforts to be more humble than anyone else that we shall persevere."

The Bard suddenly wheeled around again, causing Abel to nearly run into him. Master's Street was fairly crowded by this time with a number of centaurs pushing and pulling wagons down the muddy road from the warehouses toward the quays. Several unregistered gnomes scurried along the edges of the street with ledgers in their hands, while a number of humans carefully made their way past. Despite the Bard's remonstrations, no one seemed to take much interest in his outburst, likely because he was coming from the direction of the two taverns in the town.

"And who does that chattering hag Zoltana think she is, telling Percival his destiny!" Edvard exclaimed. "*I'm* the one who was supposed to tell him his destiny . . . a destiny that was bought and almost—*almost,* mind you—paid for! Now we'll have to *work* for it!"

The word *work* came most distastefully out of Edvard's mouth. He drew in a great breath, trying to calm himself.

They were at the intersection of three roads. Memory Lane split away from the rise of Master's Street to the left, its narrow passage straight between large boardinghouses down either side. Here the road was fitted with paving stones, and trees rose on either side before the large houses. To his left, the vast expanse of Schnib's Trading dominated the sea of smaller roofs around it. Beyond Schnib's rose the rigging of the *Ark Royal,* her sails furled and tied with precision against the yards and her footropes carefully spaced. To the right lay Gentlemen's Way, although there was nothing gentlemanly about it; it rose precipitously up the slope toward Reinard Road and was a sodden mess of churned-up mud and deep ruts. Someone had rigged a windlass at the top of the street, and several centaurs were using it with a thick cable to pull a wagon loaded with supplies reluctantly up the slope.

Fortunately, the Bard's course did not require him to attempt the muddy ascent up Gentlemen's Way. As he looked up at the carved sign above his head, he could make out the shape of a chest with a hammer and chisel crossed in front of it and knew at once that he had found his destination.

"What time do you make it?" the Bard asked without preamble.

His scribe checked the sun and the shadows cast by the signage above their heads and replied that he counted five bells past the advent of the forenoon watch.

The Bard considered this thoughtfully for a time before giving up entirely. "What hour is it?"

Abel replied it was around thirty-seven minutes past ten in the morning—give or take a half hour—by the Imperial method.

The Bard was more comfortable with this answer. "Ah! Not too early, then, for calling."

Abel found this comment amusing since the shop, Walters

Casks, had no doubt been open for business since the crack of dawn.

Edvard adjusted the rakish angle of his hat brim, gripped the door handle, firmly depressed it, and strode confidently into the front of the shop—nearly stumbling over a stack of small wooden chests with metal fittings in his rush. The casks scattered noisily across the carefully fitted wooden floorboards with a tremendous racket.

"Here, now!" the woman behind the counter boomed in a voice that threatened to shake the glass in her windows from their leaded panes. "Have a care! Those casks are expensive. Feel free to tread on them all you like after you've bought and paid for them."

"Dear madam," Edvard began with an elegant sweep of his hand. "I am . . ."

It was the most words in a row that he would manage to get out for some time.

Calista Walters was a stoutly built woman with broad shoulders. She was as fierce as a hurricane and every bit as unrelenting. Even though at her full height her head barely came up to the level of the Bard's chest, he instinctively backed away from her. She held a wailing baby firmly on one hip in her left arm and wielded the stout finger of her right hand in the general direction of the Bard like a rapier blade as she advanced. She was ferocity invincibly armored in a skirt and petticoats, her coiled hair shielded by a lace-doily helmet.

"I know very well who you are, you rascal!" Calista's voice drew all the wind out of Edvard's words against her red-faced blustering. "You're the Dragon's Bard from Eventide and the one who is supposed to have arranged the marriage between my niece Vestia and that no-good dreamer Percival Taylor, that's who!"

The Bard winced, his eyes narrowing perceptibly. Crying children were not among Edvard's favorite audiences, and this one seemed particularly shrill today. He was having trouble concentrating in the fury of the woman's assault.

"Yes, madam, and . . ."

"And nothing is what you've done!" Calista pressed her advantage in the attack, her jabbing finger pushing the Bard back up against the closed door and preventing all possibility of escape. "It's none of my affair how people conduct their lives so long as they are decent with each other and pray to the Ocathion, the Goddess of the Sea, like any good person should. I don't get involved. BUT Livinia is my sister by marriage and she is set on this marriage between her daughter and this Taylor boy . . . a marriage YOU told her that you could arrange just like you arranged that marriage between that Jarod Klump—"

"Klum," the Bard tried to wedge in the word, hoping it might lead to some leverage for further words behind it.

"Well, whatever his name is, she says you got him to marry that wishing well woman and that with a broken wishing well in the bargain," Calista continued. Several more children, having heard their mother yelling, rushed into the front of the shop. They were assorted shapes and sizes, but all of them were girls, the eldest of whom may have been as old as nineteen or twenty. This tallest of the group was wearing a leather apron and carrying a forging hammer as though it were as light as a quill. All were watching with intense interest as their mother yelled at someone other than themselves. "Livinia gave you a commission to get Vestia properly married to that Taylor boy—paid you part of it in advance—and now here you stand in my shop a good ten leagues from Eventide and from what I hear that Taylor boy is here too! So, it may be none of my business and I certainly do not put my hand to business where it's not welcome but perhaps you can explain to me how you are going to get that boy to propose marriage when he isn't even within a day's ride of where his intended lives?"

"It's interesting that you should ask—"

"I don't *have* to ask!" Calista bellowed. "The captain was in here just this morning off of the *Demeter* with a good laugh about how that lubber from Eventide was trying to talk his way onto every ship in the harbor! As if they would have him. He's such a helpless case that even the press gangs don't want him! Sooner or later that boy is going to talk his way past some drunken quartermaster. How will my niece manage to bring him before a priest if he's off drowned at the bottom of the West Ocean? If it were any of my business—which it isn't, mind you—I would have a good mind to send a message to my sister this same day demanding that she bring Vestia right to my house so that she could see what a fool she was setting her cap for!"

"YES!' shouted the Dragon's Bard as Calista took in a breath. "Do it! Right now!"

Calista had already formulated another tirade, but Edvard's response completely foundered her thought. Even the baby in her arms stopped crying at once. "What?"

"By all means, send a message to the beautiful Vestia at once," the Bard said quickly, sensing the opportunity to turn the tide. "Demand that she come to Blackshore immediately and take lodgings with you, and I promise you that within three months' time she will be wed as per my commission from your most honorable sister-in-law."

Everything might have been quickly resolved to the Bard's satisfaction had Percival simply done as he was told.

Despite the initially romantic notion of staying in a pirate's lair, Percival found these surroundings depressing, damp, and, above all, boring. He told himself that he was a man of action who was not meant to hide out in a cellar, no matter how piratical that had seemed on first blush. Real pirates, he told himself, were bounding over the sea in their pirate vessels, the wizard ports spewing mystical fire over the decks of heavily laden treasure ships. They swung by the ropes that were tied all over the masts and sail-holders with broadswords held between their teeth while rescuing the likes of Tuppence Magrathia-Paddock with their free hands. True, he had heard that they buried treasure regularly, but real pirates probably hired people to do that for them since they were so rich.

The one thing he was pretty sure of was that they did not sit around in cellars waiting for adventure to come to them behind the potato sacks.

So Percival left the rather disinteresting environs of the pirate lair, slipped through the kitchen, and climbed back up to his rooms upstairs. He quickly put on what he believed was his most dashing outfit—kid leather leggings, his open-collared shirt tied loosely at his neck, the wide-brimmed hat that Merinda Oakman had fashioned for him on a special order from his mother to be patterned exactly after the Dragon's Bard's hat—and he finished it off by draping his cape over his shoulders and tying it in a neat bow in the front. Thus attired in the best fashion of all the best stories he had ever had told to him about the sea, Percival descended the stairs and slipped unnoticed by Stoney through the front doors of the Mistral's Mistress.

He decided to reconnoiter the town, to get the lay of the land as a predator might study its prey. He supposed that if he were to pursue the life of a pirate rogue, he might one day have to plunder the town, and therefore an advanced familiarity with it would serve him well in the future. He moved with studied casualness down the quay, slipping surreptitiously between barrels, crates, and open cargo. His course was distracted for a few minutes as he noticed several mermen working with the *Mary Celeste,* a three-masted barque just coming into the harbor. The mermen were guiding the ship through the narrow channel and toward where all the boats were tied up.

Percival was fascinated by the mermen. He had heard stories about them but had never met one before. Mermaids, of course, were legendary beauties, and he half hoped to see one. So fascinated was he by the mermen pushing the large ship along that Percival passed Master's Street without a glance.

He made it as far as crossing in front of the door to Gilly's Alehouse when two massive hands at the ends of two equally enormous arms grabbed him and dragged him into the darkness.

The Traveler's Travails

CHAPTER 5

Professor Nick-Knack

I s this the one, mother?" said the hulking giant as he pressed Percival down to sit on a chair.

"Yes, he is the one," responded the woman.

"Who are you and what do you mean by—" Percival began but then stopped in surprise. "Madame Zoltana!"

"You *do* remember me," Zoltana smiled. "I am touched."

"Of course I remember you," Percival said with annoyance. "We only met last week."

"Ah, but so much can change in a week's time," Zoltana replied. "One day you think you have life all figured out . . . your future is set and your destiny within your grasp. Then the next day—poof!—you discover that everything you thought was true is suddenly only a dream and your future is obscured. Take Gilliam Gorgantua here, for example."

Percival looked up at the enormous innkeeper. Even

though he was over six feet tall, he looked as though someone had made him out of clay and then pressed down on him. He was wide, with enormous arms and stout legs. His face was block shaped, with prominent ridges above his eyes obscured by thick, bushy brows. He had a lantern jaw with a slight dimple, and his long, flowing mane of hair was tangled and matted.

"Take him?" Percival stared back at the man's deep set, dark eyes, convinced that he would never see the man blink. "Take him where? He dragged *me* in *here*."

Madame Zoltana drew in a deep, calming breath. "I mean that you should consider his story. Gilliam used to be what one might consider a freelance guard, wandering the countryside in search of places that might need someone with his qualities to enforce proper authority. Sadly, his family could not provide him with a better start in life—"

"I've told you time and again not to upset yourself about that, Mother," Gilliam said with a sincere rumble of displeasure.

"Yes, I know, but—"

"You're his mother?" Percival asked in surprise.

"Yes . . . and since his family could not provide him—"

"But his last name is Gorgonzola or something, and you're Zoltana," Percival persisted.

"It's a stage name!" Zoltana's voice rose as her face reddened. She drew in another breath. "The point is that one day he walked into this establishment looking for work. The place was run by a gnome named Phlebish who was trying to deal with a particularly tough crowd of rum runners the night he showed up. Gilliam established order in the tavern—at the expense of a number of the smuggler crewmen—and Phlebish hired him on the spot."

"And that was a big change in his life?" Percival was having trouble following the point of the story.

Zoltana blinked behind a forced smile. "No. The change was that Phlebish was so impressed with Gilliam . . ."

"Or possibly rather drunk on rum," the enormous man offered.

" . . . that the gnome wrote Gilliam into his will that same night and was found dead the very next morning."

Percival's jaw dropped. "That's terrible!"

"For the gnome, yes," Zoltana nodded. "But since gnomes do not exist, by royal decree, when the will was read it was decided best to set aside all questions about the alehouse by simply titling it to Gilliam without question."

"It's really rather miraculous if you think about it," Percival nodded. "Gnomes never write in any language other than their own. It's a wonder they found anyone at all who could read it . . ."

"Yes, it was," Zoltana forged ahead. "So, you see, Gilliam's entire life changed in an instant because of a piece of paper."

"Yes, I can see that," Percival nodded.

"And what about you, Percival?" Zoltana said, moving around the youth's chair near the center of the closed alehouse, the long fingers of her hands sweeping across his shoulders. "You are a handsome young man, with daring and an eye toward adventure."

Percival considered this as dispassionately as possible. "Yes, that is true."

"Haven't you felt that there was something more for you in life than being a tailor's son in a backwater country town?" Zoltana crooned into his ear. "That somehow you never did fit in with your own family? That you were different from them somehow?"

Percival's brows drew together. "Yes . . . sometimes . . ."

"Didn't your parents seem like strangers to you?" Zoltana continued.

"Well, I got along fine with Mother," Percival shrugged, "except she always seemed to cling to me and keep me from doing things."

"Holding you back," Zoltana urged. "Trying to make you into something that you are not?"

"Yes, now that you mention it," Percival nodded. "I don't know why I never saw it before."

"Because Madame Zoltana has discovered the reason for it," the woman said, bringing her angular face to look straight into Percival's eyes. "Because I have discovered papers that prove that you were *adopted!*"

Percival was struck dumb, his jaw slack in his shock. "Can I . . . can I see these documents?"

"Shortly, yes," Zoltana assured him.

"Yeah," Gilliam agreed enthusiastically. "They're upstairs drying right now."

"Drying?" Percival asked.

"It's the damp air so near the water," Zoltana quickly said. "It's made the ink . . . unstable . . . after so long in the dry vaults beneath the castle in Mordale."

"I see," Percival nodded with a distracted frown. "So . . . I'm not Percival Taylor?"

"That's right," Zoltana said solemnly. "You are actually Percival Merryweather, the lost son of Captain Merryweather."

"But . . . but I *know* the Widow Merryweather!" Percival exclaimed. "That doesn't make sense . . . she's known me my entire life . . ."

"Not *that* Captain Merryweather!" Zoltana snapped. "This is an entirely *different* Captain Merryweather altogether! Probably a brother . . . or a cousin."

"But why would—"

"Why do you find this so difficult to understand?" Zoltana said, Percival's head held firmly between her hands. "Haven't you felt that you were born to more than this? Didn't you know in your heart that some mistake was made? Do you find it so hard to believe that you are *not* the son of some tradesman and his wife but are, in fact, the son of Captain Edmund

Merryweather, who sailed with the most fabulous treasure known to the Five Kingdoms some fifteen years ago and never returned? And it is *you,* Percival—his true son and rightful heir—who will find this treasure, rescue your father, and discover your true destiny!"

Percival looked up suddenly at Zoltana, slamming his right fist into his hand.

"I *knew* it! I'm not just Percival Taylor. I'm someone *special!*"

"That's right," Zoltana nodded with satisfaction. "And if you're going to rescue that treasure and your true father, you need to meet the one man who can help you find them both."

The bronze plate by the gate showed the relief image of a mermaid lying in a languorous pose on a stone with breakers on either side. Below were inscribed the words "The Siren's Rest Boardinghouse, #17 Memory Lane, Blackshore." If one then looked more closely still, one would notice just below these, in much smaller letters, the inscription: "Professor Nicholas Balderknack, #17B."

Memory Lane was an island of civilization surrounded by commerce and trade. Whereas most of the streets in Blackshore might be generously described as only defined by the limits of the building on either side, Memory Lane had carefully laid setts—squared and shaped granite stones—in a herringbone pattern all the way from the intersection of Master's Street and Gentlemen's Way in a straight line until it ended at Wizard's Way and the Port Anghel Road. The sides of the street had raised gutters, which were generally known only in the finest streets of Mordale, and trees—still young and barely fifteen feet in height—had been planted at regular intervals.

The Siren's Rest provided lodgings for wives whose men had not returned from the sea. Widow Hendebruk had taken the position of managing this house after her own husband had failed to return from the sea and the years of her watch for his return had grown long and gray. This large house dominated the entire north side of Memory Lane, featuring not only a second story but an amazing dome rising above its gables on either side. The dome had a widow's walk at its crest, created specifically for women who stayed at The Siren's Rest so that they might climb the circular back staircase and make their way up to the top of the dome. There they could look out beyond the waters of the bay and Mistral Sound to the open ocean beyond.

Their eyes would peer across the waters looking for some sign that would soothe the hollow in their hearts. They never once considered what their benefactor—Professor Nick-Knack, as many of the local merchants called him—might be doing beneath the dome on which they stood.

Percival fidgeted.

Everything in the room was making him uncomfortable. It was a rotunda situated on the first floor of The Siren's Rest that rose up through the second story and to a domed ceiling overhead. The underside of the dome was a carefully rendered fresco that depicted some sort of map of the stars, with different-sized dots of white against a deep blue background all connected into shapes by faint, yellow lines. Tall columns of polished marble supported the dome, with leaded glass windows filling the arches that connected the columns at the top near the dome. Some of these were propped open, allowing a light and freshening breeze into the space.

Beneath this was a circular balcony level filled with beautifully finished wooden cases. Many of these were filled with more books than Percival had believed ever existed, while others displayed objects that were at once fascinating and frightening. There were a minotaur war-mask, polished and carefully preserved; a pair of crossed dwarven fire-axes; and several elegant versions of fairy snares. There were also numerous elegant and exotic bottles set in various niches, each with its stopper removed and sitting to the side of its matching container. There were two doors that exited the balcony level, but both of these were closed, their shining finish showing some dullness from the passage of time. The balcony itself was ornately finished with a narrow, circular staircase sweeping in a great arc down to the floor of the rotunda where Percival stood.

This level was, if anything, more confused than the balcony, for the overstuffed fading red chairs, the polished tables, and even the inlaid marble floor itself were difficult to see beneath the piles of books, papers, and assorted bizarre items that seemed to occupy every horizontal surface. Shadow puppets with strange outlines made of translucent leather leaned against crystal geodes on the left, while a seashell necklace lay draped casually over a weathered, wooden shield with strange and frightening markings on the right. Numerous statues of varying sizes stood about the room, monstrous and frightening shapes of creatures for which Percival had no name. Two full sets of armor—each radically different from the other— stood at the side of the room; one of them reached nearly to the bottom of the balcony twelve feet above the floor. No fewer than three separate book stands supported their own enormous bound collections of maps and charts. Although Percival knew his letters, his reading skills were not yet as developed as perhaps they should be, yet even he could tell that most of these maps were notated in scripts completely foreign to him. The main floor of the rotunda was nearly overwhelmed by an enormous wooden globe fixed inside a series of supporting rings in polished brass. Its original surface was a carved map, but various different parchments, hides, and cloth had been affixed to that surface with corrections to the map, some drawn over the top of other maps until the entire globe was nearly filled three levels deep in corrected map sections. The entire device could apparently be turned in any direction by a series of gears and adjustment wheels in intricate workmanship. Attached to this framework, too, was a complex series of magnifying lenses, each mounted on swivel arms so that they might achieve different combinations with which to look down onto the various maps pinned to the globe. Next to these controls stood a tall writing desk almost completely covered in papers, a quill lying on its side at the top of the desk, and the stopper in the ink jar waiting to be pulled.

The dizzying height of the rotunda coupled with its discomfiting contents left Percival feeling slightly nauseated.

"Stop fidgeting," the woman crowed, slapping Percival's hands back down against his sides for a second time.

It did not help his nerves that he was standing next to Madame Zoltana, who was eyeing everything in the room with perhaps too much appreciation. He looked longingly toward the double doors through which Widow Hendebruk had ushered them into the room upon their arrival—although not without giving both of them a disapproving inspection before allowing them inside. As he watched, one of the side doors on the balcony above abruptly opened.

Through it stepped a slight man with a rangy frame. He looked to be about forty years of age, although his peppered hair was already thinning at the top. He had a slightly receding chin and a rather prominent, hawkish nose with bushy greying brows above both eyes. His eyes were striking, a steel blue in color that caught your attention at once, for they were filled with infinite wonder and sadness. He wore a silk swordsman shirt with puffy sleeves and was buttoning a jerkin with wooden toggles on top of it and over his pants. He was barefoot as he rushed down the curving staircase toward them.

"My apologies for my dress," he said with a pleasant coastal accent. "I was not expecting callers."

"No need to apologize to us, Professor," Madame Zoltana offered with a magnanimous gesture of her hand. "I fear we must apologize to you for disturbing your rest."

"It is no matter, no matter at all," the Professor said as he came to the bottom of the stairs, quickly navigating the jumble of furniture and objects between them as he joined them in the center of the room. "Is this the boy?"

"It is," Madame Zoltana said with confidence.

"So, you're Captain Merryweather's son," the Professor said, looking at Percival in a way that reminded the young man of a butcher appreciating a cow. "Tell me about yourself."

"He was adopted," Madame Zoltana said quickly. "I've brought the patents with me, of course, all very much in order, and a number of sworn affidavits collected in Eventide at the time of his—"

"Of course you have," the Professor said, waving his

dismissive hand. "But I want to talk to the boy. What is your name, son?"

"Percival, sir," he responded at once. "Percival Taylor . . . I mean, Merrywitter—no, Merryweather, sir."

"Well, Master Merryweather," the tall man said, extending his hand. "I am Nicholas Balderknack—Professor Balderknack, by appointment of his Royal Highness King Reinard. Most people around Blackshore call me Professor Nick-Knack, but you can just call me Professor if you like. Please, sit down and—oh, sorry!"

Professor Nick-Knack quickly snatched a stack of books from the chair on which Percival was about to sit down. "I wasn't expecting visitors today."

"It was fortunate that you came to me," Zoltana exclaimed before they had settled into their overstuffed chairs facing each other over a low table near the center of the rotunda hall. "As I foretold, the son of Captain Merryweather has been found and brought before you, Professor. I am but a humble practitioner of the arts of fortune, and I would be most grateful for your advancing to me the fee we discussed for discovering the boy and bringing him to you."

"Fortunate fortune indeed when it is proven true," said Professor Nick-Knack, his hands pressed together and his two forefingers on his lips. "And you shall have earned it and more as soon as the veracity of this boy's claim is established and the expedition properly outfitted."

"Expedition?" Percival asked. "Where are we going?"

"Quite possibly . . . everywhere," Balderknack said, leaning forward with a glint in his eye.

"Everywhere?" Percival gulped.

"Son, I've brought tales back from all over the world," the Professor said, leaning back into his enormous chair. "I've seen the titans of the east in their hidden kingdoms beneath the Maruanth Mountains. I've bartered with the djinn of the sand-seas of Abrathas for the privilege of sailing across their domain. I've fought in the arenas of Minoria in single combat against their finest minotaur gladiators. I've escaped the Mermaid Grottos, withstood the siren's call, and wept at the sound of the trees singing in the heart of the Soundless Forest. I have seen the kraken in its lair at the bottom of the ocean and conversed with the Lords of Thunder in the cloud-castles above Mount Xhan. I've been a part of every adventure the world has ever known, but there is one place—*one* place to which I am desperate to return and only *you* can show me where to find it."

"Me?" Percival asked.

"Yes, you!" Zoltana urged.

"I will finance the venture entirely, and you will, if we succeed, garner the greatest treasure you'll ever know," the Professor said, leaning forward again.

Percival was thinking. If he was the son of Captain Merryweather—and not just the son of a tailor from Eventide—then this could be his chance to find his destiny, live a life of adventure, and impress the Governor's daughter with perhaps relatively little inconvenience to himself. Still, even though he was trying to talk himself into being the adopted son of a romantically tragic sea captain, there was still a practical Taylor side remaining in his thinking.

"And what about you?" Percival asked. "Where's your profit in all this?"

"You recover your father and his golden treasure," the Professor said quietly, with a little more pain showing in his eyes than he would have preferred to share. "I recover something far more precious to me."

CHAPTER 6

Djara Djinni

Professor Balderknack quite unexpectedly traveled backward twenty years through time.

His body remained in the present. He supposed afterward that to the casual observation of Percival and Madame Zoltana, his entire journey was but an awkward and prolonged pause in an already awkward and prolonged conversation. But as he sat there and answered the youth's question, he could not help but take the journey once again and remember . . . remember with painful, glorious clarity, that summer two decades before.

For though his guests in his vaulted trophy room could not see it, Professor Balderknack—the most reputed adventurer and honored explorer of their age—was standing on the aft railing of the warship *Royal Trident,* watching with painful longing the receding shoreline of Blackshore Bay and throwing up his breakfast over the side.

Nicholas Balderknack was contemplating whether or not one might be able to die from seasickness.

The rolling motion of the ship under his feet made his stomach lurch at every swell. His legs had acquired a strange, rubbery quality that no longer desired to support him in the way he had been accustomed to since he was eighteen months old. Sleep was his only relief—when it came—but the crew of the *Royal Trident* seemed to take much delight in rousting him out of bed and putting him to tasks that he could not do to anyone's satisfaction since he was constantly having to lurch to the rail in the middle of his assigned duties. When the crew tired of the spectacle of this pathetically helpless lad hanging with a green pallor over the side of the ship, they would at last roll him into his hammock and leave him alone for a while. There he could close his eyes and try to ignore the timbers that swayed dizzyingly around him and wait for his insides to stop moving as well.

Nicholas hated to travel.

He had been orphaned at the unfortunate age of eight years. His mother, Hani Balderknack, had died at the time of his birth. His father, Noal Balderknack, had been a shoemaker with a fine business in South Breakershire, or so the son had come to understand later in his life. Noal had wanted to secure a future for his lone son and moved to Blackshore with a chest filled with sample shoes and a desire to open new markets across the sea. Leaving Nicholas in town with his nurse, Noal set out from Blackshore aboard the *Nyad*, bound for the Minos coast. The sea, it seemed, took exception to the plan, for nothing was heard of Noal Balderknack or the *Nyad* again.

Nicholas's nurse, Wansey Drevan, was also Noal's housekeeper and took charge of the remaining stock in the shoemaker's workshop as compensation for raising the boy. She proved herself inept at both occupations, using the boy as an indentured servant and ultimately squandering the proceeds from the shoe stock. She also devoutly believed that she had been cursed at an early age by a traveling wizard—although she was never specific about the details—and therefore strictly forbade even the mention of magic in her household, let alone allowing it to be used. Her own husband, Burke Drevan, was a trained rope maker but much preferred pursuing a professional career as a drunkard. Wansey often would tell stories to Nicholas about how fortunate he was to be beaten only on the weekends because the world outside was far worse. She would then tell him tales of how his father had been eaten by a magically controlled kraken or how his father had been tortured by angry magical ghosts or how his father had been driven mad in the magical labyrinths while minotaur mages laughed and bet on how long his mind would last. Nicholas believed these stories through most of his youth, and they planted in him a desire to stay put and hide from the world—as well as from the Drevans, at least whenever Burke was having his increasingly frequent terrors. When this happened, Burke would beat Nicholas. As Nicholas got older, however, his reflexes improved and he learned that he could quickly move to avoid the blows. But this only infuriated Burke more, who would then beat his not-so-quick wife, and she in turn would beat Nicholas all the harder for it.

Then, in the year that Nicholas turned seventeen years of age, Burke got a little too drunk and hit his wife very much too hard. Wansey Drevan fell on the spot without a sound and would never do anything ever again. By the time the governor in Blackshore was finished with his inquiries, Burke also found his silence in Hangman's Square . . . and Nicholas Balderknack found himself with three gold, six silver, and two copper coins in the pouch tucked under his belt; two extra sets of clothes in a sack slung over his back; and six pairs of shoes. Once again, he was on his own. He remembered a little of the shoemaking trade his father had taught him in the hazy past. "Pa" Burke had unintentionally taught him never, *ever* to drink anything harder than cider, and "Ma" Wansey had instilled in him a curiosity about magic and the greater world, though he still was loath to go anywhere new or unfamiliar.

Having nowhere to go, Nicholas remembered having seen a sign outside of town for the Mistral's Mistress tavern. He managed shyly to ask several of the ladies standing around the square who had come to observe the hanging where he might find the "mistress establishment" and was puzzled at their indignation. Soon, however, he remembered the full name of the tavern and was able to get directions toward the waterfront. He started down Queen Nance's Lane before Burke had even stopped swinging.

He did not make it as far as the tavern door. A press gang from the *Royal Trident* happened to have come ashore at just this moment and decided that this tall and awkwardly moving young man would be easy pickings for their task. Beatings had become a way of life for Nicholas, and so being pummeled and rousted into the ship's jolly boat seemed vaguely like some form of greeting that he didn't understand.

And now he lay in the hammock once more.

"You lot pay attention now!" the captain shouted next to Nicholas's ear. The young man might have started completely out of the hammock if he had had any strength left to do so.

"This here is an example of what *not* to do in a press gang!" the captain snarled, his swagger stick smacking against the bulge of Nicholas's small rump at the bottom of the hammock. "This piece of jetsam isn't worth a broken peg on a backstay. He's not even good for ballast. He can't work, can't pull his weight, and though he doesn't eat much, he *does* eat, which means that he's taking up space and food that another man who's *worth* something might use. Now I'm telling the lot of you . . . the next time you press gang someone aboard a king's vessel that is as unserviceable as this piece of hanging meat, you'll have the devil to pay and that's a promise!"

Nicholas opened his eyes. The ship was moving far more than he remembered. He fought the urge to close his eyes again.

"Captain!" came a call down the ladder from the gun deck above.

"What is it, Mister Ordan?"

"Weather ahead, sir!"

"Ahead be hanged," the captain replied. "I'm feeling the swell now. All hands on deck, Mister Ordan . . . and see that the gun ports and carriages are secure."

"Aye, sir!"

Nicholas heard the rushed footsteps on the planking around him and then he realized he was alone. He rolled sluggishly to one side and fell out of the hammock, sprawling on the deck. It felt good to be facedown against the wooden planks, but he realized that those too were heaving more than he remembered. There was also a howling, shrieking sound that he had not heard before.

He pushed himself up from the deck and staggered over to the ladder leading up to the lower gun deck. He could hear the hammers battening down the main hatch two decks overhead. The air on the berth deck had ceased whatever meager circulation it might previously have claimed. It was stifling, and both his head and his stomach knew that he had to get out to fresher air. He gripped the railings on the ladder and hauled himself up.

The lower gun deck was deserted. He could see the rows of wand-cannons lining the deck, each one fixed in place. The gunnery mage for each division would be in charge of those during battle, triggering the mystical forces of each to hurl either projectiles or magical charges against enemy vessels. He had heard of such things but had never actually seen one in use. They were not entirely reliable, and an occasional misfire was inevitable. Part of the gunnery mage's job was to balance required force against the risks of something going wrong. A properly trained gunnery mage, he had heard the captain say once while Nicholas's head was over the aft rail, was the point on which victory or defeat was balanced.

At the moment, however, such glorious thoughts were pushed from his mind. He could feel a cascade of air from the overhead hatch, so he gripped the next ladder and pulled himself up in a sprint past the main gun deck and onto the weather deck above.

His feet slipped instantly from under him and he slid across the deck, smashing against the port side bulwark. He instinctively wrapped his arms around a set of block and tackle extending to the backstays and looked back across the deck.

Rain poured down on him as the wind howled in the rigging overhead. The world had gone a gray-green everywhere he looked. For a moment, the sea itself seemed to be at an odd angle, as though the deck of the ship was level and the world was tilted. The placid surface was gone, replaced by enormous, roiling waves capped in curling white, often appearing twice the height of the ship's freeboard. The crew members were climbing the ratlines into the rigging, moving along the foot-ropes to reef the sails. He could hear the sailing master shouting from the quarterdeck, his voice nearly swallowed by the wind.

The world was in motion around him.

Something inside him moved too.

He quickly pulled himself up on the bulwark railing and leaned over the side, reflecting that it was the only thing he had learned to do about the ship thus far.

He was bent over the rail when the wave reached up from the depths and dragged him, unnoticed, into the sea.

It was still.

Nicholas awoke, head laid to the side down on warm sand.

"Who are you?"

Nicholas cried out and pushed himself up from the sands with a start at the sound of the melodic voice, the brilliant white grains cascading from the side of his face.

Sitting before him on the sands was a woman. She had smooth, olive-colored skin with an elegantly wide nose set in an oval face. Her smallish mouth nevertheless had full, rose-hued lips. Her black hair was pulled back from her face and woven into a long braid that extended down her back to a narrow waist. She wore a high-collared silken blouse with diaphanous sleeves, the same material that hinted at the beautiful shape of her legs within her silken pants. She sat cross-legged on the sand, her feet bare, with her long hands pressed together and her chin resting lightly at the apex of her fingers. But it was the large, almond-shaped eyes that held him spellbound: languid, liquid pools in which he longed to become lost.

"Whuh?" Nicholas was finding it difficult to form words.

She laughed, and it was as though the sun arose in his soul.

"Whuh!" she giggled, her eyes flashing at him. "What is a 'whuh,' and how did you become one?"

Nicholas shook himself largely, if not entirely, from his stupor. "No, I'm sorry . . . my name is Nicholas. Nicholas Balderknack."

"Nicholas-nicholas Balderknack?" The girl turned her head sideways in disbelief. "Where are you from, that your people should give you the same name twice?"

Nicholas couldn't help but stare at her. "I . . . I don't! I mean . . . you can just call me Nick. I guess my name is rather long."

"Not nearly so long as mine," the woman said with a sigh. "The last time it was recited in full was my Ascendance Day ceremony, and it took five readers in shifts to complete it in one week."

"That *is* a long name," Nicholas agreed. "What may I call you, then, or will that take a month?"

The woman smiled again and the sun seemed brighter. "You may call me Djara."

"Jara," Nicholas repeated softly.

"No," the woman said, shaking her head. "Djara."

"That's what I said," Nicholas was confused.

"No, you said 'Jara,'" she replied. "Djara is completely different."

"Perhaps you can help me with that," Nicholas urged, feeling an unaccustomed confidence as they spoke.

"We appear to have plenty of time," Djara noted, sweeping her arms around them, indicating the vast horizon.

For the first time, Nicholas examined their surroundings.

They sat on a spit of white sand under a brilliant blue sky. The turquoise of the surrounding reef deepened to a cerulean blue beyond the white breakers of the surrounding coral reef about three hundred feet from shore. The white sands ran to a rise in the center no higher than two feet above the shore. The spit of sand was no more than fifty feet across at its widest point and perhaps two hundred feet long.

There was not a single plant or tree to be seen, nor even a rock outcropping to provide any hope of shelter or shade.

"Do you like my bottle?" she asked.

"How long have you been here?" Nicholas asked in turn as he looked back at the woman, not fully comprehending what she was saying.

Djara shrugged, then gathered up her knees in her arms,

her bare toes digging into the sands. "I do not know. The sands wash clean each night and it gets tiresome counting the suns as they pass by. Time becomes meaningless when you have no one with whom you may watch it pass."

Nicholas laughed briefly and then looked around once more. "But how have you survived here? There is no water you can drink . . . no food to eat. There's no shelter from the sun or the—"

"Are you hot?"

"I . . . what do you mean?"

"Do you feel the heat of the sun on your skin?" she asked with a rueful smile. "Does your skin burn?"

Nicholas thought for a moment. He realized he had been sitting in the sunlight for some time, and while the temperature was comfortable, he did not feel the warmth on his skin.

"But . . . what do we eat?" he asked.

"Let me tell you a story," Djara said, standing up.

"A story?"

"Yes, it is a good story, and it will please you to hear it," Djara continued. "It is about a kingdom far beyond the sea where the sphinxes rule beneath the peaks of the Xhai Ne Mountains."

"Where the pink what rules?" Nicholas asked, his gaze fixed on Djara's eyes.

"No . . . the sphinxes," Djara continued, her lithe arms sweeping gracefully out as she gestured. "Winged creatures of distant lands whose bodies resemble lions but with large heads looking like humans."

Djara got to her feet and began to dance as she spoke, kicking up the sands around them. "Next to a glacial lake they built their greatest city in a mountain bowl. They called it Tsaranju, and it was where the wisest of the wise came each year for a contest of wits and knowledge. They came from many different lands, from the distant horizons of the world, in hopes that they might win."

The sands flew upward around them, swirling in the air, shifting and gathering. Suddenly the sands grew denser in the air, the crystals reflecting different hues. They became walls, towers, streets stretching out beyond the lagoon surrounding the spit of sand. Clouds on the horizon shifted as well, becoming mountain peaks covered in snow as Nicholas watched in wonder.

"But it was in the marketplace—the great bazaar of Tsaranju—where the most unlikely of heroes appeared: a tired and hungry traveler from a distant land. He had heard of the fabled wealth of Tsaranju and knew that there would be great treasures brought by all those who came to match their wisdom against one another. He had been a slave of thieves, and it was all that he had been taught from his youth, but he was a good man with a good heart looking for a way to change his fate. Yet on this day, his fate would have to wait, because he was standing in the market with no money and his hunger held the better part of his conscience at bay."

The sands became the stalls of the marketplace. Nicholas could hear the muffled sound of sellers crying out their wares. In front of him, a mound of sand rose up from the ground, shaping into a stack of white-sand apples.

Nicholas smiled.

Djara continued her dance about Nicholas in the bazaar that had risen from the sands. "But though he was tempted, his heart would not allow him to steal again. He tried to think of a way whereby he might get an apple honestly, and he might have done so if fate had not stepped in and made his decision for him. For he was a child of fate and his name was . . . Nicholas!"

In the instant his name was said, the world changed.

Nicholas stood dressed in tattered rags, a knapsack leaning against his feet. The sounds of the enormous bazaar overwhelmed him. The air was cool from the snow-capped mountains towering above him. He could smell the spices, their aromas mixing from the various stalls that formed a patchwork in every direction in the large square. More remarkable still, they were attended by towering creatures that looked just as Djara had described them; their bodies those of lions, with large, human-looking heads. They wore coats of bright colors ornamented with golden brocade woven into the cloth from which the brilliant feathers of their multicolored wings emerged. The spindly towers of the city rose above the bazaar, magnificently delicate and decorated in intricate patterns of blue, green, and golden tiles.

He turned back to the apples. They no longer looked like they were made of sand but gleamed in the morning light with a polished shine. As he moved closer to examine them, a small imp darted out from beneath the table. He glanced at Nicholas, then at the sphinx fruit vendor who had turned his back to the table.

It was all the opportunity the imp needed. The little creature snatched an apple from the cart and tossed it at Nicholas.

Surprised, Nicholas caught the apple.

"Thief!" screamed the imp, pointing at Nicholas.

The sphinx fruit vendor wheeled around at once.

Nicholas looked at the sphinx.

The sphinx looked at the fruit in his hands.

"Run!" yelled Djara, grabbing Nicholas by his free hand and dragging him away.

The sphinx roared in outrage, leaping over the fruit cart in a bound.

"This way!" Djara cried, gripping Nicholas's hand as he ran as fast as he could between the stalls. The sound of the sphinx crashing behind them was closer with every step.

Djara tugged on Nicholas's arm. "This way! Hurry!"

Nicholas struggled to keep up as Djara ran in front of him down a narrow alley between the buildings. They were dashing through a maze into an ancient part of the city that had, by the look of the failing walls, been abandoned.

Suddenly, the ground beneath them gave way. Nicholas cried out as they tumbled down into a steeply slanting shaft, sliding farther into the darkness . . . deeper below the mountain.

At last Nicholas and Djara came to a halt. His eyes were slowly growing accustomed to the darkness and he was relieved that he could no longer hear the sound of the sphinx in pursuit.

"Are you all right?" Nicholas managed to say between gulping breaths. "Djara?"

He could barely make out the outline of her figure as she stood a few feet ahead of him. "Behold, Nicholas! The lost Palace of Time!"

Nicholas took a few steps forward and then stopped.

Light grew from an unseen source, illuminating a vast cavern before them. Nicholas could not see the bottom of the chasm despite the growing glow. The space was over a mile across, and there, suspended as though flying in the center of the cavern and emitting the growing luminosity, was a temple of magic and power. Its towers sparkled with countless gems, untouched for millennia.

"It is said that the greatest treasure of the ancients awaits the one who can conquer its challenges," Djara whispered.

Nicholas took another staggering step forward, his jaw dropping in wonder.

"But that," Djara said, "is a story for another time."

Nicholas's jaw was still slack as he stood once more on the white spit of sand in the midst of the ocean.

Djara was smiling, gesturing toward Nicholas's hand. "You said you wanted something to eat."

Nicholas looked down.

He had forgotten about it, but he still held the apple.

He raised it to his lips. Its surface was smooth and cool.

He bit into it.

The juice ran down his chin.

"Do you like my bottle?" Djara asked.

Nicholas could only nod.

"I am pleased," she said with a sad smile. "But there is a catch . . ."

CHAPTER 7

Lost Shores

Nicholas stopped short of his second bite of the apple.

"A catch?" he asked as the apple hovered just past his lips. For all he knew, it had been sand only moments ago, and he had the suspicion that it could all too easily be sand once again with equal felicity.

"Yes, my Sayyid," Djara said, the sunlight dimming as her eyes became downcast. "There is a balance in the realms of fire, earth, water, and air, the foundation of our magic, which it is forbidden to violate. Our lives and our existence are bound to its very laws. No power can take from the celestial creation with one hand without giving with the other."

"I see . . . no, I don't," Nicholas said, still holding the apple in front of his face. "I mean, we just went somewhere, didn't we? I brought back this apple, didn't I?"

"Well, that depends upon where you stand." Djara smiled back at him with a breeze that was fresh and pure.

"I'm standing on an island of sand in the middle of the ocean," Nicholas answered. "But not a moment ago you and I both were running through a marketplace. That's where I got this apple . . . if it *is* an apple."

Djara frowned. "Does it not taste delicious?"

"It is perhaps the most perfect apple I have ever tasted," Nicholas replied, shaking the partially eaten fruit in emphasis as he spoke. "But, please, I'm very confused. Just answer my questions and I think I can understand what is happening here. Now, that marketplace we were running through . . . did you take us somewhere or was the place entirely an illusion?"

Djara considered for a moment then answered, "No."

"No?"

"No."

"No to which?"

"No to both."

Nicholas drew both his hands up to the sides of his head in frustration, apple juice sticking to his hair. It gave him an idea. He held out the apple toward Djara, who was once again sitting cross-legged on the sands before him.

"This apple," Nicholas said carefully. "Is it a real apple?"

Djara giggled sunshine. "Yes, of course it is an apple!"

"A real apple?"

Djara nodded.

"And there are no trees on this island?"

Djara nodded again, enjoying the game.

"And you say we didn't go anywhere?"

Djara giggled and nodded again.

"So," Nicholas asked through another bite from the apple, "where did this apple come from?"

"From a stall in the bazaar of Tsaranju," Djara replied at once.

"But you said we didn't go anywhere, including the bazaar of Tsaranju!"

"Hah! Of course not. I brought the bazaar of Tsaranju to us," Djara responded, slapping her hands down on her knees.

Nicholas had no reply.

"Such a fine diversion!" Djara said, standing quickly and rushing toward him. She threw her lithe arms about his neck, the curve of her body pressing against him with a familiarity that both thrilled him and panicked him at once. "I knew when I saw you passing in the storm that you would be a fine companion. Did I win?"

"Yes . . . you win!" Nicholas knew with despair that he was sweating profusely and was equally aware that there was nothing he could do about it.

"Oh, Sayyid!" the unworldly beauty said as her soft, long fingers felt along his brow. "You are over warm! Here, I have been an ungracious host. Let me tell you a story."

"No, I don't think—"

"But it is a good story and I think it will please you to hear it."

The sands of the atoll began shifting once again.

"Well," Nicholas began, trying hard to swallow a piece of apple that was threatening to stick in his throat. "I don't know if you really should . . ."

"It is of an ancient place deep within the forests of Hutanbaru," Djara said, her husky, warm voice speaking in honey tones. "There a civilization once arose that was the envy of all the kingdoms of the Tanah-aier. It was said that their gardens were lush with sweet and fragrant flowers whose colors were more vibrant than those anywhere else in the world."

Trees erupted from the sands, strange with clustered green spikes instead of leaves, towering over his head to impossible heights. The sand beneath his feet erupted into a carpet of soft, evenly hewn grasses. The turquoise waters swirled into a suddenly formed lake, darkening as the sands congealed into dark river stones beneath the clear waters. Beyond, a rising wave of sand solidified into a stone cliff face as waters began cascading clear and pure down its face. At its crest, obscured by the erupting dense foliage all around them and entwined around their bases stood a pair of elegant towers. One stood as an impossibly narrow spindle of alabaster and gold ornamented with enormous rubies. The second had broken, its top fallen down into the lake at the base of the waterfall, its tear-shaped pinnacle broken open.

"But one night, all the people of Hutanbaru vanished," Djara continued, standing by the water's edge as she spoke. "The land, it was said, was haunted by their ghosts, and none of the neighboring kingdoms dared enter to challenge the greatness of the fallen empire in their midst."

Nicholas smiled. Without thought, he stepped into the shallow waters of the pool. The water was cold around his feet, splashing about him as he rushed toward the fallen tower. He stumbled once, losing his footing on the smooth rocks and falling face first into the water. He pushed himself up, his mouth open and tasting the waters. The salt he expected was absent, with pure, fresh water in its place. He stood upright, forging ahead into waist-deep water as he came to the side of the fallen pinnacle. The broken stones of its crest lay shimmering beneath the surface under his feet. He reached down into the waters, his fingers wrapping around smooth contours.

He pulled upward, the object shining in his hands. It was unusually heavy, he thought, for its size.

"The ancient and glorious land was shunned as generation passed to generation, and the stories of the forbidden kingdom became legend." Djara's melodic voice came to him clearly across the waters despite the rushing of the waterfall nearby. "All remained hidden behind a wall of fear and folktale until one man came from far away who had not heard the stories of the fearful place. He knew no language of the Tanah-aier and so could understand none of their warnings as he crossed into the ancient gardens still mysteriously kept in pristine beauty. He alone had the courage to challenge the dead for their tragic secret."

Nicholas stared at the golden mask in his hands. Rubies, diamonds, and sapphires fitted into its crown.

"But," Djara continued with a sad edge to her voice, "that is a story for another—"

"Djara!" Nicholas cried out. "Wait!"

"Sayyid?" Djara asked, smiling.

"This is a good story," Nicholas said, gazing at the mask in his hands. "Have I a place in this tale?"

Djara laughed with unbounded joy. "Yes, Sayyid! You are the traveler who discovers this land."

"And you?" Nicholas asked, staggering back toward shore with the mask in his hands. "Are you also in this tale?"

"Do you wish it, truly, Sayyid?" Djara asked, her eyes wide with hope. "May I take a part as well?"

"I wish it," Nicholas said, flashing what he hoped was a winning smile in her direction. "We will take our part to-gether."

Nicholas had forgotten all about the "catch" . . .

They were approaching the Temple of Souls in the heart of Hutanbaru. Nicholas could see the broken dome of blue crystal piercing the jungle canopy beneath a golden sunset when, with downcast eyes, Djara turned to Nicholas. They stood atop a pinnacle of stone as she took his hands in hers.

"Sayyid," she said, shaking her head, "I have never had such joy as I have had this fortnight in your company. I would continue on with you with all my heart . . . but I fear that is a story for another time."

The twilight faded. The jungle collapsed into white grains about their feet. Once again, Djara and Nicholas stood on the flat dome of their island.

"No!" Nicholas insisted. "Take us back . . . I mean, *bring* it back! There is more still! We outwitted the serpent men and have been in touch with the spirits. We know how the curse may be broken and this land freed again. All we need is to get to the temple and fulfill our vow. It cannot be more than another day's journey as we will—"

"Hush, my Nicholas," Djara said, pressing her fingers to his lips. Her sadness was deep as an ocean. "There are rules, Sayyid, that must be obeyed. I am here under punishment, but even my captor must obey those laws—and so must I."

"Captor?" Nicholas asked. "What do you mean?"

"Do you like my bottle?" Djara asked, leaning into Nicholas once more. "Will you come back?"

"Back?" Nicholas laughed. "I'm not going anywhere."

"Yes, you are going," Djara sighed. "You must."

"No," Nicholas said, holding her by her beautiful round

shoulders so that he could look again into her large, enthralling eyes. "I'm staying here with you."

"A fortnight," Djara said, tears filling those same eyes. "For a fortnight each year, a mortal may come into my bottle and listen to my stories. But then he must leave me. That is the catch, my Sayyid: I might have joy for these fourteen nights so that I may spend the remainder of my time reflecting upon my past trespasses in loneliness and solitude."

"No, Djara!"

"I do not mind now, Sayyid." Djara looked at him with a wistful smile. "I have such great memories of our time and our stories. They will keep my heart warm and my spirit light. And, if you wish it, there is a way for you to return to me."

"Tell me," Nicholas begged. His eyes were fixed on her, but in that moment he thought, too, of the golden mask and jewels he had gathered that remained in the woven sack he had bartered from the natives of Hutanbaru. "How may I come back?"

"This ring," Djara said. She took the silver woven band from her finger and slipped it into his hand. "This is the key to my bottle. I can use it only to bring mortals in and send them back . . . but if you have it with you, all you must do to find me is set sail again in one year's time with this ring on your finger. Twist it thrice at sea and my bottle will open to you. The storm from the open bottle will then find you and bring you back to me."

"But if I have the key . . ."

"Then only you can come to me," she said as she looked up. The sands were beginning to blow across the island. The sky was darkening before the speed of the unnatural storm. "You take my heart and my hope with you!"

"But . . . what's the catch," Nicholas called out. "You said there is always a catch!"

"Come back to me, Sayyid!" Djara shouted above the gathering wind. It was already difficult for Nicholas to see her. "I've another story to tell . . ."

"I will come for you!" Nicholas shouted into the howling wind.

"Beggin' your pardon, Captain!"

Captain Shumach reluctantly opened one eye in his swaying bunk. A minotaur towered over his bed, his outline etched starkly by a flash of lightning from the aft windows of the captain's cabin. "This had better be important, Quartermaster. I've been fighting these seas all day and I'm in no mood to take you on as well."

"Sorry, Captain," Master Grobak rumbled. Both he and the captain knew that any physical match between them would have been entirely to the minotaur's advantage. Still, discipline had to be maintained even if it were illusory. "We've fished a human out of the water."

"Overboard?"

"Not one of ours, sir." Grobak shrugged his huge shoulders.

"Where away?" The captain's questions were difficult to hear above the crashing of the raging sea beyond the great cabin's glass and the whistling wind in the rigging coming through the planks above.

"To larboard, sir," Grobak answered. "It's a man, sir . . . he was clinging to a piece of jetsam."

"In these seas?" the captain said, struggling to put on his boots. The bunk was mounted on swivels so that it would remain relatively stationary while he slept, but the floor was another matter. It pitched violently beneath him.

"He was waving at us, sir," Grobak said. "We cast a line to him and hauled him aboard."

"We're only two days away from Blackshore," the captain grumbled. "This storm couldn't wait until we got to port and now we've got to deal with this . . . this . . . well, who is he, Grobak?"

"Answers to the name of Nicholas," the minotaur said as he left the cabin. "Don't know who he is, but he's got a bag full of right valuable swag, he has."

Nicholas returned to Blackshore with his woven sack filled with treasures from beyond the horizons of the known world.

To his astonishment, he discovered that a year had passed for everyone in the town since he had been press-ganged aboard the *Royal Trident* and fallen overboard—though to him it had barely been three weeks. His wealth of treasure could not be denied, and he was at once acclaimed as a great adventurer and supreme explorer . . . though he knew that he had actually gone no farther than two days out to sea. He had wanted to tell the truth, but once the crew of the *Helena*—the ship that had fished him from the storm-tossed sea—carried him into Gilly's Alehouse, they started asking about the golden mask. Suddenly Nicholas realized just how good a thing it was to know Djara—how profitable it most certainly could be—and how some good things one needed to keep to oneself. So he began to tell of Hutanbaru, the temples of that distant land and its enchantment, while carefully omitting any mention of Djara, the island, or the bottle in which all this had taken place.

He remembered, however, her words to him, and so with some trepidation, Nicholas bartered passage a year later aboard the *Barbarie Anne* to sail westward from Blackshore. The captain was suspicious, as Nicholas seemed unconcerned about the ports of call the ship would make on its journey, but as Nicholas had barely argued the price, greed had won out over the captain's curiosity. Nicholas weathered his stomach, which still lurched as it had on his first voyage, seemed relieved when the ship encountered a heavy storm on the third day out, and was dutifully at the rail when a wave once again swept him overboard.

It proved, indeed, a most profitable arrangement. He came to recognize the rules though Djara never explained them to him in a manner in which he could properly understand. He could never take more of the treasures from around the world than he could carry in his own hands. Once or twice he nearly drowned returning from the bottle when he misjudged the amount he could carry and it nearly dragged him to the bottom of the sea upon his return through the storm. Captains and their crews who retrieved him from the water were always handsomely compensated, and word got about to those who made port in Blackshore to be on the lookout for a man flailing about in a storm.

The wealth and fame of Nicholas Balderknack overflowed the bounds of Blackshore as the years passed. He was summoned to court and so impressed Their Majesties with his tales and his treasures that he was granted the title of Professor and an honorary chair in the Royal Lyceum Celestial as the King's Explorer. Still, he kept his home in Blackshore despite the urgings of the court to take his residence in Mordale. His treasures were so eclectic—and never very large—that he became known among his neighbors in Blackshore as Professor Nick-Knack.

Nicholas accepted these honors and accolades with grace and a smile—although he secretly knew that the "greatest explorer of the age" still got terribly seasick on ships and had actually never voyaged more than three days out from shore.

He set out on his fourteenth voyage aboard the *Mary*

Ann, a trade ship under the command of Captain Edmund Merryweather. His fortnight with Djara was supremely sublime as they sailed across a sea of glass to the Cavern of Sighs. He would forever remember her face beneath the full moon: the soft smile on her full lips and the peaceful adoration in her eyes. In that moment he forgot the treasures and the wealth and the honors and knew that after all he had come to truly love her.

But there are rules that must be obeyed, and fate would not afford an imbalance in the world of magic.

So it was that fate arranged for Nicholas to be picked up at the end of his fortnight in the bottle by that same ship, the *Mary Ann,* from which he had fallen overboard the year before. This fact was not lost on the captain's son, Ransom Merryweather, who made a few inquiries of his own upon reaching port in Blackshore.

And when the following year arrived, Ransom Merryweather paid a call on Professor Nick-Knack. It was too late when the Professor discovered that his ring was missing, for the *Mary Ann* had set sail with the tide a day earlier than expected and left a storm full of trouble in her wake.

Every year since that day, Professor Nick-Knack had searched the world, revisiting every place Djara had taken him, but he could not find his way back to her. He had come to know that the only way he could find his beloved again was to find the key to her bottle, and that meant finding Merryweather and the *Mary Ann.*

CHAPTER 8

The Dueling Buccaneer

"Now, isn't that just *ducky*," Madame Zoltana spat as they exited the front of The Siren's Rest and back onto Memory Lane. It was the word of last resort for her, a curse she reserved only for when all other curses failed her.

"What do you mean?" Percival asked, genuinely perplexed by the statement.

"He won't pay me until you actually set sail on this expedition of his," Zoltana seethed. "You would think that a man of his stature could afford a little more trust in his fellow human beings!"

"But I *am* the lost son of Captain Merryweather," Percival said. "You said you had the documents . . ."

"And so I do, deary, so I do," Zoltana said quickly, grabbing the boy by the arm. "But that's not enough for this untrusting man. He has money and power, and that always turns people to strange and suspicious ways. What you need to think about is your future. Do you want to go back to being the adopted son of a tailor or to reach for that destiny that called you here in the first place?"

Percival balked. "I really want to find my fate, Madame Zoltana . . . now more than ever. But this Professor Nick-Knack seems to think I'm some sort of buccaneer who's sailed all the waters of the Five Seas and—"

"*Nine* Seas, you idiot! There are *Nine* . . . oh, never mind," Zoltana said, dragging Percival behind her back toward the quays in her viselike grip. "If you ever want to claim your destiny, then you had just better figure out a way to be a buccaneer and it had better be *soon!*"

Percival sat at the small table in the middle of the cramped cellar room that comprised the "Pirate's Lair" and checked the list he had inscribed in pencil on parchment—both items having been borrowed from the scribe Abel's backpack.

Percival considered that his first true act of piracy.

He had been pondering, for the previous three days, what would be required of him to fulfill the obligations he was acquiring as a result of his presumed status. If he were to win the heart of Tuppence Magrathia-Paddock, there was no help for it: he would have to be a buccaneer. This suited well, he thought, the expectations of his newly acquired patron, Professor Nick-Knack, because, he had reasoned, a buccaneer by definition would have to travel by sea and know all about driving boats over the water.

The center question, for the last three days, had been *how* to become a buccaneer. He had been tossed off of every ship currently in the harbor and the King's Marines had not wanted any part of him either . . . which was all right with Percival, as their profession looked entirely too much like actual work and, besides, seemed contrary to the expected profession of buccaneer. His mother had taught him . . .

Percival frowned at the thought. Winifred Taylor had raised him well and had done her best to teach him some sense, which in Percival had somehow not been all that common. She had doted on him, cherished him, and seen to it that he could at least read and write a bit, with the hopes that it would improve his station in life. It was a shame, Percival realized, that she was not his real mother, for he suddenly truly missed her and wished he were home with her and Joaquim where life was simpler and where he wouldn't have to deal with fates and destinies all on his own.

His sniffled slightly and then focused again on the stolen parchment in his hands.

He had made a list, as Winifred had taught him to do when he was having trouble getting his thoughts organized.

The title stood proudly at the top of the parchment, its script large and bold.

HOW TO BECOME A BUCCANEER

It had taken him nearly an entire day to find the correct spelling of the word, and in the end it had come down to a narrow consensus, but Winifred had taught him to be thorough. He considered the list.

1. GET CUTLASS
2. GET PIRATE BOAT
3. GET OR MAKE PIRATE FLAG
4. GET PIRATE MAP
5. GET A CREW WITH SHOVELS & CUTLASSES
6. ABDUCT TUPPENCE

Percival nodded with satisfaction. Here was a series of achievable steps toward acquiring his goal. He had a plan.

Moreover, he had already made considerable progress on the list. He had not listed a buccaneer costume because, thanks again to his adopted mother, he already had a suitably striking costume. And, thanks to another visit to Professor Nicholas's residence the day before, he had acquired not only a fine cutlass but also a rather striking parrying dagger as well. Both complemented his outfit and added tremendously to his appearance. He had considered growing a rough beard as well but gave up on the idea after a few days of rather unsatisfactory progress. Nevertheless, he had been able to check off nearly at once the first item on his list.

Getting a pirate boat was now perhaps not nearly as difficult as he had once presumed. Thanks to the beneficences of Professor Balderknack, he should have access to sufficient funds to acquire such a vessel. All he felt was necessary was to make a few inquiries among the pirate captains as to which of their boats might be for sale and barter for a price. His father Joaquim had taught him how to barter even with the fairies, so he knew this would not be too difficult.

The pirate flag presented a more ticklish problem, as he was uncertain whether one had to register such a thing somewhere like a coat of arms. Did one purchase such a flag or make it oneself? He hoped it would be the latter since he was quite good with needle and thread and rather looked forward to making his own flag.

Item four gave him pause. He knew he would need a proper pirate map, especially since Professor Balderknack seemed to have a particular destination in mind. All pirates that he had ever heard of had their own maps that led them to their destinations, and, truthfully, the professor expected Percival to take him wherever it was he wanted to go. Percival had no idea where that might be or how they might arrive there. This item, he knew, would take more thought.

Percival was absolutely certain that he could be a rogue

buccaneer captain of a pirate boat—so long as he did not have to steer it, make it move, know where it was on the sea, or stop it when it came to the shore. He then would need to get a crew for those incidental jobs, if the boat did not already have sailors when he bought it. Percival decided that the crew members would have to bring their own cutlasses in order to save expenses—and their own shovels, since pirates in all the tales he had read were constantly digging up or burying treasure.

Finally, he knew from most of the stories he read that the rogue always abducts his girl from the clutches of a terrible fate. He was not sure yet what fate Tuppence was suffering under, but if abduction was what was required by custom, who was he to question it?

Percival nodded in satisfaction at his list. Then, inspired, he picked up the pencil once more and wrote along the bottom of the parchment the days of the week, circling Pentaday . . . one more day away. It was the day upon which Tuppence Magrathia-Paddock had so sweetly mentioned precisely where she would be and at what time—warning him not to find her there in that secret spot.

Which, Percival knew, was *exactly* where a rogue buccaneer was always supposed to be.

Vestia Walters stood on the threshold of her aunt's house, both anxious and decidedly piqued.

She could no longer hear the incessant chattering of her aunt in the house behind her or the less constant noise of her brood rolling from small room to small room and up and down the narrow staircase. She looked out on the steep incline of Gentlemen's Way, watched the wagons filled with goods being winched up the street, and wondered what would happen next.

Vestia Walters was the daughter of Eventide's leading matron and patroness, Livinia Walters. Jep Walters, the town cooper, was her father. She was the pampered princess of the village, a prominent lily in something of a rather small pond. Her long golden hair and green eyes were easily dismissed as mere beauty, having the depth of a sheet of parchment—and a blank sheet at that—but those few who knew her well understood that this was something of an illusion. She possessed considerable cunning and an uncanny sense when it came to all things social. Her mother certainly had instructed her well in what to expect out of life and made her aware of how best she might invest her statuesque appearance.

It was to protect that investment that she had appeared at her aunt's door.

She had arrived that same morning on a wagon hired by Harvest Oakman from Eventide to bring a shipment of his furniture for trade in Blackshore. She was accompanied by Melodi Morgan, the only suitable companion available on such short notice. Melodi had chatted all the way, and Vestia had evinced as much interest as possible under the circumstances—which, to be truthful, was not much.

The match between Vestia Walters and Percival Taylor had, so Vestia understood, been contracted and all but signed. Following the successful marriage of Jarod Klum and Caprice Morgan three months ago, it had been made known by the Gossip Fairy herself that the Dragon's Bard had been the facilitator of the entire affair. Percival and Vestia had been an item in the town for some time and the subject of both of their mothers' plotting for longer still. That Winifred Taylor could not seem to get her butterfly son to settle down and ask Vestia for her hand had been a matter of frustration both for Vestia and, to a greater extent, her mother, Livinia. It was, in fact, Livinia Walters who had quietly contracted with the Dragon's Bard to do for her daughter what he had so successfully done for the Klum boy—arrange matters to a satisfactory matrimonial end.

All had seemed to be going well . . . until Percival had vanished one day, leaving a ridiculous letter that broke Winifred Taylor's heart and left Joaquim Taylor to somehow deal with the pieces.

Then Vestia's mother got word from her sister in Blackshore that the Dragon's Bard was at her door . . . and that Percival was to be found in port as well. Moreover, the Bard had asked that Vestia come as quickly as possible. This news had been of some comfort to Winifred Taylor, as she now knew that her son was alive and not far away. Joaquim had wanted to go and fetch him home at once, but Livinia interceded, saying that it would be better for everyone if he were not driven home with an oak stick but lured home with honey.

Vestia, it seemed, was to be the honey.

As for Vestia, her own feelings were ambivalent. Percival had embarrassed her and not for the first time. He could be such a dolt sometimes and yet utterly charming at others. His smile was winning and his manners impeccable. He always dressed extremely well and was well spoken even if sometimes what he said was not terribly sensible. Above all, they were a good match, offering Vestia perhaps her best hope of leaving Eventide and finding a bigger life for herself than could be afforded by the little town that had gotten smaller to her as the years passed.

"Vestia!"

She turned in the doorway, looking up the street as she held her hand to shade her eyes. "Melodi. Where have you been? You went to the market nearly an hour ago."

Melodi Morgan flounced down the steep cobblestone street, her arms swinging freely as she moved. Her raven black hair bounced in its curls as she approached. She had an upturned nose in her heart-shaped face with beautiful cheekbones, her mouth drawn into a perpetual mischievous smile. Melodi was one of the three sisters in Eventide who supplied the local wishing well with its wishes. Since the breaking of the curse in the town some months back, the once-broken wishing well was functioning again, and Melodi's prospects had improved to the point of making her worthy of Vestia's notice. "Well, I've *been* to the market . . . and I've been farther than that still so that I might bring you a bit of news."

Vestia drew in a deep breath. Melodi liked guessing games, but the well-reputed fair-haired beauty of Eventide was in no mood to play. "What is your news, Melodi?"

"Well, as you said, I was at the market—there's a rather nice one on the edge of Hangman's Square—and I got distracted by a perfectly charming shop called 'Sea Spells Seashells,'" Melodi giggled. "Did you know that sea magic is entirely different from wood and stone magics? The shopkeeper there was so helpful and—"

"Melodi," Vestia said, clearing her throat. "Your news?"

"Oh! Well, as I was coming out of the shop—I mean, I really didn't have enough coin to actually buy anything although things really are going quite well right now with the wishing well working again and all—"

"Melodi!" Vestia urged.

"Sorry . . . I was coming out of the shop and that's when I saw him."

Vestia leaned against the doorjamb. This was going to take some time. "Saw . . . who?"

"Him . . . Percival, of course!"

Vestia stood upright. "You did? Where?"

"I told you, in Hangman's Square, but . . ."

Vestia stepped out at once, looking up to the top of the street.

" . . . but he isn't there now."

"Where is he?" Vestia asked in a rush. "Where did he go?"

"Well, that's what I was trying to tell you!" Melodi giggled again. "I tried to call out to him, but he must not have heard me. He was walking very fast, and I had a hard time keeping up with him."

"Where, Melodi? Where did he go?"

"Out of town," Melodi blinked. "There's a road to the north and he took a trail off to the west. I came right back . . . I even asked about it for you."

"You did?" Vestia said, a smile playing on her lips. She gripped the shorter young woman by her shoulders with both hands. "Tell me!"

"It's a place called Prow Rock—it's the first trail to the left of the Port Anghel Road once you leave town," Melodi said. "But . . . Vestia! Wait! We're supposed to stay here until the Dragon's Bard comes by!"

But Vestia was already running up the street.

She knew she didn't need a Bard to tell her how to interest a man.

Percival adjusted his puffed-sleeve shirt, opening the collar slightly so as to expose more of his hairless chest. He tugged at the tops of both his boots, checked the weapons scabbards, and ran his hand back one more time through his hair.

Prow Rock was an outcropping of stone that resembled the bow of a ship. It projected out from an open meadow surrounded by trees and dense undergrowth. The area had been a small lake not many decades ago but had since filled in with sediment. The feeding stream still wandered through the meadow, cascading down both sides of Prow Rock, giving something of the look of the stone cutting through the sea. The sun was settling toward the west as the afternoon lengthened.

There, near the rock, stood Tuppence. She was wearing a dress with gilded brocade panels in the bodice and satin sleeves. The dress was elegant and beautiful, expensive and carefully tailored to her form. Percival's heart swelled in admiration of the immaculate handwork, the choice of fabric, the perfect beadwork, and the fine weave.

Percival strode purposefully out of the shadows directly toward the Governor's daughter.

"You have discovered me, Rodrigan, in my secret sanctuary!" Tuppence turned her pale face toward him, the back of her hand rising in shock to her red lips as she spoke. In truth, everyone in Blackshore knew about Prow Rock and there were none of the local citizenry who had not utilized the spot for a rendezvous at one time or another. It was an unspoken law that one always checked to see if the meadow was occupied by anyone else before entering.

"So I have!" Percival said, making sure his voice sounded husky and piratelike as he crossed toward her. "How could I not? My heart called me here, for I could not be deprived of my feeling at the sight of you!"

Tuppence made the calculated move of her hand to her forehead. "Oh, Rodrigan! My heart bursts open to you!"

Percival blinked uncertainly at the mental image this evoked but pressed on. "Where now is your guard dog?"

"My fierce Triton is, alas, being bathed at the house!"

"And your handmaiden?"

"Alas! She is gone to bathe my dog and shall not return for yet another hour and a quarter at the least!"

"Oh, really?" Percival stopped in midstride in front of Tuppence. He had always been taught that it was improper to be with a woman of court without an escort and suddenly was uncertain as to how to proceed. "Well, if you think we should wait . . ."

Tuppence, a woman well versed in the Dragon's Bard library, took the initiative. She swooned, most carefully, in Percival's direction.

The young man had fine instincts and caught her in his arms, bending over her as she had planned . . . their faces close together.

She opened her eyes with perfect timing. She leaned her lips toward his, murmuring, "Rodrigan!"

"PERCIVAL TAYLOR!"

Percival, shocked at the explosive and commanding shouting of his name, released Tuppence at once. The Governor's daughter fell the remaining two feet flat on her back into the grass of the meadow with a dull thud and a pinched "Oof!"

"Vestia?" Percival stammered in disbelief.

"Oh, how very good of you to remember!" Vestia said as she charged across the meadow, her blonde hair flying behind her and her fists gathered at the ends of her arms. "Since we're dealing in introductions, perhaps you can introduce me to your new little play-friend here?"

Tuppence was still floundering slightly in her dress as she got to her feet. Her storybook moment had been spoiled and now her tone was imperious. "Who *is* this person?"

"Ah, Miss Vestia Walters," Percival stammered. He had fallen into uncertain territory and his mother—or adopted mother—had always told him when in doubt to fall back on good manners. "May I introduce Miss Tuppence . . ."

"Tuppence Magrathia-Paddock!" the dark-haired woman corrected. "And I shall certainly NOT be introduced to this strumpet!"

"What did you call me?" Vestia seethed.

"Strumpet, of course!" Tuppence sniffed her disapproval as she stood with all the dignity that her leaf-covered dress could afford. "My Rodrigan, being a buccaneer, has no doubt fallen susceptible to your portside wiles and cunning artifices of temptation! Such, I understand, is the way of rogues, to be preyed upon by scheming wenches . . . but I shall redeem him from the likes of you!"

Vestia's face deepened into a bright red as her eyes widened. She glanced at the ground, found what she suddenly needed, and picked up a broken branch almost a thumb's length wide at the base. She started breaking smaller branches off of it with her hands until it was a stout piece of wood about an arm's length long. "Oh, you have *so* got this coming to you, puff-ball!"

Tuppence reached down and pushed back both her sleeves up to her elbows. "I shall not give up my Rodrigan to such a base house cat as *you!*"

Percival stood between them, holding up his hands. "Now, dear ladies, perhaps we should—"

Vestia swung first with a wild cry. Tuppence jumped backward, out of reach of the improvised club.

"Ow! Vestia!" Percival took the blow.

But Vestia was not listening to him. She pressed her attack forward.

Percival drew his cutlass in his own defense. Tuppence carefully kept Percival between her and the crazed Vestia, the result of which was that most of the blows were falling around him. He had to use the side of the cutlass to parry the club swinging down around him.

"Vestia!" Percival tried again, blocking yet another blow with his sword. "I wasn't expecting you here."

"Obviously!" Vestia growled, holding her club back as she tried to maneuver around Percival.

Percival turned to the black-haired woman. "Perhaps it would be best if you were to go back to your—"

That was when Percival saw the wand in Tuppence's hand.

"No! Wait!" he cried out.

Tuppence reached forward with the wand to discharge its magic directly at Vestia.

Vestia swung with all her might for Tuppence's waist.

Percival tried to get out of the way.

None of them succeeded.

The wand had been a gift to Tuppence from her father the governor as a means of protecting her from "bad men." Her father would have approved of the result.

Vestia's swing caught the wand, pushing it off to the left. Tuppence had never actually used a wand before, and the release of its power not only shattered Vestia's stick, knocking the blonde to the ground, but threw the Governor's daughter back once again flat on her back. The discharging magic, however, caught Percival squarely in the chest, knocking him over the edge of the meadow and sending him cartwheeling down the steep side of a ravine.

Percival's tumble was a strange experience for the young man because his entire body, cutlass still in hand, was paralyzed, locked in the surprised pose he had struck at the moment the magic enveloped him. And so it was that he tumbled like a tossed statue, feeling every bump along the way before sliding to a stop near the ravine's bottom.

For quite some time he watched the dappled sunlight through the fixed vision of a particular set of overhead trees and listened to the two women at the top of the slope continue their combat fist and claw. After a time, silence finally came, and he wondered if either of them had won.

Vestia returned to her aunt's house with a bloodied nose, bruised fists, disheveled hair, her dress torn in a number of places, and in generally dirty condition.

The Dragon's Bard was waiting for her as she came to the door. "I see the direct approach was not entirely successful."

Vestia glared at him.

"I believe there are more subtle means at our disposal," the Bard continued, holding up a piece of parchment with a scribbled list on it. "I found this not an hour ago among Percival's effects. I believe his next move will be to acquire a ship . . . and I personally know that there is only one available that would fit his bill."

Long after sunset, Percival regained the use of his arms and legs. In the dark he found his way out of the ravine and was pleased to find the Port Anghel Road and the lights of Blackshore below.

"Now I know," he said to himself as he staggered back toward town, "why men go to sea."

Shipwrights and Wrongs

CHAPTER 9

The Widow's Walk

T his is the ship?" Vestia said skeptically.

"Yes," the Dragon's Bard nodded in appreciation as his eyes followed the elegant lines of the craft's hull. "She's called the *Revenge*. Isn't she a beauty?"

"It's not even in the water," Vestia replied.

"Temporary condition, I assure you," the Bard replied through a grin.

Vestia cocked her head to one side, her eyes squinting slightly as though the enormous hulk in front of her would improve if seen less clearly. The ship might have looked reasonably fashionable in the water, but as it lay careened to one side, the bloated bulk of its hull presented itself in aspect more like a beached, pregnant whale. The top masts and bowsprit had been removed, as had most of the rigging, before the ship had been dragged up on shore for repairs. Vestia could not see the weather deck from where she stood, but she could see light through the missing planks in several places along the ship's keel.

"Would you mind explaining to me once more how this wreck of a ship in any way helps me with my problem?" Vestia asked, rubbing her neck. She was still sore from her altercation with that "painted harpy" the day before, and her hands still looked puffy despite the careful application of powders by Melodi that morning to cover up the bruises on her knuckles.

"Assuming that Percival is your problem—and I would be the first to agree that he is your problem—our plan of attack is subtle and simple," the Dragon's Bard replied. "You must be where he is, appearing mysteriously by chance. You will be constantly before his eyes and on his mind. It will work on him, your ever-present beauty, your charming smile—you do have a charming smile, don't you?"

Vestia bared her teeth.

"Well, we'll work on softening that up a bit," the Bard continued, "but with you always there, the spark you ignite in him will kindle into a raging blaze of devotion."

"And what about the Governor's daughter?" Vestia asked. "It seems to me something's already burning."

"Smoke, my dear Vestia," the Dragon's Bard replied. "A great deal of smoke but not all that much heat, I'll wager. *Wanting* something isn't the same as *having* it. The chase can be very exciting, but *catching* Miss Magrathia-Paddock may be something far different from what young Percival expects. You recall the last thing on his list?"

"It was 'Abduct Tuppence,'" Vestia shrugged. "What is the point?"

"After your confrontation yesterday," the Dragon's Bard said with raised eyebrows, "would *you* want to try to abduct the Governor's daughter? More to the point, would you want to try hanging onto her?"

"So, I'm supposed to just flounce about in front of him and he's supposed to eventually remember that I'm here?" Vestia scoffed. "*That's* your great plan?"

"Only a very small part," the Bard assured her.

"What's the *large* part?" Vestia asked, her voice rising.

"I want you to become a pirate," the Bard responded.

"A pirate?" Vestia stared at the Bard as though he had just stuck a pair of carrots up his nose. "What is it with pirates? Everyone around here is obsessed with pirates! Is there anyone in this entire town who *isn't* a pirate?"

"Look, all I'm saying is that if you look the part of an adventurous pirate woman, Percival will see you in a different light," the Bard shrugged, taking a step backward as Vestia appeared likely to do to him what she had intended to do to Tuppence the previous day. "Stand you next to Tuppence and he'll know you're the best choice."

Vestia felt herself relax slightly. "Fine! What am I supposed to do?"

"You are . . . you are Brenna Raven—the Seawitch of Torgantha!" the Bard declared.

"Seawitch?" Vestia lowered her eyebrows in disapproval.

"Merely a title, I assure you," the Bard replied. "Brenna Raven was a crafty woman of the sea, legendary for her ruthlessness and cunning, who has been hiding these many years in—"

"What are we doing here?" Vestia interrupted.

"We need to find the shipwright," the Bard replied. "He can tell us how quickly the ship can be put to sea. It's vital that we know the time for repairs so that we can make the rest of our plan to win you back your Percival. The wright must be around here somewhere."

"Perhaps inside the ship?" Vestia suggested.

"Excellent suggestion," the Bard replied. "Come quickly, for we may not have a moment to lose."

Vestia looked again at the missing planks from the bottom of the ship's hull. Her words lacked enthusiasm. "Of course . . . not a moment."

Edvard passed quickly around the bow, stepping over the thick logs supporting the hull above the packed ground that sloped back into the bay. Vestia followed with less enthusiasm. Several large capstans with enormous chains held the boat from rolling back down the logs and into the water.

"There is access here up onto the deck. I think from there I can enter into the hold," the Bard exclaimed, scampering up the ladder.

"You do that," Vestia urged with as little interest as possible.

As she came around the bow, Vestia saw the long, enclosed shed that ran along the side of the ways. There were several large doors in the side of the shed, each carefully padlocked.

She raised an eyebrow in amazement.

Beyond the work shed, across a carefully kept green lawn, stood a tidy square home rising two stories above a surrounding garden. In Vestia's eyes it was the most charming building she had ever seen. The walls were clapboard, painted in an ocean blue with bright white trim at the corners. The windows were also trimmed white with flowerboxes filled with red and yellow flowers beneath each. The roof at the corners of the second story all rose toward a large, glassed-in cupola in the center surrounded on the outside by a railed walkway. Vestia had seen similar walks and cupolas on many of the roofs in the town, especially on the east side, and had asked her aunt about them. She had replied that they were called "widow's walks" because the wives of sailors from the town would often climb up the staircase to this pinnacle of their homes and look out over the bay and the waters beyond, searching for some sign that their husbands had returned from the sea. Despite their name, these were places of hope, for the women's hearts and longings were cast from those "widow's walks" out across the sea, calling their loved ones home.

There, standing on the widow's walk, was the tall figure of a man leaning on the rail as he looked out to sea.

Vestia watched him for a moment. A trim man with broad shoulders, he stood nearly motionless in thought. Vestia shifted slightly to her right but still could not see his face.

"Hulloo!" came the Bard's hollow voice echoing from within the canted cargo hold. "We are looking for the shipwright of this fine vessel. We've a proposition which I think you'll find most profitable . . ."

Vestia stepped quickly away from the beached ship, taking her eyes off the man on the widow's walk from time to time only as required to be sure of her path and footing. She passed around the locked work shed and onto the lawn, circling the house to the far side. There was a small back porch attached to the house overlooking a finger inlet from the freshwater cove just beyond.

Vestia raised her hand to shield her eyes from the morning sun, now rising behind the cupola and making it hard to see the man's face regardless of where she moved. His hair was tied back into a ponytail behind his head, though she could see wisps of it that had escaped confinement shifting brightly in the background sunlight.

"Excuse me, good sir!" Vestia called up in her most genteel voice.

The man did not move at all.

"Pardon my intrusion!" Vestia tried again.

Her existence was again ignored.

"HEY!" Vestia bellowed.

Shaken from his reveries, the man looked down from his railing.

"Would you mind coming down, sir?" Vestia called up.

"Yes," responded the man in a deep, resonant voice. "I would."

He turned back to gazing over the bay.

Vestia considered for a moment. She was not a woman accustomed to being so ignored or easily dismissed by anyone. It seemed that the entire port of Blackshore was determined to irritate her.

"Then I have no choice but to come up!" she announced firmly, stepping up to the porch and thrusting open the back door.

The gale of her anger carried her through the kitchen space and into the center of the house. There she noted a strange feature, for there was a large pool constructed in the center of the room. Potted plants were set in the corners and a pair of narrow bookshelves graced two of the walls, adorned with a meager selection of tomes. The curiosity of the room threatened to distract Vestia, but she was determined, circumnavigating the masonry-rimmed pond to the staircase at the far side. As she passed the open door to a bedroom on the second floor, somewhere in the back of her mind she realized that she had come into the house without any invitation and had left the public areas well behind and below her. However, the impertinence of the man had left her with sufficient momentum to grip the railings of the last ladder and propel her up into the windowed cupola of the widow's walk. She stepped onto the teak flooring and through the open door onto the railed walkway beyond.

"Sir, I have come to . . ."

Her voice failed.

The view from the walk was magnificent, presenting the best aspect of Blackshore Bay Vestia had yet seen. The town stretched along her right in the morning light, nestled back in its large cove against the rising hills, slightly hazy in the morning light. The *Ark Royal* lay at the far end of the quay with her dew-draped masts and rigging shining. The long stretch of Tobin's Point carried her sight to the lighthouse and the Mermaid Grotto beyond. Then outward, where the bay emptied into Mistral Sound between the lighthouse and the Troll Cliffs and the great ocean beyond—a horizon that something within her found compelling. Where the sky met the sea she could just make out a slight discoloration leaning with the wind.

"Is that . . . a ship?" Vestia asked in wonder.

"Yes, milady, it is indeed." The man remained where she had last seen him, only now she had a much clearer view. He had a narrow jaw, closely shaven. Considering the depth of the dimple in his chin, so close a shave, Vestia thought, must have taken considerable patience and skill. His hair was a deep brown in color, long and tied back firmly out of the way. He had an aquiline nose and prominent forehead with deep-set eyes that she could not yet quite make out. "She's outbound though . . . we'll probably lose sight of her within the hour."

"It's . . . it's wonderful," Vestia murmured, a smile playing at the corner of her lips as she stood next to him at the railing, gazing toward the horizon.

The man turned to face her. "May I ask the lady if she has come to break into my household and trespass upon my property for the sole purpose of enjoying the view?"

"Certainly not!" Vestia turned to face the man with indignation.

It was his eyes that stopped her this time. They were a pale gray, like the sky before a storm, she thought, but it was not just the color that had taken her aback but the soul somehow behind them. They reflected a well of pain, loss, and longing the likes of which she suddenly knew were beyond her experience.

"I . . . I am sorry for entering your house," Vestia said, feeling suddenly too warm despite the morning chill. "I've been too bold."

The man smiled slightly. "It's quite all right. The truth is that I prefer a bit 'too bold.' However, if you're going to make a habit of charging into my home, we should at least be introduced. Would you happen to know someone who might oblige us?"

"Given the circumstances," Vestia offered her hand and smiled, "perhaps not. My name is Vestia Walters . . . pleased to make your acquaintance, sir."

"Bold, indeed." The man chuckled slightly, then nodded, gripping her hand carefully and shaking it. "Adrian Wright, at your service, milady."

"The shipwright . . . I am delighted, sir," Vestia nodded slightly.

Adrian turned back to look at the horizon once more.

"Clear again," he said, shaking his head, his brow furrowing slightly before he looked up. "Now, Miss Walters, perhaps we may get down to the *Revenge* quickly before that friend of yours finds some way of doing serious harm to himself inside my work."

"It has been a most . . . educational afternoon," the Dragon's Bard said, doing everyone the courtesy of standing a good distance off as he spoke. "What was that part of the ship you said you found me in?"

"The bilge, Master Bard," Adrian answered. "It is called the bilge."

"Ah, yes, I shall have to remember that," the Bard replied.

"I think we shall all remember for you," Vestia said, holding her handkerchief over her nose and mouth.

"And you are quite certain that the *Revenge* can be readied within a week?" the Bard pressed.

"The work is largely completed now," the shipwright answered. "The sparring is all cut and the hull planks fitted. The ship will need to be rigged, but that should take only a few days once she is back in the water. Finishing the work is not the problem."

"Indeed?" the Bard coaxed.

"The problem is getting Captain Swash to pay for the work," Adrian responded. "He's not likely to do so anytime soon, and until he does, his ship stays where it is—taking up space on my ways."

"Might you be open to a better offer, then?" the Bard asked. "If I were to take the ship off your hands, for example."

Vestia looked at the shipwright hopefully.

Adrian glanced at her and then said, "I might."

"Thank you, my good man!" the Dragon's Bard responded. "We shall be getting back to you quickly. Take no action without consulting us first!"

"Your first action should be to find Kami's Baths," Adrian said. "It's up on Three Sisters Road—I'm certain anyone will be happy to direct you."

Adrian watched the Bard and Vestia as they walked toward the town up Sailor's Walk Road. When he was certain they were on their way, he turned back to his work shed, drew out a heavy iron key, and, with a sigh, unlocked the door.

The interior of the long building was illuminated by light streaming down from windows set in the northern side of the roof. These formed slanting square shafts of brilliance in the dust-laden air between the columns supporting the crossbeams overhead.

Adrian stepped into one of the shafts, the overhead light casting his features in stark relief. His head hung bowed as he looked at his open hands, considering them as they moved in the light. Then he reached forward toward the workbench in the shadows. It was still difficult for him to see, as it was each day when he first came into the shop, but his hands knew better how to find what he needed. The right hand rested on the carver's mallet while his left passed over the assorted gouges and knives, all carefully arrayed on the bench before him. His hand found a v-parting tool of just the right depth and he fastened upon its handle.

Taking in a deep breath, he stepped forward into the shadows.

She was there.

The figure was one of exquisite beauty, a delicate chin rising to beautiful cheeks beneath luminous, laughing eyes of seafoam green. The nose was small and slightly upturned at the end. The lips were full, with a mischievous turn at the right corner. She had a high forehead sweeping backward into luxurious curls rendered in spirals that cascaded backward down her elegant neck and draped down over her shoulders, covering her breasts as they swept down to her narrow waist. Her lithe arms were held forward, hands extended as though reaching for someone before her.

She was crafted and carved entirely from a single piece of wood . . . a ship's figurehead of unparalleled splendor.

Adrian Wright knelt down before the figure, setting down the mallet and gripping the v-parting tool by the handle with both hands. Still, he hesitated, glancing down into the shadows of the long shop interior beyond the light.

She was there, too, in dozens of silent, wooden incarnations. In some she held her hands crossed in front of her. In others her head was turned differently. In some she looked fierce; in others, sublime. Each was unique in some way, but all were alike in that they depicted the same woman, the same full lips, the same upturned nose . . .

Adrian Wright blinked and then turned back to the figurehead before him. He looked up into the face above where he knelt. The figure stared out over him, its arms reaching for something beyond Adrian.

It was the same every day he came to the shop.

As always, tears streamed down Adrian's face, mixing with the shavings from the wood as he began to carve once more.

CHAPTER 10

Nyadine

A drian, what are you doing?"

Adrian looked up from his work. The years rolled back to a different time though the place was not so far removed. He was again sitting next to the shores of Naiad Cove, the freshwater pond situated just south of the ways where he built and repaired the ships of Blackshore. The house and its widow's walk existed only as vague shapes in his hopes and dreams. It was a time before . . . when Nyadine was still here.

"I am carving," Adrian answered with a smile. The driftwood turned in his left hand while he worked the knife with his right. A glance at Nyadine's furrowed brow and he corrected himself. "I am shaping this wood into a pleasing shape using this tool of humankind."

The displeasure in her face vanished with her comprehension.

"Then you must shape it in my image," Nyadine teased. "Am I not a pleasing shape?"

Adrian stopped, grinning as he looked at her. "You certainly are."

To look upon her was to smile. Nyadine's waist-long, pale-green hair was braided in a crown that met in the back and coiled down her left shoulder back into the water. Her long, elegant body was largely submerged among the reeds and lily pads. The narrow chin of her flawless face rested on the beautiful sweep of her arms and long-fingered hands, crossed on the wide stone at the water's edge. She wore the peculiar, diaphanous gown so preferred by the naiads. The garment flowed about them when submerged but clung tantalizingly to their lithe forms whenever they ventured to pull themselves higher out of the water. Like all naiads, she had no feet, her legs melding into the water around her of which she was very much a part. Her full lips seemed forever in a pout occasionally accented with a teasing smirk at its corners, as though everything and nothing were serious all at the same time. Her large, liquid eyes were of jade hue that could change to the color of a storm at sea with her displeasure . . . and he had seen that change often.

Nyadine was a naiad—a freshwater or river nymph—who with her sisters occupied Naiad Cove and harvested the reeds for Bryan Chanter, the paper miller and bagpipe maker in Mordale. The Wanderwine River emptied into this wide, reed-and-lily-rimmed pond before passing beneath Tide Bridge and cascading down a short waterfall into Blackshore Bay. Among those reeds and lilies, the naiads lived their lives, occasionally abandoning their pond and rushing upstream with the fairies each spring. What they did on these journeys, none of the naiads had ever told. Some speculated that their naiad males were all only to be found far upstream in the Lake of Souls. Others—most notably the ladies on Molly Highstreet— believed that there were no males of the naiad kind at all, that the freshwater nymphs got their children by seducing human men and then traveled upstream to give birth. A third minority opinion believed that the naiads simply felt confined in the pond and regularly traveled the rivers out of a simple desire to see something new.

Adrian held the second opinion, but he, being human, had hopes of convincing Nyadine to remain with him.

"Wood!" Nyadine exclaimed. "Oh, how I love wood! Our cousins the nymphs travel the ways of wood. They melt into the bark and the fibers of their trees, moving with them and among them at their will. Oh, how I should so very much like to see the woods as our cousins see them!"

"You cannot see the woods," Adrian said with trepidation. Nyadine's eyes were still bright and he dreaded saying anything that might turn them to storm.

"And why should I not?" Nyadine demanded.

"Because the woods run deep from the water's edge," Adrian

said softly. "You are not a woodland nymph, you are a naiad, and you know that you cannot leave the water far behind."

"But I long to see the woodlands!" Nyadine pouted, the water roiling with the naiad equivalent of stomping her foot.

"I could plant some trees for you," Adrian offered. "Here along the edge of the pond so that you could see them as your cousins see them."

"Could you do that for me?" Nyadine asked, her beautiful eyes pleading with him. "And could you make for me a water passage beneath the ground so that I might have my own pond in the middle of the trees?"

"Well, I don't know," Adrian stammered. "That's an awful lot just to . . . couldn't I just plant them here where you can see them from the shore?"

Nyadine blinked her eyes; her pout deepened. She pulled herself farther out of the water, her gown clinging to her figure as she lifted up her face toward him.

Adrian dropped his knife and carving, leaning toward her.

"It's not that much more to ask, is it?" she murmured to him. "Just this one thing more . . . and you will make me happy."

Nyadine raised her supple hands to caress his neck, drawing their lips together.

"Just this one thing more . . ."

Adrian began work on the channel that evening. After an extensive—and far too extended—conversation with Blinsa Plurgarf, the gnome rat catcher in Blackshore, Adrian had a fair understanding of the construction techniques used in the kingdom's sewer tunnels. Some additional input from a local mason allowed him to gather materials and begin construction of the channel. He built a dam where he wanted the inlet to be and began by draining the water behind it. The soil was rather porous, but eventually, after a number of setbacks, he managed to stop most of the flow behind the dam and began work digging a channel that one day would become Nyadine's access to her private pond. He started with the pond area itself and, once he was satisfied with it, began digging a deep channel toward the dam he had built at the edge of Naiad Cove. It took him six months and every moment that he could spare, but he was driven on by the luminous green eyes and the promise of a naiad's kiss.

He covered over the tunnel, smoothed over the land, and planted trees around the small pool he had created inland just south of his shop for his Nyadine. At last satisfied in the spring with the blossoming of the trees, he broke the dam, allowing the waters of Naiad Cove to run down the buried channel and fill Nyadine's pool in the middle of the garden he had built for her.

The sound of Nyadine's laughter rose from the water of the pool as she swam the length of the tunnel. Adrian watched her as she leaped straight up from the surface, cascades of water falling from her as she pirouetted in the air, her laughter ringing among the trees of the garden. She fell with a great splash back into the water, soaking the amused shipwright as he stood watching at the edge of the pool. He was delighted as Nyadine rose at the edge of the water, her elegant arms crossing along the top of the fitted stones.

"It's wonderful, Adrian," Nyadine exclaimed, her jade green eyes flashing. "It's just what I had asked for . . . but . . ."

Adrian's face fell. "What is it, my dearest?"

"Well," Nyadine pouted slightly, "I cannot touch the trees and know the wood from here. Besides, I have heard that among the women of your world there are those who dance . . . and I so long to dance."

"I . . . I don't see how I can . . ."

"I know," Nyadine interrupted at once. "If you could carve a likeness of me— a likeness with *legs* like the women of the humans—I could occupy that likeness for a short time . . . and I could touch the living wood and we could dance!"

"Nyadine," Adrian protested, "I don't know if that will work at all. I thought that some part of you always had to be connected with the water or you would die."

"Superstitions and stories!" Nyadine glared at him, her eyes darkening. "I could be out of the water long enough for us to dance . . . and you *do* want to dance with me, don't you, Adrian? You *do* want to hold me in your arms, don't you?"

Adrian was lost in her darkened jade eyes.

"It's not that much more to ask, is it?" she whispered. "Just this one thing more . . . and we can dance. Just this one thing more . . ."

Adrian began carving a wooden figure of Nyadine at once. His hands were not used to the detailed work and the wood, for the first time in his life, felt awkward in his hands. He abandoned his first two attempts as the figures simply did not look enough like Nyadine to please him. He completed the third and brought it to the pool in the middle of the garden.

"No," Nyadine sulked. "It's not good enough. Do it again."

He went back to the shop and began again and yet again. Three weeks had passed and at last he felt the likeness worthy of her. He once again brought the likeness to her and, to his great relief, she was pleased with it.

To his wonder, her body became transparent in the pool before him. She rose upward from the surface, her form flowing into the wood. The wood itself was transformed, became supple and smooth. The carved clothing began to shift and move. The toes and feet stretched.

The wooden face drew life, and the familiar eyes became liquid and focused on him. She opened her mouth . . . and sang.

Tears came to Adrian's eyes. The music of her voice was more achingly beautiful than anything he had ever heard. It was joy and freedom and triumph on a scale he had never before imagined possible. He shared in the emotions of the song, knowing that his own feeling would only diminish it should he too give it voice.

Nyadine threw her arms around Adrian. Instinctively, he wrapped his arms around her narrow waist, thrilling at the chance to hold her.

"Isn't this marvelous, Adrian?" Nyadine asked with a giggle filled with sunshine. "You are wonderful!"

"Are you really pleased?"

"Oh, yes!" she responded at once, gazing up into his face. "It's just . . ."

Adrian's face fell slightly. "What? What is the matter?"

"Well, it's these trees."

"What about the trees?" Adrian demanded. "You said you wanted the trees."

"Well, I thought I wanted the trees but *all* the nymphs have trees," Nyadine said. "What I really want is a house."

"A *house?*" Adrian exclaimed.

"Think of it, Adrian," Nyadine said. "If you took out all these silly trees . . ."

"Silly trees! But you said you . . ."

"You're not listening," Nyadine said, her eyes darkening. "If you took out these trees and built a *house* over my pool

. . . then it could be *our* house, Adrian. It could be our private place, just for ourselves and without the prying eyes and ears of Blackshore or their wagging tongues to talk about us. Wouldn't you like that, Adrian? Don't you want to be with me?"

"Well, of course I do, Nye," Adrian said. "But a house?"

"It's not that much more to ask, is it?" she pouted. "Just this one thing more . . ."

The trees were cut down. The garden removed.

He built her the house above her pool. She was gone from the cove as he built it, up the Wanderwine River, having followed the fairies when they left in the spring. The colors she had chosen. The style she had approved. The gardens were replanted and the furniture arranged as she had explained it to be done. Adrian worked long hours at the ways, taking on more work in order to offset the expenses of building the house and acquiring the furnishings. The home was completed, including the tower and the widow's walk at the apex of its roof.

Nothing was left for Adrian to do but wait for the return of his Nyadine.

One evening, he sat in his chair staring into the pool at the center of the house that was too large for him. The wooden carving he had so meticulously made of the naiad stood across the room on the far side of the pool. He was about to look at it when Nyadine's head suddenly appeared over the stone edge of the pond to rest as he had dreamed it would on her crossed arms. Her smile brightened the room, and Adrian suddenly felt his cares float from his shoulders.

"Nyadine!" he exclaimed. "At last!"

"It's marvelous, Adrian!" Nyadine exclaimed as she looked around at her surroundings.

She rose out of the water toward the sculpture, melding herself into the form, bringing it to life. Nyadine stepped carefully around the pool, her every movement beyond any grace that Adrian could conceive of in his dreams. She moved to his chair, curling up on his lap with her head nestled against his shoulder. He could feel the chill of her firm flesh in his arms as he held her.

"My Adrian," Nyadine said. "It is exactly as I hoped it would be. This is a place where I could be safe; where I could settle down with you into a life of bliss that would never end . . . if only . . ."

Adrian closed his eyes in fear. "What is it, my love?"

"There's just one thing more."

"One thing more?"

"Yes," Nyadine said. She rose to sit upright in his lap, holding his face in both her hands as she spoke to him. "I have seen the river and I have seen the cove, but I have come to know that there are lands far across the sea that I have not seen. I long to see them, my dear Adrian, before I return at last to this home you have made for us, to remain with you here forever. It is just one trip, my darling man—one last journey before I come back to you, and when it is done, it will be enough."

"But you cannot cross the seas," Adrian said. "You cannot abide the salt of the sea. I do not see how . . ."

"But, my dearest, you *do* know!" Nyadine said with a beaming smile. "Carve for me a likeness for a ship's prow . . . those figureheads attached at the bow! I will use it as I do your likeness here. The ship will touch the water for me and abide its salt as I sail above it!"

"But Nyadine," Adrian protested, "you could be lost at sea. There is no telling when or even whether your ship will return to Blackshore."

"Then choose a ship, a local ship, and fix my likeness there," Nyadine said, dismissing his reasoning. "Adrian, you must do this for me or I shall never be content, never be happy. It is just one thing more . . . one last thing more."

"Then you will return to me?" Adrian asked with all the impossible hope that love demands.

"Yes, my dearest man," Nyadine assured him, drawing her full, cold lips closer to him. "It is just this one last thing that must be done."

The figure of Nyadine was affixed by Adrian to the prow of the *Nereid,* a local merchant ship bound with cargo for the west. Before the ship left the ways, Adrian brought his beloved Nyadine to it in a large barrel, neither of them able to think of a better means of conveyance. There in the darkness Nyadine merged with the figurehead of the ship—carved into an uncanny likeness by Adrian.

Her joy was full as the ship moved down the ways and slipped into the water. Adrian watched anxiously for some sign of distress from his beloved naiad, but all he could hear was her singing with joy.

The seamen wondered at their new figurehead. It did not move, but it made this marvelous song in port. The tide being right and the cargo already aboard, the crew made at once for sea.

Adrian mounted the stairs in his home and climbed to the widow's walk at the peak of his roof. He watched the *Nereid* as the mermen brought the ship out of the harbor, its sails set as it came into the Mistral Sound beyond.

He heard his beloved Nyadine singing all the way.

Six months later, the *Nereid* returned to Blackshore, her hull low in the water, full of trade goods. Adrian saw her approach from the widow's walk of his home and rushed down to the docks as the mermen brought the ship into port.

The beautifully crafted figurehead was still fixed to the prow. Adrian wildly considered what he would tell the captain of the ship that might persuade him to bring the vessel back to his shop—some pretext of repairs, perhaps, that would allow him to reclaim his beloved companion.

But when he arrived, the ship was not singing.

He stared at the figurehead from the dock. It was weathered and cracked in places but unquestionably his own loving craft. Yet he knew at once that the life was gone out of the wood.

Nyadine had fled the work of his hands.

His mind ran in fevered circles. Had she fled this figurehead for that of another ship? Or had the ship sailed into fresh water and she had been lured up some distant river? Had something terrible happened to her, or had she been taken by some power he did not know?

Then tales began being told in Blackshore about different ships at sea whose figureheads could sing.

He questioned her naiad sisters in the cove. Each of them persuaded him that if he should do likewise for them . . . carve their likeness into a figurehead . . . that they would search the seas for his Nyadine. He carved more and more figureheads, each in the hope that this time the naiad would find his beloved and bring her home.

But naiads are selfish creatures, and none of them returned.

At last he fixed on her promise. She had said that when it was enough she would return. He continued to carve the figureheads because it was the only way he could bring her back to his hands and his craft. He wept when he did because it would never be enough to touch only her likeness.

And he climbed the stairs each day to the widow's walk, desperate to hear a song across the waters that would never be sung.

A Little Piracy, Please?

CHAPTER 11

Captain Swash

The brilliant moon sailed across the swiftly moving night clouds. Percival slipped like a ghost among the trees and ferns beside Apple Lane, his cloak held across his lower face and the enormous plume feather of his broad-brimmed hat fluttering behind him. His cutlass occasionally banged against his thigh, and the hilt of his dirk occasionally gouged him, but he was otherwise perfectly comfortable with his stealthy approach. The cloak also caught on the underbrush from time to time, hampering the grace of his movement, but on the whole, he was convinced that he cut a roguishly dashing figure in the night.

It was not yet the sounding of the First Watch—a full four hours past sunset—when he looked up from his hidden approach to see the imposing outer walls of the Governor's House set at the crest of a hill. The main gates were closed, but such a direct approach was not his objective. He turned instead around the western corner of the edifice, passing as a shadow among the trees at the edge of the shorn grass between the towering curtain wall and the orchard's edge that hid him in its shadows. Very quickly, his objective came into view: the balcony and patio of his beloved Tuppence protruded some twenty feet above a small flock of sheep lying at the base of the wall, their energy having been spent during the day pulling at the grasses of the lawn surrounding the mansion.

Glancing furtively about, Percival reached down about his feet. Within moments he found a likely small stone. It was not quite the pebble he had hoped for, but even in the moonlight it was difficult for him to see anything much smaller that presented itself as readily available.

The railing of the balcony had several flower pots seated on the top rail. He would have to be careful of them. Stepping to the edge of the orchard trees, he drew back his hand and let fly the stone in the direction of the balcony.

It missed the balcony entirely, clacked against the masonry wall, and bounced down onto the grass.

Several of the sheep bleated pathetically in protest.

Percival reached down, found another stone, and hurled it with somewhat better force and aim. The stone sailed as a barely perceived shadow against the stars and over the edge of the balcony.

Thud.

"Ouch!" came the squeaking exclamation from above.

"Tuppence!" Percival whispered hoarsely as he stepped forward quickly from the shadows to stand beneath the balcony among the sheep. "'Tis I, Percival . . . uh . . . Rodrigan!"

Tuppence staggered to the edge of the balcony, rubbing the back of her head. Percival was pleased to see that she quickly composed herself, knowing sensibly that moonlight such as occurred this night was not to be wasted on a little pain.

In the silver moonlight, Tuppence was radiant as she stood at the railing. Her hair was down about her shoulders, framing the beautiful shape of her face in rapturous splendor. Her delicate hands were clasped to her breast. The diaphanous nightgown was cloaked in a robe that hinted at the treasure of her figure beneath. Percival's heart leapt once again at the sight of her.

"Rodrigan! You rogue!" she whispered down to him from above. "Your being here risks the wrath of my father and the terrible justice of his guards' blades! Why have you risked so much to come?"

"But . . . your note said that . . ."

"And yet you came anyway, knowing the risks involved," Tuppence mewed in gratitude. "How can my heart be kept safe when you have stolen it from me? And now I fear that in your boundless passion you have come to abduct me from the protection of my father and all my good friends."

"Actually . . . no," Percival replied in a loud whisper.

"No?" Tuppence squeaked a bit too loudly for Percival's

comfort. "What do you mean coming to my balcony on a moonlit night like this and *not* abducting me?"

"Well, abducting you certainly is on my list," Percival replied, "and, I assure you, a very important step on the list, but I thought that I might sail away with the pirate ship, return with treasure, and *then* abduct you when I got back."

"When . . . when you got *back!*" Tuppence straightened up on the balcony.

"Well, I thought it might be dangerous out there on a pirate boat and all," Percival answered, confused at why his beloved Tuppence seemed to take umbrage at what he had thought to be a really good idea. "You could be here safe and when I get back from the voyage—THEN I could abduct you. It just seemed more practical."

"Rodrigan!" The night might have been a gentle one but Tuppence was working herself up into a gale. "What kind of a rogue are you? Everyone knows that damsels are abducted *before* the voyage in every case that has ever been documented. Their honor is at stake and their virtue put to the test—although not too much to the test—while they are imprisoned aboard the rogue's ship in his flight to the freedom of the seas! And now you want to go against an entire tradition in literature just because you think it impractical and . . . and inconvenient?"

Tuppence's guard dog had awakened at the sound of his mistress's increasingly distressed voice. Fiercely determined to protect her—or at least to join her in her outrage—the tiny Triton scampered onto the balcony and began bounding around Tuppence's feet, yapping loudly.

"Shush!" Percival urged, imagining the Governor's guard rushing out to apprehend him. More sheep, awakening at the noise, started bleating around his feet.

"It's that . . . that Vestia woman, isn't it," Tuppence chirped. "*She* put you up to this!"

"Vestia?" Percival said incredulously. "That's ridiculous!"

"I wouldn't put it past her after I so thoroughly trounced her in the glade," Tuppence exclaimed over the yapping of her fearless guard dog. "She absolutely ruined my dress and bit my leg . . . bit it, mind you! As it was, she gave me such bruises about the face and arms that I had to hide for days from my father or he would have given you the short drop in Hangman's Square for certain."

"Me?" Percival exclaimed "What did *I* do?"

"Now, you'll be abducting me before your voyage and I don't want to hear anything more about it," Tuppence said, stamping her feet with such vigor that Triton yelped trying to get out of the way. As it was, several of the flower pots shook precariously on the edge of the balcony railing, threatening to add to the rising level of tumult in the night.

"Fine!" Percival said in a hushed voice, his hands gesturing his surrender, "but not tonight. I've a few more things to do before I abduct you."

"Oh, really?" Tuppence said haughtily. "I suppose they have something to do with your friend, Vestia . . ."

"No they do not," Percival answered. "I've just got a few more pirate things to pick up, is all, and I'm having trouble finding them."

"Pirate things?" Tuppence sniffed. "What kind of 'pirate things'?"

"You know," Percival said, although he himself barely had any idea at all what those things might be beyond the list he had made for himself. Still, he was loath to mention that those things included such basic necessities as a ship and a crew. "Things that all rogues need before they set out on their adventure voyages."

"I suppose Captain Swash is unwilling to help you, then," Tuppence pouted. "No doubt, you were rivals on the high seas and he holds a terrible grudge against you."

"Captain Swash?" Percival urged.

"Yes, the terrible Captain Swash. If there is anything a pirate needs, Captain Swash would have it," Tuppence said, leaning over the balcony toward him. "Look for him in the Laird's Lair, my beloved Rodrigan, and convince him to part with what you need."

"And then?" Percival swallowed.

"Then I'll wait for you by the moonlight," she said, and her smile brightened the night.

Percival stood outside the Laird's Lair, his arms crossed in front of him and his stance questioning.

The shop was adjacent to Gilly's Alehouse. In fact, you could enter the shop directly from the alehouse through a second door from the tavern's main room. This door and the front door were often open during late morning, afternoon, and early evening hours. Percival had not bothered to go into the shop, nor had he even taken much notice of it, although he had passed it often enough. There always seemed to be someone coming or going from the door, however, and as he watched it from the quay in the late morning sun he could see that the people entering the shop were diverse, although they largely could be categorized into two groups: scalawags who came occasionally from the *Ark Royal,* and merchants, tradesmen, and occasional courtiers who were all from out of town.

It took nearly half an hour after the shop was opened for Percival to deem it clear of any patrons who might overhear his business. His expedition on behalf of Professor Nick-Knack was one of confidence.

Besides, there was something odd about this establishment.

A loud bell clanged overhead as Percival stepped through the door and came almost at once to a stop.

The floor was almost completely obscured in stacks of pirate-themed objects and crafts. Small wooden sailing ships with black pirate flags affixed to their masts were piled on a table, while colored glass beads overflowed the sides of their casks on a second table. Ratlines and tarred shrouds were rigged to the wall with no other purpose than to provide a place to hang a number of tunics, black baldrics, and sashes. Other shelves about the room were filled with collapsing telescopes, sextants, bone dice, card decks, flutes, bagpipes, and concertinas, which stood in ranks of shelves some five deep in places against the walls. A number of cutlasses hung from their hand guards on wall pegs behind the counter at the back of the shop with a large pirate flag draped across them.

Behind the counter, a portly man sat in a tall chair leaning into the corner, his booted feet propped up on the counter and his arms folded across his chest. He had long, wavy black hair that was tied into a ponytail at the back and a long, thick beard that was braided in the front. His nose was large and bulbous. His dark eyes lay beneath bushy brows and followed Percival as he navigated through the cluttered shop.

"Mornin', traveler," the man said in a gruff, gravelly voice.

"Good morning," Percival replied. "I'm looking for a Captain Swash."

"Aye . . . and so is the King's Navy," the man answered. "The way I hear it, he is the most fearsome captain what ever sailed the Nine Seas. He were a man of terrible reputation whose appearance on the horizon would strike fear into any sailor's heart. His ship were the scourge of every port from here to furthest Arquebia. Is that the man ye seek?"

Percival thought for a moment. "That sounds about right."

"Well, when I sees him, I'll let him know yer looking fer him," the large man said, pulling himself upright on the chair. "Until that time, I see that ye be a man of discernment and adventure. Perhaps you have an interest in the buccaneer's trade . . . and would like to be taking with you some remembrance of them days what's gone past?"

"That won't be necessary . . ."

"These here cutlasses, for example," the man with the braided beard went on. "They were taken during the Battle of Zhumad, where King Reinard himself pursued the ships of the Five Brethren after their tragic raid on Port Anghel . . ."

"I'm not interested in—"

"I see that you are a discerning and educated man," the bearded man continued. "I've some artifacts from Captain Swash's personal collection here behind the counter that I rarely show to anyone except—"

"No, thank you," Percival interrupted. "I really need to speak with Captain Swash."

"Indeed," the portly man sighed. "And now what would you be wanting with the good Captain that would be worth his time listening to you?"

Percival looked around and then, leaning over the counter, motioned the portly man closer.

"I need to hire his ship and his crew," Percival said in a low voice.

"Do you now?" the stout man asked as he leaned forward. "And why would you be needing the Captain and his ship?"

"Can I trust you?" Percival said in even quieter tones.

"There's no man you can trust more than I," he answered.

"I'm in charge of an expedition . . . but I need it to appear as though I'm a pirate," Percival confided. "So I'd like to hire a pirate ship and crew to help me."

"You want to *hire* a pirate ship and its crew?" the stout man asked.

"Yes," Percival nodded. "And I understand that Captain Swash and his crew are available."

"Well, now, they are and they aren't," the man said, straightening up and running his right hand down the length of his braided beard.

"What do you mean?" Percival asked.

"Lad, old Captain Swash would be only too glad to help you with your problem," the man said, looking quickly around the shop as though to discover if anyone had slipped in unnoticed. "If you're a man of daring, of vision and adventure, then perhaps old Captain Swash can help you after all . . . if you're willing to help old Captain Swash out with his problem first."

Percival's eyes narrowed. "And just *what* would Captain Swash's problem be?"

"Well, lad, 'tis a strange tale," the man said, straightening up and slapping his hand against his protruding belly. "Captain Swash swept the seas, plundering distant ports and taking the cargoes of the king's treasure ships from the northern routes. He returned here to Blackshore with his ship, the *Revenge,* hull low in the water from the weight of the treasure she held in her hold. Yet in that terrible night when they first made their approaches, his first mate, by the name of Bore—a man he had trusted with his own life—struck a bargain with that crafty Klestan, king of the merfolk, and managed to offload the cargo in the middle of the night and bury it somewhere ashore where no man would find it. Bore went with them to bury the treasure and then used a wand on them when their backs were turned. Erased their memories of the day, he did, but old Bore were no expert with a wand and managed to erase his own memory as well. He were found the next day, poor man, wandering the shore mad as the moon. All that were left with him were the map what he drew, the strange clues he left on it about the treasure's location, and his wand. Since then, old Captain Swash and his crew have been hiding out here in this town, searching fer the treasure. But if you, lad, can find it . . . if you be a man of destiny . . . then you could be the one to find the treasure."

"Me?" Percival was surprised. "How?"

"I've got something here that I've shown to *no one,*" the portly man said, grinning through his beard. He reached down under the counter and opened a cabinet door. Slowly he drew his hand upward, pulling from the cupboard a roll of brown parchment tied with a string and a wand. "I've not shown these to a breathing soul before now, but I can see that you are just the man to break this curse and bring that treasure home."

"What is this?"

"This here's Bore's Map," the man said with a half wink of his eye. "It tells where the treasure may be found . . . if a man be smart enough and wise enough. The wand was found with Bore and may help you decipher the map's true meaning. And it's all yours . . ."

Percival reached for the parchment, but the man snatched it back.

" . . . for one hundred gold crowns," the man finished.

"A hundred crowns!" Percival exclaimed loudly.

"It's all that I'll be getting from the treasure!" the stout man said indignantly. "Sure as you'll be finding the treasure yourself and that's the last I'll see of you!"

"I'm not interested in the treasure," Percival said in frustration. "I want to hire the Captain and his crew!"

"Aye, and so you will when you release them from this curse!" the bearded man replied. "And one hundred crowns is nothing compared to the treasure you'll find when you decipher the map."

Percival slowly pulled out his coin purse. "I've got ten gold coins on me now. It's all I have."

"For the key to inestimable wealth?" the stout shopkeeper shouted. "Ten coins would be theft!"

"More like piracy," Percival agreed, shaking the bag so that the coins could be heard clinking loudly together. "But you should be familiar with the concept in this fine shop."

"I'll not be robbed in my own shop!"

Percival shrugged and started to put his coin purse back on his belt as he stepped toward the door.

"Thirty!" the shopkeeper said behind him.

"Fifteen," Percival replied.

"Not if your life depended on it," the shopkeeper snarled.

"Thirty, then," Percival nodded, "but Captain Swash and his men have to agree to be hired for two months as my crew."

"*If* you break the curse," the shopkeeper stipulated.

"Done," Percival agreed, spilling the thirty gold coins into his hand and measuring them out to the shopkeeper.

"And here is your map and Bore's Wand, lad," the shopkeeper said, handing Percival the tied parchment.

"And if I find the treasure?" Percival asked, taking the map.

"Then I personally guarantee that old Captain Swash and his crew will be at your disposal," the man said.

"And how are you in a position to guarantee that, sir?" Percival asked, already knowing the answer.

"Because, Master Percival," the man said, "I most certainly AM Captain Swash himself."

CHAPTER 12

Wooden-Leg Smith

Percival sat alone in the corner booth of the common room in the Mistral's Mistress. The room was completely empty of its clientele, the last of the sailors having left shortly after Rhenna MacKraegen had announced that the bar was closed and she was retiring for the night. Stoney had urged the emptying of the bar with as much haste as possible. He had agreed to let Percival remain behind only on the promise the boy would complete his business by the time Stoney had finished banking the kitchen fires and cleaning up.

Percival sat staring miserably at his treasure map spread carefully open on the surface of the table. He rested his chin in the palm of his right hand, his elbow on the table as he idly rolled Bore's Wand back and forth across the map's surface with the fingers of his left. A carefully trimmed lamp sat on the table, shining brightly down across the wand's ornate and intricate surface, illuminating the words *Reliable Wand Co.* inscribed on the handle that flashed briefly into view with every revolution.

He had been studying the map—and digging at various locations—for several days. Each time, he believed that he had ferreted out the intricate mystery of the map and that Bore's Wand had led him directly to the location of the Blackshore Treasure—and each time had disappointed him.

The problem with the chart didn't seem to be a lack of identifiable clues but rather a preponderance of them. That the map itself was of Blackshore Bay was evident by the contours of the coastline and the town clearly labeled as Blackshore on the map. The obligatory "X"—which, as any frequenter of such legends knows, is supposed to mark the spot—was not immediately evident. There were circles all around the border of the map, each one containing a different number in what initially appeared to be completely random sequence. There were a square of different numbers in a nine-by-nine grid in the upper right corner of the map and a strange poem in the lower left corner that appeared to be in a standard rhyming form but with certain lines of the verses breaking the form altogether. Some of the named locations on the map were embedded in the poem's words, as were the written forms of still more numbers, which did not match the numbers on the edge of the map. Then there were the numbers on the map itself, which were placed over specific locations but in no obvious arrangement.

It wasn't that he couldn't decipher the map—for if there were anything that Percival was good at, it was deciphering puzzles—but the problem was that the map could be reasonably deciphered in a number of different ways.

The first day had led him to Chanci's Fall. The name had leaped out at him from a phrase in the map's poem: "her heart with Fancy's Call." Taking the number corresponding to Chanci's Fall on the map, he realized quickly that when he laid the wand between the numbers on the border and added up the numbers appearing under the ends of the wand and included the number under the wand in the cover, the sum equaled the number of lines in the poem. Knowing that it could not possibly be a coincidence, Percival had followed the map around the southern end of Naiad's Cove and then struck out west. He discovered a coastal inlet with steep cliffs where a small stream cascaded down at the end of the narrow canyon and into a shallow pool that emptied into the encroaching waters of the bay. Bore's Wand had led him to a path that brought him to the bottom of the falls. Behind the falls was a shallow cave filled with dark sand. "Behind the lace," the poem had said, and so he had started digging. He had managed a considerable excavation before the hole began filling with water and he realized that the treasure could not possibly be here.

The second day he studied the map again, and this time

Bore's Wand illuminated new features for him. He was thrilled to discover why he had been mistaken the previous day and, shovel once again in hand, set out for the Cragsway Road out over the Mystic Peninsula in the direction of the Wand Foundry. There, under the shadow of the wand manufacturing abbey, Percival found Skullbreaker Cove, the three towering island monolithic stones rising up from the water and pointing to a hidden stretch of sand behind the half-sunken ruins of a beached ship. Bore's Wand assured him that this was, indeed, the place of the treasure, and he dug with determination into the wet sands—until he struck bedrock just before nightfall.

Each day it was the same: he would discover a new set of clues on the map, he would set out for a new indicated location—Willow Marshes or Deadfall Bog or Snowlace Beach—with his shovel in hand, and he would return with nothing except a tremendous appetite, an aching back, and sand seemingly in every possible extremity of his clothing.

On two occasions, he thought that someone had gotten to the treasure ahead of him. There were always people who had come down from Port Anghel or even Mordale who would suddenly appear about town with a shovel or spade. They too would rush furtively down Sailor's Walk Road toward Cragsway or Southshore Road. He followed one suspicious man all the way back to Chanci's Fall, only to watch him slip behind the waterfall and attempt digging in the same location Percival had mistakenly tried days before. It amused Percival for a while to watch the man struggling, his rising curses erupting from behind the waterfall as the morning went on.

The second time, he followed a man and a woman who were in a wagon. He gathered from Stoney MacKraegen that they had come up the Southshore Road originally from Meade and were on their way to Port Anghel for the man to take up a position as a cooper's apprentice. Percival had followed the newly discovered clues on his map and had gone west down Old Tobin's Road. He followed Bore's Wand down the western slope to the Siren's Breakers, a rocky section on the eastern shore of Mistral Sound. There he was just checking the angles from the five dead trees indicated by the map when he heard two people arguing as they approached. Percival quickly hid himself in the only available cover by wading out into the sound and holding onto the rocks called the Siren's Throne. The tide was fortunately low, and the waves were breaking shallow over his waist. The undertow pulled at him, but he was out of sight and could hear the couple as they continued their argument just a few feet away.

"Arnold, what pirate would bury a treasure here?" the woman yelled.

"A smart one, Alice," the man replied testily. "What better place to hide one's treasure than where no one would expect it to be hidden?"

"It just seems to me that if *I* were a pirate, the last thing I would be doing would be burying my treasure anywhere!"

Alice continued. "What good does it do anyone—including the pirate—to leave their plunder underground? Wouldn't it be smarter to spend it or maybe invest it in some guild-backed business . . ."

"Alice, you don't know anything about pirates!" Arnold said. "It's tradition! If you knew anything about pirates—"

"I know enough not to go back to that shop again!" Alice cut in.

"Shut up, Alice!"

Alice shut up and Arnold dug and Percival's teeth started to chatter as he stood in the water. After a considerable time, Arnold abandoned the dig, and Alice and Arnold again started arguing. When their voices had retreated far enough, Percival came out of the water and looked down into the rather large hole in the ground that Arnold had left behind.

Empty . . . like all the others he had dug.

Now, late in the evening, Percival was again exhausted. He thought that he had found a breakthrough, combining several of the locations and discovering a hidden key to a new location on Crossbone Shore. But after a day of digging in the shadow of a broken statue, he had trudged back to the Mistral's Mistress, where he now sat dejected in the corner booth.

Percival folded up the treasure map and slipped it inside his leather case. He then pulled out his list and checked it once again. He had been making remarkable progress. In addition to his cutlass from Professor Nick-Knack, he had now acquired both a pirate map and a pirate flag from Captain Swash. The pirate flag was the daring image of a winking and grinning skull fixed above crossed wands. It had an air of both menace and whimsy that appealed to his romantic side. Captain Swash had insisted, in fact, that he purchase the flag in two sizes: a large one for use on the ship, and a smaller, more convenient personal size for plundering coastal towns. Percival had also purchased a shovel to go with his treasure map, as Captain Swash had rightly pointed out that one could hardly dig up a buried treasure without one's own spade. The Captain had even thrown in a pirate scarf for Percival to wear on his head just because Percival had been such a good patron.

The conditions of Captain Swash, however, had necessitated adding an item to his list: "Find Blackshore Treasure." That was the key to his getting a captain and crew. All that would remain after that would be to find a ship. That would round out his ambitions to become a pirate, fulfill his destiny, and take the beautiful Tuppence in his arms. Admittedly, it seemed a bit backward to him that he needed to dig up the pirate treasure *before* he set sail for adventure, but thus far things had not gone strictly according to any book he had read.

Percival slipped his list into his case and turned down the lamp until the flame was extinguished. He leaned back in the darkened booth weary in mind and body. He did not think it possible for someone to be that tired. Surely, he thought, tomorrow the answer would present itself to him; he would see something in the map that he had not seen before and it would lead him to the treasure.

He closed his eyes, just for a moment.

There was a banging on the door.

Percival opened his eyes with a start. He realized at once that he had fallen asleep in the booth at the back of the Mistral's Mistress. Somehow he had slipped down to lie on the bench.

"Coming!" Stoney MacKraegen shouted as he moved through the doorway behind the bar. The great ship's lamps at either end of the bar were trimmed low and barely glowing. The coals were all that remained alight in the great fireplace on the opposite side of the room. "Belay that noise, you swabs, or you'll be waking the missus!"

Percival slipped as quietly as he could down under the table in the booth. *If he finds me still here, he'll kill me!*

Stoney moved to the door of the inn. "Who be ye?"

"Smith and company!" came the muffled reply. "Clear the way, MacKraegen, we've a night ahead of us and that's sure."

Stoney glanced again around the common room's interior. Percival held his breath, but Stoney took no notice of him. The innkeeper threw open the two steel bolts securing the door, then drew out his large key and turned it in the lock. The door swung wide.

"Welcome, lads," Stoney said, stepping aside. "Always glad to open for a few of the brethren."

More pirates! Percival thought. *But I've never seen these men before. They must be Swash's crew!*

The pirates flowed into the room through the door, moving at once to the bar. Percival counted twelve of them in all, each one of them carrying a spade slung over his shoulder as he entered the bar room. But it was the first man through the door who riveted his attention.

He was a full head taller than the rest, with broad shoulders and enormous, powerful arms. He had dark skin—darker than anything Percival had ever seen before—and long black hair. A gruesome scar extended from his forehead down to the side of his jaw, interrupted by an eye patch over his left eye. He wore no shirt but a long coat and a brightly colored scarf. He moved strangely as he walked, with something of a stiff gait with one heavy boot on his right foot and . . .

Percival's jaw dropped.

The man's right leg was wooden. It had been carved out of ebony to resemble the shape of the man's original leg, although even in the darkened room Percival could see that there were strange figures and symbols carved into the wooden appendage.

"What will Mr. Smith be having tonight?" Stoney said

from behind the bar to the enormous dark man standing in front of him.

The tall, black-skinned man said nothing.

"The usual," answered a wiry little pirate standing next to him. "And quickly, as we've thirsty work tonight."

"Taking care of the treasure are you, then?" Stoney said as he began filling the mugs he had distributed along the bar.

"That we are," rumbled the enormous black man, his voice resonant throughout the room. "Keepin' it safe. Keepin' it hid."

Stoney nodded. "Well done, lads. The town's grateful to you for all that you've done—and what you continue to do."

"We do not do it for the town," the black pirate responded with a sneer. "It's our treasure. We earned it and we keep it safe for ourselves."

"True enough," Stoney answered. "But we're grateful all the same."

The pirate with the wooden leg quaffed down his ale in a single draught, banging the mug back on the bar top. Stoney refilled it, and the dark-skinned pirate drained it once again.

"Hollow, is it, Mr. Smith?" Stoney asked with a smirk, pointing to the pirate's wooden leg.

"Just thirsty," answered the wiry pirate next to him with a wink.

"We've dirty work to do, mates," boomed the wooden-legged pirate after downing his third mug of ale. "We're to be done by morning's light and all back at sea before the sun's up."

The gigantic pirate looked at Stoney.

"I'll put it on your tab, boys," the innkeeper said, holding up his hands. "As usual. Take care of the treasure . . . that's all I ask."

Percival swallowed, then licked his lips. These pirates were out for the treasure, and if they found it before he did, then his plan would suffer a significant setback. On the other hand, according to his agreement with Captain Swash, all he had to do was *find* the treasure, not necessarily come back with it. This appeared to be not the first time these pirates had gone out on this chore. Maybe *that* was why he never found the treasure—because they kept *moving* it! MacKraegen and who knew how many others in the town were in on the secret . . . he didn't know who he could trust . . .

And he *had* to find the treasure.

Percival glanced around him and saw his free pirate scarf sticking out of his leather case. He quickly pulled it out and tied it around his head. He crept out from under the table, taking up his own shovel as quietly as possible. He moved quietly to the back of the pirate band at the bar just as they were putting down their mugs and picking up their own shovels.

"Where do we go tonight, Mr. Smith?" called out the wiry pirate.

"Siren's Breakers," came the deep voice in reply. "Let's go, you dogs!"

Thirteen pirates pushed out of the door of the Mistral's

Mistress that night, the last of them carefully turning his face away from Stoney MacKraegen as he passed the threshold.

The moon shone brightly down on the bay as the pirates moved through the silent and deserted streets of the town up the hill toward Port Anghel Road with Percival, a pirate at last, among them.

CHAPTER 13

Buried Treasure

"How bad is it tonight?" asked Dead-Eye Darrel as they passed beyond earshot of the last small house on Old Tobin's Road. The party of silent pirates had resolutely made their way along the quays and then turned west out of town. Percival had given a glance behind him as they walked. He could just make out the Governor's House in the moonlight atop the hill that overlooked the bay. It lay in the other direction, and he felt himself getting farther and farther from the enchanting Tuppence.

Percival clutched his shovel more tightly and tried to look casual. He was beginning to get the hang of the pirate names, but what he knew was hardly comforting.

"Bad enough," Cutthroat Karka grumbled. She was a goblin and short for a pirate, but Percival sensed there were none among the group who dared cross her. "I hear that there have been maybe ten or twelve of them fortune seekers this last week alone. Old Swash has done brisk business of late, I can tell you that."

"And that makes more work for us," whined Silent Sasha. For the life of him, Percival could not figure out how that pirate had gotten his name. "You mark my words—and many a day has gone from sunrise to sunset when I've said this very thing—that Captain Swash is abusing each of us in a most reprehensible manner and if he were brought up before the Brethren of the Gold Coast they would not be remiss in calling down the full weight of the pirate code on the Captain and most likely keelhaul him at a minimum or perhaps even some more dire fate for the crimes he has committed against each and every one of the—"

"Silence, Sasha!" grumbled the rest of the pirates in an enraged chorus.

Silent Sasha stopped speaking at once.

"How about you, mate?" asked Hook-Hand Horvath, turning toward Percival.

"How about me?" Percival answered, trying to pull his head down further into the collar of his coat.

"Aye, what think you of our chances of being finished with our little chore before sunrise?" Horvath sported a bristly beard that stuck out at a length that might have reached his chest. The hair of his head was bound up tightly in a bandanna. He had leveraged the weight of his own pickax through the hook that served as his left hand, letting it ride on his shoulder. The ax itself had a steel ring embedded in the end of the handle, presumably to accommodate the pirate's special circumstances.

"I think our chances are . . . right good," Percival answered in his best grumbling pirate voice.

"Do ye now?" Horvath asked with a frown. "Now, why would you be saying such a fool thing as that?"

Percival shivered. He dreaded being found out by these cutthroats but his course was set and he would not turn away no matter what. "Well, you asked the question . . . all I did was answer it."

"Answer it wrong!" snarled Hook-Hand Horvath. "We've been doing the Captain's dirty work for him nigh on all these years and it only be getting worse! And now yer telling me that it be some kind of pleasant stroll in the night!"

"Oh, let the man be," Silent Sasha chirped. His voice was high and had the irritating quality of cutting through everyone else's conversations. "You did ask him a question and he gave you an answer and what is the harm done if he should voice an opinion that you do not share and that the rest of us may be in disagreement with in the first place simply because you don't know the youth and have no possible basis for taking his words as insulting especially since you hardly know the man . . ."

"Silence, Sasha!" groaned the group around him. Percival belatedly joined in the chorus in an effort to blend in with the group.

Mr. Smith suddenly turned off the road, plunging them all down among the trees. The moonlight that had been so bright in the open grew suddenly distant, and the darkness of the woods closed around him. He could barely see the pirate in front of him—Karka, he thought—and the sounds of Horvath's grumbling that seemed too close at his heels. He imagined the sharp pick of his ax swinging forward just out of spite. He was no longer certain that he had taken the right course.

"Since the subject has been broached," Karka remarked without turning her head, "I don't recall your name, friend."

Percival knew the answer even as he blurted out his automatic responses. "Who? Me?"

"Aye, you," Karka said with what was, for her, unexpected patience. "What is your name?"

Percival's eyes widened in the darkness. He certainly could not give his real name. He remembered when the Dragon's Bard had taught him about how to lie . . . that a bigger lie was easier to believe than a small one, and that every lie goes down easiest with a story wrapped around it.

"You want my name?" Percival's mind was racing, searching for an alias. He suddenly remembered a seaman who had come through Eventide several years ago. His name had been Jonas Grumby, but that didn't sound like much of a pirate name.

"Are you deaf, then, as well?" Karka growled.

Deaf? he thought. Would it be helpful to him if he claimed he were deaf? Could he work that into a story? "No, I don't think so . . ."

"Well, then?"

"Wall-Eyed Pike," Percival blurted out.

"Wall-Eyed Pike?" Karka was dubious.

"Argh, that's right," Percival responded in his best imitation of a pirate voice. Panicked, the words flowed out of him before he could think. "Got my name off the coast of Margo Largo during a terrible storm. I was on the after quarter of the Captain's deck holding the rudder hard abeam when the jib gaff broke free and swung across the flying dunsel. Hit me in the back of my head. Fortunately, my face ran into a wall before that loose jib gaff threw me over the keel."

"Sounds like you were in terrible danger," sniggered Hook-Hand Horvath. "Them jib gaffs can be nasty. How ever did you survive it?"

"I was saved at the last moment by the powder monkey pulling me back onto a loose batten before I was lost," Percival said.

In front of him, Karka snorted.

"Oh, aye," Horvath chuckled. "That explains it, then."

They were winding their way down a circuitous path. Percival could hear the waves breaking beyond the dark trees around him.

"Honestly, Horvath," Karka said through a sigh. "Where

is the Captain recruiting crew from these days anyway? You would think he would be more selective about who he entrusted with this treasure business."

Percival held his breath for a moment, an idea flashing through his mind. What if these pirates *moved* the treasure every night? That would explain why he had such trouble finding it! All he had to do was stay with these rogues and *they* would lead him to the treasure even as they were moving it.

It was a brilliant plan, in his estimation, and he was just congratulating himself on it as he followed Cutthroat Karka out of the tree line and stepped on to the sands of the beach.

The clouds raced in overhead, partially obscuring the brightness of the moon. Five dead trees stood silhouetted against the moonlit clouds, and the all-too-familiar finger of stone jutted into the night sky just off the rocky shore. Percival knew the place at once as the Siren's Breakers . . . the very spot both he and the disappointed couple had dug up the previous afternoon.

Indeed, the holes they had dug here still remained as ragged scars in the sands of the shoreline.

How did we miss it? Percival thought. *We were right here!*

Mr. Smith stepped toward the largest of the holes and pointed to it. His deep voice rumbled over the surf nearby. "Start with this one—and put your backs into it. The moonlight won't last, mates."

The pirates all stepped forward quickly, bringing their shovels to hand alongside Mr. Smith.

Percival moved with them, anxious to see the treasure that had eluded him.

The pirate band pressed their shovels into the sand . . .

. . . and at once began filling in the hole.

Utterly confused, Percival joined in with them, moving the sand from the mounds he had made with such effort yesterday back into the hole he had created. The pirates around him worked with a fervor, shoveling sand into the pit as though driven by a demon at their backs. When at last the crater had vanished, Butcher Bill Volnak, Dead-Eye Darrel, and Silent Sasha worked over the spot, smoothing the sand with the backs of their spades until all traces of the previous dig had disappeared.

"That be about it," muttered Hook-Hand Horvath to Mr. Smith.

The giant man with the wooden leg nodded his approval. "You know what's to be done, mates. Hook-Hand . . . you do the honors."

The group of pirates quickly scampered back across the sands, retracing their steps as they came again to the trail leading upward away from the beach. Percival was next to last among them, pausing at the line of trees to look back across the beach. Horvath was coming up behind, a great leafy branch cut from a tree caught in his hook as he walked backward, sweeping the sands behind him and erasing their footprints from the sand.

"What are ye waiting for, Wall-Eye?" Horvath growled as he passed him on the trail. "We've dark work to be done."

The beach again looked flat and pristine beneath the moonlight, as though none of them had ever been here.

There, in the night, something inside Percival Taylor changed. He could not have explained it at the time because it was a new sensation for him and one that he could not recall having had before. It was as though something pure, clean, and fragile had suddenly popped like a bubble and was replaced by something real and sad. He had lost something in that moment and he knew that he would never have it back.

The pirates had buried his innocence in that sand.

It was midmorning when Percival again entered the Laird's Lair next to Gilly's Alehouse. Though the shop was indistinguishable in its appearance from his last visit, the young man saw it in a completely different way. The bell clanged above him as he passed through the entry, carefully closing the door behind him.

Loud snoring collapsed into a snort from the direction of Captain Swash. He was leaning back into the corner behind the far counter, his arms folded across his ample chest. His dark eyes struggled to focus as he blurted out, "Mornin', traveler."

Percival, his face still dirty and his light hair stained and plastered flat against his head, said nothing. He simply walked over to the side of the shop, carefully closing the door that opened onto the common room of Gilly's Alehouse and making sure the latch caught.

"If ye be looking for adventure, you're making port in the right harbor, mate," Swash continued with a wide gesture of his arms. "There be all sorts who come to trade here in the Lair from across the Nine Seas. I can see that ye be a man of discernment, with adventure crying out in your blood. May chance ye be in need of some token of yer travels—"

"We've already met, Captain," Percival said, stepping over toward the counter.

"Aye?" The Captain's dark eyes narrowed.

"Aye," Percival replied, stepping up to the counter. "We made a bargain, you and I."

"Oh? OH! So 'tis yourself returned, is it? I know ye well, lad," bellowed the blinking Captain Swash, his eyes focusing at last. He flashed a broad, gap-toothed smile. "Ye be the adventurous lad who wanted to hire on old Captain Swash and his cutthroats to paddle you about Mistral Sound a bit to impress the Governor's daughter."

"We had a bargain," Percival insisted.

"Oh, aye, and that we did," the Captain replied, leaning

back again into his corner, his grin still bright from behind his braided beard. His booted feet once more swung upward, casually crossing as he rested them again on the counter. "Have you managed to find my treasure, then, lad? I suspect it may be more difficult than you expected, but I have something I've shown no other man that might help you. For just a mere few gold coins, I could trade you for—"

"I've found it," Percival replied.

The dark eyes blinked. The great bulbous nose quivered slightly as the broad grin fell slightly at the corners. "You've . . . what?"

"I found the Blackshore Treasure," Percival said in a calm, low voice as he leaned slightly across the counter.

The Captain's eyes widened. "You *did?* Where?"

Percival suddenly grabbed the boots of the Captain with both hands and, with all his strength, pushed upward. Captain Swash struggled to keep his balance but it was too late; the tall chair on which he was perched slid with the shifting weight, squealing and then shooting out across the floor from under him. Captain Swash fell straight downward, his back slamming against the floor, the air rushing out of his lungs with a "whuff" sound.

Percival grabbed the edge of the counter and vaulted over it, landing on his feet on the opposite side. The pirate floundered at his feet, trying desperately to pull air into his lungs. Percival quickly surveyed the boxes behind the counter, found what he was looking for and dragged it out, and then spilled its contents across the countertop.

"Here it is," Percival declared.

The counter was littered with dozens of identical treasure maps and a like number of wands.

Captain Swash tried painfully to sit upright on the floor, but Percival planted his own booted foot on the chest of the pirate captain, pushing him back down against the ground. Swash glared up with fury in his dark eyes.

"So, last night," Percival continued in casual tones, "I was surprised to find a group of pirates going about with shovels in the middle of the night. I said to myself, 'They must be out looking for the treasure.' So I followed them so that I could find that treasure I promised my good friend Captain Swash that I would recover for him. What did I discover—to my surprise—but that these pirates were in the business not of burying treasure but of covering up the holes made by other people who were trying to dig up a treasure. Imagine my astonishment as the night wore on to find that these same pirates visited every one of the places where I—and no doubt hundreds or perhaps thousands of others—had been, all of whom had dutifully dug their holes, found nothing, and left thinking that it had been their fault for reading the map incorrectly or interpreting the wand the wrong way. And imagine my abject astonishment when I discovered those pirates filling in every last hole that I and who knows how many others had dug so that the next fool to step through your door could be sold another map and another wand and dig up the same empty hole all over again."

"Yer in dangerous waters, lad," Captain Swash croaked.

"Not if you're willing to be reasonable," Percival said.

Captain Swash held suddenly still.

"My dear Captain," Percival continued, leaning over to look down into Swash's face. "Tell me, was there *ever* a buried Blackshore Treasure?"

"Are you daft?" Captain Swash wheezed. "What good is a buried treasure to a buccaneer? That's just what we tell folks so they'll go off digging holes and leave us alone!"

"And I understand that you are a pirate. I also think I understand that you have discovered a means of piracy that does not require you to risk your life either in combat or at sea. You've discovered a kind of . . . well, let's call it 'soft piracy,' where you have found the means of getting people to pay you money because they believe that they can find a treasure that you never actually buried. It's a great deal safer and a more sure way of separating people from their coin purse than having to fire a broadside."

"The waters are getting deeper beneath you, boy," Swash grumbled.

"Of course, I could explain all of this to the magistrate in Mordale, I suppose," Percival mused. "Or perhaps have that letter delivered that I penned and left in safe hands. But why should I ruin everyone's day? So many people in this town make such a fine living off of its reputation as a pirate haven. Why not keep everything simple? I believe I have completed my half of the bargain here, and all you have to do to keep everything the way it is now is fulfill your half of the bargain."

"What do you mean?"

"I *found* the Blackshore Treasure, Captain Swash," Percival said. "Provide a crew, take me on my little voyage, and you can *have* your treasure safely 'buried' once more."

Percival felt the pirate go limp beneath his foot.

"At your service, sir," groaned Captain Swash.

All at Sea

CHAPTER 14

Plundered

The morning was cold, with a low-lying fog blanketing the still surface of Blackshore Bay as the *Revenge* slid down the shipwright's slipways stern first into the waters. The ship's momentum was checked by the drag chains until she floated quietly in the bay beneath the brightening light of an orange dawn.

"Aye, she's a fine sight still," grinned Captain Swash from near the top of the slipway. "Fine lines about her hull and the yarest I've ever sailed."

"Yarest?" Percival questioned as he stood with his arms folded, hunched over against the bitter morning. His shirt and vest were stylish in their cut but hardly proof against the frigid morning air. Not even his long greatcoat seemed to help block the seeping chill. He kept shifting his weight between his feet in an effort to bring feeling back into his toes.

"Aye, she's yar," Captain Swash repeated a little louder, as though he thought Percival must have been hard of hearing. The Captain was in his own greatcoat bound together with a broad, colorful sash. An enormous hat on his head sported a wide blue feather, reminding Percival somewhat of the Dragon's Bard. "*Yar* means she's easy to handle and forgiving to those that treat her right. She'll tack tighter than you might expect and respond light and quick in even a breath of wind. As fine a craft as ever plied the Nine Seas and the envy of many a sailor's eye."

"Do you think it's safe?" Percival asked, snuffling against his complaining nose.

"Safe!" Captain Swash bellowed his effrontery. "Safe enough—leastwise, I'm sure she is after Master Wright has finished with her. We left her a bit the worse for wear after our last encounter with the King's Navy, but see how even she sits in the water. No worries there, mate. She may not be the youngest girl in the village but she's still the best. Come on, now, lad; there's barter to be done and it's best you leave that to me."

Captain Swash strode down between the slipway rails that had only moments before supported the hull of the ship. Now the slipway seemed somehow bereft and forlorn without any ship for it to cradle. Percival followed with a start, trying to keep up with the long strides of the pirate captain. The drag chains were slacking slightly as, down the slipway below them,

Percival could see the shipwright gathering up the mooring lines from where they lay on the ground. He slipped them in quick loops over a capstan near a long, narrow pier that extended over the water just north of where the ship had been launched.

"Is that him?" Percival stuttered slightly in the cold.

"Aye, that's Adrian Wright," Captain Swash affirmed. "Finest shipwright between Southcape and Port Anghel. Could have made a fortune building ships up north. Why he stays here is a puzzle and no doubt. We've known each other these long years. Just let old Captain Swash do the talking."

"Why?" Percival asked, his eyes narrowing. "I'm providing the money."

"You be providing old Nick-Knack's money if what I hear in town be true, and if you'll want to be keeping any of it you had best let me handle this here parley," the Captain said with a wink of his eye. The stout pirate was approaching the pier near the end of the slipway and called out. "Ahoy there, Adrian! That's a fine job you've done on my ship there! Can we lend a hand bringing her in proper?"

Adrian Wright slipped another loop of the long cable around the capstan. "Thanks all the same, Francis. We don't need your help."

"Oh, there's no need to be like that!" Captain Swash said, striding onto the planks of the pier, his footfalls resounding in the still morning air. "I've come to settle accounts with you after all and pay you a good wage for your honest work."

"I doubt you have ever paid a good wage in your entire life," Adrian replied, stretching his broad shoulders. "And I doubt you have enough experience with honest work to recognize it when it were properly done."

"Ah, there you have me, me boy," the Captain grinned. "Still, the *Revenge* is no harbor longboat. She's floating free and easy now, but you'll need help bringing her to the pier. I wouldn't want you scratching that fine fresh paint you've laid to her sides."

"I've a merman team below, and the new owner's on board," Adrian said with a casual air. "Thanks all the same."

"Oh, them mermen are fine enough for—" Captain Swash stopped abruptly, the words of the shipwright suddenly impacting his thoughts. "New owner? *I'm* the owner!"

"Not since I sold her yesterday," Adrian said, taking his thick leather gloves off and stuffing them into the front pocket of his leather apron.

"Sold her?" the Captain sputtered. "Sold my ship from under me?"

"She was hardly your ship in the first place," Adrian said.

"I won her at sea," Swash bellowed. "Took her off the coast of Okinos from Red-Shanks Roberts with a hold full of plunder in the midst of a fearsome gale! Many a lad paid for that ship with his blood and his breath that day!"

"You won her in a dice game from John Aubrey after he drove her onto the rocks off Skullbreaker Cove," the shipwright countered. "He tore up her bottom, fouled all her rigging, and broke the main mast. The entire ship wasn't worth the cost of fixing her, and Aubrey swindled you when he put her up as a guarantee against your bet."

"But I won her all the same . . . 'tis much the same thing," Swash complained. "Point is that she's my ship!"

"I'm the one who put her back together," Adrian said, folding his powerful arms across his wide chest. "You signed a note to pay for the repairs, and I've not seen a silver sovereign since."

"Well, we're here now, ain't we?" the Captain shouted. "We've come to square accounts with you."

"But, as I said, I've already sold the ship," Adrian shrugged.

"Where are they, then?" Captain Swash bellowed.

"As I said," Adrian smiled, "they're aboard right now."

The sun was cresting over Mount Molly to the east, its light igniting the overcast clouds in a flaming sunrise.

"Ahoy the *Revenge!*" Captain Swash called. "Show yourself, scoundrel! We'll have words or steel between us!"

The masts and rigging of the *Revenge* stood tall against the brilliance of the sunrise beyond. A single figure of a woman leaped up onto the gunwale of the ship, her form silhouetted against the fiery clouds, her legs wide as she steadied herself. She dressed in men's high-cut breeches cinched tight against her narrow waist. Her tall boots were turned down at the top just at the knee. She wore a man's shirt, open at the throat. She held the shrouds with one gloved hand, the other hand resting on her hip. Her blonde hair was tied back into a ponytail whose loose ends whipped about in the freshening morning breeze. The warm light of dawn brightened upon her striking features, bathing her in a warm glow.

Percival's jaw dropped.

It was the unexpectedly incredible sight of Vestia Walters—new owner and captain of the pirate ship *Revenge*.

Vestia sat in the grand chair of the captain's cabin at the back of the *Revenge*, her crossed ankles resting on the desk, thoroughly enjoying herself.

Percival stood opposite her looking as uncomfortable as she could ever have hoped. "Vestia, just what do you think you're doing?"

"Me?" Vestia asked, batting her eyes at Percival. "Why, I just saw an excellent business opportunity, Percival. I saw this ship and thought, 'My goodness, wouldn't this be an ideal investment for my dowry?' My mother thought it would be a good investment too, and so she was more than willing to see to it that my father would provide the money to acquire it."

"But I *need* your ship!" Percival sputtered.

"*My* ship!" Captain Swash piped in. "This is *my* ship, and you're sitting in *my* chair, you brazen little . . ."

Adrian Wright stood just behind the chair on its left side. The glowering shipwright with the deep-set eyes raised the index finger of his large, powerful hand in warning.

" . . . young woman," the Captain finished, backing slightly away from the desk. "It seems to me that a woman of your sensible thinking should know better. Having the *Revenge* and keeping her, it seems to me, are two different things. The ship's just so much carved wood without a crew—and the crew is mine."

"Why, Captain—Swash, isn't it?" Vestia said through a tight smile. "That wouldn't be a threat, would it?"

"Just sensible advice," Captain Swash replied quietly. "There's no profit for anyone in you getting hurt.'

"How kind of you to be so concerned for me." Vestia nodded, then swung her legs down off the desk, leaning forward. "But there's no need for anyone to be concerned. I'm only too delighted to help."

"I saw a goblin once tell me he wanted to help me," Captain Swash grumbled. "It were right before he drew a knife on me. Smiled that same way, too, he did."

"You're not helping," Percival said to the Captain, frustration seeping into his voice. "We had a deal, Captain . . . your crew and your ship."

"The crew I've got!" Captain Swash whined. "But

this—person—has plundered the ship right out from under me!"

"Well, that's half a bargain, then," Percival complained. "Which means, I guess, that I'll only tell *half* the people I meet about the true nature of your business! The crew is no good to me without the ship!"

"Well, the ship is no good to you either without my crew!" raged the Captain.

The heavy captain's chair scraped suddenly against the decking.

Captain Swash and Percival both turned toward the woman who was now standing. She leaned forward, placing both of her gloved fists on the surface of the desk.

"The Captain is right," Vestia said quickly.

"I am?" the Captain asked.

"Look, Percival," Vestia said, her eyes suddenly liquid and large above her formidable pout. "I don't understand every-thing that you're going through or what went wrong between us. Whatever it is that I've done, I'm very sorry for it and I'm trying to make it up to you. You have your crew under Captain Swash. Let me offer you the use of my ship."

"Why, Vestia," Percival smiled. "That's . . . that's wonder-ful! Thank you!"

"I only have one condition," Vestia said, holding up a single gloved finger.

"Sure! I'll be happy to—"

"I must come with you," Vestia said through a demure smile.

Adrian Wright stood on the forecastle of the *Revenge* next to Vestia. The mermen had secured the ship to the pier and had departed, leaving them both to watch as Captain Swash and Percival made their way back up the long slipway to Sailor's Walk Road. Vestia stood with her feet planted wide on the deck, her arms folded across her chest as she watched their visitors depart, a thoughtful look on her face bright in the morning sun.

"I have yet to thank you for your help," Adrian said. "You are very talented at woodworking. Wherever did you pick up the craft?"

"Did I not mention that my father was a cooper in Eventide?" Vestia said, raising her eyebrows. "I grew up with the craft around me. Father taught me some when Mother was not looking. I rather liked fashioning things with my hands, bending the wood into useful shapes and pleasing my father with them. Of course, that's not the sort of thing a proper woman does—not one who is destined for a place at court in Mordale and proper society. I haven't had the opportunity in the last few years to work at all in my father's shop, my mother seeing to it that my time was occupied with more tradi-tional and acceptable activities. Still, there was something very satisfying in fitting a few planks for you in this ship, Master Shipwright."

"Then I am grateful indeed," Adrian bowed slightly. "Besides, I think this is a good look for you."

"Men's clothing?" Vestia scoffed. "You are a strange man, Master Shipwright. You needed help to get the ship finished in time and I could hardly be expected to fit planks in a dress and binders! My appearance is hardly conducive to a proper courtship. My mother would faint at once were she to see me in this condition."

"It is a good thing that it is not your mother you are trying to impress. It seemed to intrigue your friend Percival," Adrian commented. "Which, if I am not mistaken, was the point in your purchasing the ship from me in the first place, was it not?"

Vestia frowned. "Not entirely. It *is* a fine ship and a good investment at the price."

"But that is not why you bought it," Adrian observed. "Nor why your mother agreed to release your dowry to you in order to do so."

"You don't understand," Vestia said, turning toward the shipwright. "Everyone in our town knows that Percival is supposed to marry me."

"Everyone except Percival, it seems," Adrian said.

"He is just confused, is all," Vestia said as much to herself as to the shipwright. "A few days away from that painted peacock he has been ogling and he'll come back to his senses."

"You do realize that his crew is made up entirely of pirates?" Adrian said. "Once you're out of port, it isn't going to matter to a single one of them whether you paid for this ship or not. Taking ships that don't belong to them is what they do."

Vestia turned away from him, biting her lower lip. "I know. It's just . . . it's just that I don't know any other way to win him back. Don't you understand? I've just got to make him remember what he's promised me."

Adrian raised his chin, pain flashing in his eyes for a moment before he turned and looked out to sea.

"Yes, I understand," the shipwright replied. "So much so that I'm joining this foolish expedition."

"You are?" Vestia asked. "Why?"

"Because you and Percival are both sailing into deep waters," Adrian said, shaking his head in disgust, "and someone needs to come along who knows how to swim."

CHAPTER 15

Abducted

T uppence Magrathia-Paddock stood at the low wall surrounding the balcony outside her rooms, her parasol in
hand to guard her against the sunshine beating down overhead.

She was most displeased.

Tuppence had watched the *Revenge* take a berth alongside one of the long wharfs extending out from the town
into Blackshore Bay earlier that morning. She knew that the
Revenge was the ship of her beloved Percival—just as she knew
that so fragile a name as *Percival* must actually mask his secret
identity as *Rodrigan*. Tuppence knew these things in her heart
and would hold fast to the beliefs against the less-certain argu-
ments of reason and fact. So, assured at last that her Rodrigan
was preparing for his adventurous voyage, Tuppence decided
that she too must be prepared.

Accordingly, she had spent the morning packing for her imminent abduction.

Truthfully, preparing to be kidnapped, Tuppence observed, requires considerable consideration. One must pack lightly since the person abducting you almost certainly will not have thought to bring a wagon in order to carry off your wardrobe and accessories. In the case of Tuppence, packing lightly limited her severely to a single trunk, two traveling chests, and a valise, each of which she had the house servants carry down into the courtyard and set in the back of her carriage. For good measure, she also had them harness the horse to the carriage, thereby saving her rogue the trouble of having to do so in the midst of stealing her off. Tuppence then returned to her chambers, congratulating herself on having been so thoughtful in her preparations. She selected an appropriate abduction ensemble from those outfits remaining in her wardrobe, freshened her look once more, and then waited with wilting patience on her balcony for her Rodrigan to come for her while her father was conveniently away dealing with some nonsense regarding a visiting nobleman complaining about a treasure map.

As the morning wore on, Tuppence's temper climbed with the sun. She could see activity on the pirate ship from her vantage point above the town but was increasingly upset at Rodrigan's discourtesy. He was late. The Governor's daughter was perfectly willing to be stolen away by the roguish Rodrigan, but to keep her waiting for her abduction when he was obviously preparing to leave was careless on his part. She was forced, at last, to send her lady's companion, Eunice, into town to find out why she had not yet been carried off into romance and adventure.

Almost an hour later, she continued to stand on her balcony, the delicate fingers of her hands angrily tapping the handle of the parasol in her impatience. The sun had grown warm overhead and she was beginning to feel that she might "mist" or "glisten" or possibly, horrifically, "sweat."

At last she spied Eunice rushing up Apple Lane toward the house, her face red with the effort, holding her skirt up slightly with both hands so that she might run a little faster.

"And about time!" Tuppence said to Triton, her long-suffering and loyal guard dog.

"Muph!" Triton chuffed in agreement from where he appeared to be a small mop of long fur splayed against the floor of the bedchamber.

Eunice burst in through the door, out of breath and barely able to speak. "Milady! Oh, I . . . I have . . . Oh! I have . . . it's such . . . I have to . . . to tell . . ."

"Eunice! Calm yourself!" Tuppence commanded as she stepped back into the room, grateful for the shade at last. She had tired of striking comely poses on the balcony long before, having settled on one, though so far she had not had the opportunity to employ it. "Catch your breath and tell me the news from town."

"Oh! Lady Tuppence!" Eunice tried to speak. She was blinking furiously in her excitement. "I fear . . . I fear the news . . . the news I have to bear is . . . is just too . . ."

"Too? Too what?" Tuppence demanded, stamping her foot so hard that Triton raised his head from the stones in surprise. "Eunice! Tell me!"

"Oh, milady!" Eunice gulped and then, unexpectedly loudly, belched. The lady's companion, horrified by the sound that had exploded from her lips, quickly clamped both hands over her mouth, her eyes widening in embarrassment.

"It's all right, Eunice," Tuppence said, reassurance in her voice as she tried to calm down her companion. "Just tell me what you have learned."

"I am sorry, milady," Eunice said, the red in her face now increasing in its hue by her embarrassment. "It's just I'm so worried for your ladyship!"

"Eunice, please," Tuppence asked, taking her companion by both shoulders as she looked into her face, "where is Rodrigan?"

"They've gone out to the Mermaid Grotto," Eunice said. "They need to hire some pilot mermen to guide the *Revenge* out of the harbor, and it seems they're in a rush with the tide cresting at noon and all. As soon as they hire those mermen, then they'll leave."

"They'll . . . leave?" Tuppence gaped. "Perhaps they intend to abduct me on their way back to the ship and . . ."

"I fear not, milady." Eunice squinted as she spoke, which Tuppence had long since understood to mean that she was holding back something unpleasant.

"Why, Eunice? What do you know?"

"Who your young rogue went with to hire the mermen, milady." Eunice sounded slightly like Triton on those rare occasions when Tuppence scolded the dog. "It was that Vestia woman. It seems now she's a pirate of sorts and owns the ship."

"And *she's* going on the voyage?" There was a sudden, dangerous tone in Tuppence's tightly controlled voice.

"Yes, milady!" Eunice said. "The men I spoke to . . . oh, and a rough-looking lot they were, milady . . . they said that the Captain had no choice in the matter, seeing that this Walters woman owned the ship and all."

"So *she's* the one keeping my Rodrigan from abducting me!" Tuppence declared. She scooped up Triton and headed for the door. "We're taking the carriage down to the ship at once, Eunice."

"But, milady!"

"Sometimes, Eunice," Tuppence said with fierce determination in her features, "if you want to be properly abducted, you just have to do it yourself!"

To the satisfaction of Captain Rodrigan, preparations for the Revenge *to slip silently out of the dark, midnight waters of Blackshore Bay with its pirate crew were nearly complete.*

Except, of course, that Rodrigan was actually named Percival, he was not actually a captain, and, while it was true that preparations for the ship's departure were almost complete, slipping out of the bay silently was impossible since it was nearly noon and the docks were crowded with townspeople who had turned out to watch with a mixture of disbelief and amusement.

Abel the scribe stood on the afterdeck of the *Revenge* and scratched the back of his head, his pencil still in hand. He stared at the leaf of parchment upon which he had been chronicling the events in the town. The first sentence he had scrawled there was full of romance and adventure but completely wrong. He just was not sure how one should describe this particular departure of the pirate ship. His discomfiture may have been affected by the fact that the delightful Melodi Morgan, the sister of Caprice Morgan of Eventide and the traveling companion of Vestia Walters, was standing on the docks. Her otherwise charming countenance was looking somewhat distressed by the increasingly loud argument taking place not two feet in front of her between Vestia Walters and her Aunt Calista.

Calista stood with her feet firmly planted on the wharf at the base of the boarding plank for the *Revenge,* her arms folded across her chest. "I will not allow it! I would never be able to look your mother in the face and tell her that I permitted you to sail off on this . . . this . . . pirate ship!"

"It's *my* pirate ship," Vestia asserted, standing firm against the gale of her aunt's bluster. She wore a pair of new breeches she had fashioned for herself, tapering the legs to a better fit inside her tall boots. The loose-fitting blouse was cinched with a wide belt at her waist that accentuated her figure. She wore leather gloves to protect her hands, her golden tresses pulled back into a long ponytail. "I paid for it, I'm its owner, and I'll sail on it anytime I want!"

"If your mother knew what you were up to . . ."

"My mother *does* know what I'm up to," Vestia countered. "She's the one who provided the funds for me to acquire this old derelict and she knows better than most why I need to be on this ship."

"Well, I don't!" Calista huffed.

"Look down at the end of the wharf," Vestia said, folding her arms across her chest. "Do you see the carriage there?"

Calista and Melodi both turned. Standing on the quay in front of the Mistral's Mistress was a black, covered coach. A figure could be seen in the shadows just beyond the opening, holding a lace cloth to its lips.

"That is why this ship is leaving with me aboard," explained Vestia. "I just need to get Percival away from that peacock for a few days. With a little fresh air and with that stale confection out of the way, Percival will come to his senses. It's the Bard's idea, and this is exactly why mother hired the Bard in the first place. He's coming along too, to help make sure that everything goes according to plan."

"Is he taking that scribe of his with him?" Melodi asked suddenly.

"Yes, I think they're both aboard now," Vestia answered with a quizzical look on her face. "Why would you ask?"

"Oh, no reason in particular," Melodi said with a shrug.

"Miss Walters," Adrian called down from the top of the gangplank. "You had better come aboard now. The mermen are alongside."

"Yes, thank you," Vestia nodded, then turned back to face Melodi. "Give Aunt Calista what help you can and she'll take care of you until I get back."

"How long will that be?" Melodi asked.

"I don't think it will take long," Vestia said through a smile that held worry at its corners. "It isn't as though we're crossing the world to the Lycandric Ocean! We'll sail about only long enough for Percival to come to his senses."

"It might take less time to sail to the Lycandric Ocean," Calista grumbled.

Vestia ignored the remark and, turning, rushed up the gangplank. She had barely set foot on the deck before the crew hoisted the plank aboard.

"Are you prepared for an adventure, sir?"

Abel was startled to see Professor Balderknack standing beside him.

"I have always dreaded this part," the Professor went on. "The leaving home . . . but it was much easier for me when I knew that something was waiting for me out there. I hope it's waiting for me still."

A sudden shout caused both the Professor and the scribe to turn around.

"Ahoy! First Mate!" Captain Percival stood on the after-deck, the picture of heroic poise. A stout man stood just behind him. Percival glanced back down the pier to where the carriage was parked, hoping that he looked sufficiently grand in the broad-brimmed hat he had purchased from the Laird's Lair earlier in the day.

"Aye, Captain!" answered the stout man behind him.

"The wind is freshening and the tide is ebbed," Percival called out in his best commanding voice. "Mister Johansen, let's jib the luff and secure the hoist! It's time to launch the boat!"

Professor Balderknack raised an eyebrow. A number of seamen on the pier laughed heartily, but none of the crew aboard so much as broke a smile.

"Aye, Captain," answered Mister Johansen, pressing his right knuckle to his head in salute. "Single lines fore and aft. Riggers aloft. Mister Volnak, give the word to the mermen to ease us out when the hawsers are clear of the moorings."

"Aye, Captain . . ."

"Belay that talk, Mister Volnak!"

"Beggin' yer pardon! Aye, Mister Sailing Master Johansen!"

Percival looked splendid in his rogue costume and new pirate hat. He stood with his feet apart, his flaxen hair blowing in the light breeze, both fists set on his hips, and a cape that he had put on just for good measure billowing about him on the afterdeck. His voice called out clearly over the deck: "Avast! Clear away the rigging! Man the steerage! Let's come about lively, lads!"

The crew stopped at once what they were doing and looked at Mister Johansen.

"You heard the captain!" Johansen yelled. "Clear the moorings, Mister Morkie, and stow the bow hawsers, if you please.

The deck crew began moving at once. Several men dragged the aft mooring line aboard while Mad Morkie the minotaur hauled in the heavy forward mooring line onto the forecastle deck on his own.

"Will you be taking the helm, Captain?" Mister Johansen asked Percival.

Percival blinked. "What?"

"Will you be steering the boat, Captain?"

"Oh, yes!" Percival answered, striding forward to the large ship's wheel, grasping its handles firmly. "Where away, men? We're off for adventure!"

"Off indeed," commented the Professor, his brows knitted.

Abel turned back around to lean against the stern railing. Below him he could see the mermen working against the hull of the ship, pushing it away from the wharf and then forward into the waters of the bay. The town of Blackshore was receding behind them slowly.

"Isn't that Madame Zoltana?" the Professor said, pointing toward the end of the pier.

Abel looked. Both Madame Zoltana and her son, Gilliam, were standing at the end of the pier, the smiling gypsy woman waving enthusiastically at the departing ship.

"That's odd that they should be here," the Professor said, then stepped away, making his way toward the bow.

The scribe wondered what Edvard would make of that, but his master was below deck for some purpose of his own and Abel was just as glad for his absence. He turned his attention to the carriage parked on the quay, wondering for a time why the lady within remained hidden from view. But as the town grew smaller, so, too, in Abel's mind were its problems and concerns.

Abel turned around and leaned over the rail to watch the mermen taking the ship out through the shoals past the ruined tower of old Fort Gar. The Wand Foundry stood atop the Troll Cliffs ahead and to the left. He could see past Mermaid Grotto on his right now to the open expanse of Mistral Sound and the beckoning horizon of the open sea beyond.

All the while, Captain Percival held a white-knuckled

grip on the ship's wheel, moving only when Mister Johansen reached over and nudged it.

Twilight was waning. A thin line of light still demarked the horizon and a number of stars had yet to appear overhead. The afterdeck was awash in the golden glow of the two large ship's lamps mounted at the stern corners of the deck.

"It's time to change the watch, Captain," said Silent Sasha, who was acting helmsman for the watch.

"I'm Mister Johansen," grumbled Captain Swash. "What is it going to take for this crew to get that simple deception straight?"

"Aye, Mister Johansen," answered Sasha with a wink. "The glass says it's time to change the watch."

"Aye, time enough, and you be sure and turn the glass on time, Sasha, but I'll be holding off on changing the watch just yet," the Captain said. "Are our passengers properly stowed?"

"Aye, Mister Johansen," Sasha answered. "The shipwright's found himself someplace in the forepeak. We're not sure exactly where but we'll find his nest right enough. That Vestia woman is below and aft in the quartermaster's closet, with His Lordship Captain Percival in the captain's great room along with that Professor Nick-Knack. That Bard and his servant are portside aft in the cook's room."

"And what about that other woman?" Captain Swash asked with a grin.

"That one? I've got her hid aft behind the powder magazine in the smuggler's hold. She even thanks me for me service and give me a gold coin for puttin' her there," Sasha snickered, but then his countenance grew more somber. "Begging your pardon, 'Mister Johansen,' but what are you doing taking her aboard? She's dangerous cargo. Her father will be coming for her on the next warship he lays his hands on."

"Exactly," nodded the Captain. "We'll get to sea just long enough to let the fun of this game tarnish a bit. Then we'll play this wench of a Governor's daughter as a trump card. Even Captain Percival will understand that returning at once to port with this woman is the best and safest course. She's our ticket to getting this ship back to port—and us with it."

"But how did you manage to kidnap her?" Sasha asked in wonder.

"I didn't!" chuckled Captain Swash. "That's the best part of it. She bribed me to sneak her aboard and made me promise to claim that she was actually abducted by our valiant Captain Percival!"

"You mean she paid you to abduct her?" Sasha gaped.

"Tuppence Magrathia-Paddock," Captain Swash grinned. "It's always a pleasure doing business with the upper classes."

CHAPTER 16

Maelstrom

Vestia stood on the quarterdeck of the *Revenge,* her boots planted wide on the deck as she held the ship's wheel in both her hands. The wind crossed the deck from the larboard bow, heeling the ship to starboard. It washed its freshness across Vestia's face. She felt the ship moving under her feet, rushing across the ocean to rise and fall with each wave breaking against its bow.

It filled her with a joy and vitality she had never before thought possible.

The taut mainsail started to flap loudly in the wind, and she could feel herself pitch slightly forward as the ship slowed.

"Ease her a little to starboard," Adrian urged, standing behind her. "We're close hauled and need to keep a little more to leeward or you'll lose the wind."

"How much?" Vestia asked.

"Three points, I should think," Adrian answered. "Do you see that left dial in the binnacle?"

"Yes." Vestia leaned slightly around the wheel. The binnacle was a wooden pedestal supporting two brass housings with fitted glass panels on either side of a shuttered lamp. Inside were two dials fixed to specially crafted wands.

"The dial on the left is the compass dial," Adrian explained. "That one points to the roof of the world—the truest of north. Try to keep the ship heading on two-oh-five."

"What is the other one?" Vestia asked. This one pointed nearly directly behind them.

"That is the home-port dial," Adrian explained. "It always points the shortest course back to the ship's home port."

"So you can always find your way home!" Vestia nodded.

"Yes, in part," Adrian answered. "But it also helps you cross the expanse of the ocean. A good navigator with a chart can compare the two readings and determine with reasonable accuracy where he is almost anywhere in the world."

"How poetic," Vestia sighed.

"Poetic?" Adrian asked.

"Yes," Vestia answered with a wistful smile, "that one should be lost without knowing their way home."

Adrian chuckled, then pointed at the encased compass. "Two-oh-five."

Vestia shifted the wheel in her hands, feeling the satisfaction of the bowsprit swinging slightly to starboard. The mainsail went rigid once again and the ship surged forward. The low-lying clouds were racing above the masts on a warm southern breeze. It had whipped the sea into whitecaps, but she reveled in it all. She turned her head around toward the larboard quarter of the deck, strands of her golden hair from her ponytail whipping about her beaming face as she called out, "Captain! Is this the course you wanted?"

Percival gripped the railing on the larboard side of the quarterdeck with both hands. His face was a peculiar pale color and his mouth unusually grim. He seemed to be having difficulty talking. "It's the course the Professor indicated. Just . . . just follow his directions."

"How long until we arrive?" asked Tuppence Magrathia-Paddock. She had changed into a matching dress and peplum jacket, her third ensemble for the day. Unlike the captain, she seemed completely unfazed by the motion of the ship. Her dog, Triton, lay in her arms, craning his face out into the wind so that it blew the hair away from his eyes, his small, pink tongue poking from his mouth as his fluffy tail flapped merrily about. "I mean, it seems as though we've been at sea for ages! Aren't we there yet?"

"We've been at sea . . . for two days," Percival responded with an edge of despair in his voice. "Mister Johansen? If you would be so good as to take charge of the ship for a while as I am feeling rather . . ."

"Aye, Captain," answered the stout first mate through his

gap-toothed grin. "And may I suggest that you be taking Miss Tuppence to join the Professor on the forecastle. The air be fresh in that locale and the motion of the ship less pronounced. She may find it more agreeable there."

"An excellent suggestion, Mister Johansen," Percival blurted out, followed, unfortunately, by a rather large belch.

"Oh, that would be wonderful," beamed Tuppence. "And am I to be imprisoned again afterward?"

"Yes, milady," the first mate said quickly, noting that if Percival were to speak again, something less decorous than a belch might be forthcoming. "We shall be delighted to imprison you at your leisure."

Vestia rolled her eyes. After their first day on the sea, Tuppence had become dissatisfied with the location of her imprisonment. Being abducted in a secret compartment of a pirate ship had soon become tedious, and so she had emerged to inquire what other prisoner accommodations might be available. Percival had concluded that the only cabin appropriate for their abducted prize was his own captain's cabin. Thus both Percival and Professor Balderknack were relocated from their former assigned lodgings while Tuppence forbore her trials and tribulations in the largest and most luxuriously appointed rooms in the ship. The Professor found a suitable area with Adrian Wright in the forepeak, while Percival, feeling it unseemly for the ship's captain to be bunking with the crew, took up Tuppence's original compartment behind the powder magazine. He claimed to prefer it there, especially since it was located lower in the ship and the apparent motion was not as noticeable.

Vestia had been quartered in the first mate's cabin just off the gangway to the captain's quarters, and there she adamantly remained. It afforded her an excellent position from which she could observe any and all approaches to Tuppence's now more palatial dungeon. From this cozy lair Vestia could guard the prisoner from being disturbed and, for that matter, ensure that she was accompanied everywhere on board should she choose to wander. Her very presence had largely foiled Vestia's original plan of having Percival to herself for a week or so on the confines of the ship, but Vestia was undaunted. She would impress Captain Percival yet and find some way of showing up the peacock of a girl—and that meant making sure that Tuppence had no opportunity to corner Percival without Vestia being cornered with him.

Not that Vestia thought Percival was feeling much in the mood for romance so long as the motion of the ship was a problem for him.

The first mate reached forward to steady Percival. He moved with extreme caution to follow Tuppence as she flounced down the ladder to the well deck forward of the quarterdeck.

"Are you feeling all right?" Adrian asked the erstwhile captain.

"Oh, he's just getting his sea legs, is all," answered First Mate Johansen. "I'll make sure the Captain doesn't disgrace himself before his lady. Perhaps the both of you might join us. Carmen would be only too happy to take the helm for ye."

Vestia frowned. "I'm fine where I am, Mister Johansen."

"But it's a wearisome task helming the *Revenge*," the first mate pressed.

"And it's still *my* ship to helm," Vestia added.

"That it is, ma'am," the first mate acknowledged with a half smile, then turned to Percival. "Will you give an old sea dog a hand with the ladder, Captain? I'm feeling a bit unsteady today."

Tuppence, despite the rolling of the deck, made her way with surprising grace down the length of the well deck with her guard dog in her arms. She left a number of the pirate crew scattered in her wake while Captain Swash—still playing the part of First Mate Johansen—firmly steadied Percival by the arm as he tried to keep his uncertain legs beneath him.

"Why do you bother with that jellyfish?" Adrian asked, nodding toward the staggering Percival.

"Jellyfish!" Vestia exclaimed. "I'll have you know that's the handsomest, most desired man in all of Eventide! There's isn't a girl in all of Windriftshire that wouldn't do anything for a smile and a nod from that man!"

"We're not *in* Eventide," Adrian asserted. "We're not even in Windriftshire, for that matter. He didn't see your worth while you were both living in that backwoods village, and now he's chasing after that ridiculous daughter of the Governor who has no more brains than he does!"

"He's just been charmed, is all," Vestia stammered. "She's put him under some kind of spell. But I'll snap him out of it and he'll remember his obligations to me!"

"Obligations?" Adrian was having trouble following her argument. "What obligations? Did he ask you to marry him?"

"No, of course not!" Vestia snapped. "But it was all arranged! My mother had contracted the match. The parents were all in agreement. The entire village knew about it."

"And how do you feel about him?" Adrian demanded.

"What do you . . . feel? How do I feel about him?" Vestia sputtered.

"Yes, how do you feel about him?"

"Why, that's none of your affair, Master Shipwright!"

"Perhaps not, but it has everything to do with you, Vestia. Just answer the question: How do you feel about him?"

"I won't answer that!"

"Do you love him?"

"What has that got to do with anything?"

Adrian turned his head away from her, gazing angrily toward the bow. "I thought so. Here you are, chasing this man across the countryside and now across the ocean, too, and is it for his love? No. For the sake of your own heart? No, not even that. You're doing it because of your pride. You cannot stand to lose. You think he's the trophy that you are due. You don't care about him. You care that everyone else will think you're something less than you are supposed to be because you couldn't even hold on to this pretty, petty little man. Now you'll chase him across the Nine Seas just so no one else can claim him as a prize ahead of you—a man who doesn't see you at all."

"You're wrong!" Vestia shook her head. "He loves me."

"He has no clue what love really is," Adrian said sadly. "You are a great woman, Vestia, but in every way that Percival will *never* see. You're strong, smart, cunning, and you've got a good heart and a will like steel. You get what you want, Vestia, but do you really know what it is that you want? There's a truly beautiful woman inside that false face you put on every day . . . and you're going to pursue this pretty-faced jester because you're afraid to fail—you're afraid that if you *don't* win him you will be less than invincible, you'll fall off your perch, and the wild dogs that have been waiting for that day will come at you."

"You don't know anything about me!" Vestia shouted, her eyes stinging.

"I know more about you than you think," Adrian said, folding his arms across his chest, pain filling his deep-set eyes.

"Really?" Vestia snapped. "At least when I lost something that was mine, I didn't just stand on top of my house waiting for it to come back! Why did you come along on this voyage, anyway?"

Adrian stared at her for a moment, the pain a fire behind his eyes. Then he pointed at the binnacle.

"Two-oh-five," he said.

Vestia shifted course slightly to starboard again, then stared at the binnacle. "Wait, Adrian. Something's wrong."

Both the compass and the home-port dials were turning even though the ship was holding a steady course. Both arrows on the dials slowly settled to parallel directions three points to larboard. Vestia looked in the direction both dials were pointing and, in the distance, she could see towering storm clouds building above a dark horizon.

Percival staggered across the shifting deck toward one of the tables fixed to the bulkhead. The lantern hanging from the low ceiling swung precipitously over the figures gathered around the table, casting rolling shadows against the walls.

The young man from Eventide had never so much as been on a rowboat on the Wanderwine River before coming aboard the *Revenge,* and the motion of the ship had rapidly gotten the better of him. He had spent most of his time below decks trying desperately not to embarrass himself in front of anyone who might see their "Captain Rodrigan" unable to keep down much in the way of food and with a most sickly pallor to his countenance.

But now, having left Tuppence to resume her imprisonment, he was feeling remarkably better and was beginning to believe that he might continue living after all. So, with cautious steps, he brought himself out into the middle gun deck of the *Revenge* and made his way over to the cheering group gathered below the swinging lantern.

"Percival, my good man!" The Dragon's Bard looked up from the bench on which he sat, his face pulled upward with his glorious smile. He shuffled the deck of cards in his hand with practiced skill. "Or, shall I say, 'Captain Rodrigan' whilst among your gallant crew?"

The crew gathered at the table laughed heartily. Mad Morkie sat at the far end of the Bard's bench, his enormous minotaur form hunched over as his horned head occasionally bumped against the beams overhead. The cards looked diminutive as he held them carefully fanned out in his massive hands. Across from him sat Dead-Eye Darrel squinting at his own cards. Hook-Hand Horvath was seated across from the Bard, his usual shining hook replaced with a strange contraption of wires, springs, and clamps that allowed him to hold his own hand of cards without punching holes in them. Surrounding this group stood a number of other crewmen, watching the game with interest.

"By all means, call me Percival," the boy sighed. "As long as Tuppence is nowhere nearby."

"Then, Percival," Edvard said as he split the deck of cards

using only his right hand, "come join us as we pass the more tedious hours of our voyage in a charming game of—"

"Zoltanair!" Percival cried out.

"Bless you, sir," said Silent Sasha at once.

"No, it's . . . it's Zoltanair!" Percival said, the pallor threatening to return to his face. "The Game of Fates! It tells you your future and seals your destiny!"

"Game of Fates?" Edvard frowned. "What are you talking about?"

"It's all there in front of you!" Percival gestured toward the rough-hewn table top beneath the swinging lamp. "The Five Towers of Destiny . . . the Fate-dragon . . . the Mystic Deck of Zoltana . . ."

"Zoltana!" Edvard slapped his cards facedown onto the table. "Is that what that old crone told you?"

"This isn't the ancient art of divining spirits?" Percival blinked.

Mad Morkie snorted next to the Dragon's Bard.

"Uh, no," Edvard said, rolling his eyes as he picked up his cards again. "It's a game called Bard's Court. All the bards play it wherever they go. Abel will most gladly sell you an exquisite set of your own and you can 'divine' your own 'fate' whenever you like." The Bard looked up from his cards. "Who has the lead?"

Everyone at the table pointed back at the Bard.

"Sorry," Edvard shrugged. He reached out and moved the

small dragon figure to stand next to a stack of heavy round tiles. "We'll play for Sea Tales worth five points. Mr. 'Dead-Eye,' would you mind turning trump?"

"It's a Wizard," said Dead-Eye Darrel as he flipped over the top card from the deck. "Yellow is trump."

Percival stood at the end of the table, staring down at the Dragon's Bard. "You mean . . . it's just a game?"

"Well, not *just* a game," the Bard replied. "It's a very good game . . . and all the rage in King Reinard's court, I understand." Edvard slapped a card down on the table. "Brown seven."

"But, you mean . . . she lied to me?" Percival said, his seasickness suddenly vanishing in his rising outrage.

"Zoltana?" the Bard chuckled. "If that woman ever told the *truth,* the sun would fall out of the sky from shock."

"Then I'm *not* the lost son of Captain Merryweather?" Percival gaped.

"Merryweather?" chirped Silent Sasha. "Aye, he had one son, but the young man were with him aboard the *Mary Ann* when she were lost. That be the only lost son that old salt ever had. That were the very same *Mary Ann* that became the cursed ghost ship of the seas, with her captain and his cursed crew sailing eternally through a storm. That ship has been seen by many a crewman, though not by my own eyes, but I've heard it told that—"

"Quiet!" bellowed Dead-Eye Darrel. "Let the men play!"

"Three of green," growled Hook-Hand Horvath as he fought to remove his own card from the clamp on the end of his arm. "We're changing trump!"

Hook-Hand Horvath struggled to reach for the deck of cards but Dead-Eye Darrel turned the new trump for him. "Red trump now, lads. The hand's taking a new tack."

"Then everything I've done was for nothing!" Percival sighed.

"Nonsense, boy," Edvard continued as Dead-Eye Darrel played a brown two and took consolation from the white stones on the side of the table. "Everything you've done has brought you here."

Mad Morkie played a brown five into the trick and scowled.

"You don't have to let other people tell you where to find your fate, Percival," Edvard beamed as he pulled in the cards and snatched the blue stone disk from the top of its stack. "Choose your own path—and let fate find you."

"You mean like Tuppence?" Percival said, a new thought rising in his countenance like the dawn.

Edvard had gathered up the cards again and was quickly shuffling them, only half his mind on the conversation. "Tuppence Magrathia-Stocks?"

"Paddock," Percival corrected.

"Well, what about her?" Edvard scowled as he dealt out the cards.

"Zoltana didn't predict Tuppence with her fake mystic card game—that was a fate that I found on my own," Percival explained with increasing conviction.

"Now, wait a moment, boy," Edvard said quickly as he chested his hand of cards. "That's not what I said at all! Vestia has always been your destiny . . ."

"But you said I could choose my path and let fate find me," Percival replied in earnest.

"Are you going to lead?" Morkie said in a rumbling voice next to the Bard.

"Well, yes," Edvard said, his eyes blinking quickly as his thoughts tried to recover from the sudden turn of reason. "But you *had* chosen—you had chosen Vestia!"

The deck shifted suddenly underfoot, leaning toward the bow as the ship drove into a deep swell. Percival gripped the table just as the booming sound of a wave broke against the hull.

"No! Don't you see?" Percival said. "Everyone else has always chosen for me. The town and my mother and my father and even Vestia . . . everyone else wanted to choose for me who I was going to be. The only thing I ever chose for myself was what I could *pretend* to be, but I never once chose for myself who I could *really* be."

The hull groaned with the rising bow, a shudder running through her timbers.

"I've got to stop this," Percival said, looking up the ladder leading the main deck above. A thin cascade of water plashed down the rungs. "We've got to go back! I'm ınıı Merryweather's lost son. We've got to turn around before it's too late."

Percival reached for the ladder, but fate was not amused by the young man's sudden challenge. The ship leaned precipitously over, the howling of the wind above rising. Edvard and the others at the table quickly reached out, trying to steady all the pieces of the game, but several of the disks skidded off the table and across the floor. Percival lost his footing as the deck shifted, sliding with the disks across the sharply canted gun deck and crashing headlong against the enormous wand-cannons fixed on their carriage mounts.

"Percival?" the Bard asked.

The youth lay still on the floor.

The Bard and crew hurried over to where Percival lay. His head was bleeding, so Morkie removed the large kerchief from his thick neck and began winding it around the youth's head, binding the wound. The erstwhile captain of the *Revenge* remained unconscious.

The deck hove over in the other direction. Edvard held Percival with one arm while wrapping his other arm around the gun mount.

"There's a storm coming," said Dead-Eye Darrel as he looked up.

"And it's getting worse," added Hook-Hand Horvath.

"It always does," agreed the Bard.

Shouts from the forecastle carried toward the quarterdeck on the wind. Vestia could see Professor Nick-Knack rushing back across the deck, pointing at the distant storm. Mister Johansen was already shouting orders to the crew, each of whom was spurred at once to action, some climbing the ratlines while others moved to the deck rigging.

"We've found it!" the Professor shouted. "I knew that lad would find a course that would bring us here!"

"Found what, Professor?" Vestia asked. The wind was picking up, and she gripped the wheel tighter to hold course.

"The way in!" the Professor cried out as he climbed the ladder up onto the quarterdeck. "Steer for the storm, Mistress Vestia!"

"You want to go *toward* the storm?" she gaped.

"All hands," Mister Johansen shouted from the deck below. "Ready about!"

An explosion of activity erupted on the deck and in the rigging. Pullies squealed, cables hauled over capstans, and the crossbars shifted. The sails suddenly made cracking sounds.

"Tack ship!" Mister Johansen shouted.

"Turn the wheel to larboard!" Adrian said urgently to Vestia.

She began to shift the steering.

"Faster!" Adrian commanded.

She turned the wheel with a will. The ship was slowing, but the bow was definitely swinging straight into the wind and beyond, with the strengthening wind now on Vestia's right.

The sea was angry, and Vestia was in no position to argue.

The storm-driven waves formed sharp, frothy mountains around the ship, pitching it one moment toward the lightning-streaked clouds pouring rain down on its deck and slamming it into valley-deep troughs in the next. Waves crashed over the gunwales, threatening to engulf the ship and drag it into the depths. Mister Johansen had the crew rig lifelines fore and aft along both rails and batten the hatches. Most of the sails had been furled and the yards squared away with just enough canvas to maintain their headway in the howling wind. Nature had diminished the *Revenge* to a pitifully small comparative state.

Still, Vestia had refused to give up the helm, and Adrian had refused to leave her on deck. He had secured her as well as himself by a safety line to the binnacle, a precaution that had saved both of them several times from being swept overboard. Her arms ached from the constant pressure against the ship's wheel, shared by Adrian, who grimly stood fast on the other side of the wheel.

In front of them, lashed to the forward railing of the quarterdeck, Professor Nick-Knack stared out into the storm, searching its terrible flashes as he constantly tried to wipe the rain and seawater from his face.

"Stay on course!" the Professor yelled.

Mister Johansen pulled himself up the ladder from the quarterdeck, a rogue wave crashing over the starboard side and knocking him to the deck. He quickly righted, pulling himself down the lifeline to the binnacle. "This is madness! We've got to turn back! You're wrecking my ship!"

"It's *my* ship!" Vestia yelled against the fury of the storm.

"It's no one's ship if we're all dead!" Johansen shouted back. "Half of them what's below wish they *was* dead as it is. Our most temporary captain has a lump on the noggin and a mortal case of seasickness. That Tuppence woman, on the other hand, is probably getting ready to try to serve him tea and biscuits in her cabin. Never seen a woman with such an iron constitution, though her dog's not doing as well. The crew's aloft clinging to the rigging for their lives or on the deck praying for the safety lines to hold. So we all need to be reasonable, now, and find our way out of this storm!"

"How?" Adrian shouted. "The compass and the home-port dial are both useless!"

"Then we follow the wind and have it blow us clear of—"

"THERE SHE IS!" screamed the Professor.

Mister Johansen turned about. Adrian and Vestia looked up.

The bow had fallen down the side of the wave, water crashing over the forecastle and rushing back across the well deck. The crew on deck held fast, bracing against the onrushing water.

The wave dissipated before it reached the bulkhead aft, sliding off the camber of the deck out through the scuppers in the bulwarks on either side. The bow rose with the next wave, and it was then, through the spindrift of its crest, that they saw it.

"It can't be!" Mister Johansen shouted.

"Do you see it too?" Adrian called out.

Vestia's eyes widened. "It's a ship!"

Across the crests of the waves, obscured through the sheets of rain, appeared the dark form of a three-masted carrack merchant ship. Her sails were ragged and torn, the canvas flapping in the gale.

"It's the *Mary Ann*," Adrian cried.

"Catch her!" bellowed Nicholas Balderknack, straining against the ropes that held him fast to the rail. "We've got to catch her!"

"Catch her? Are you insane?" Johansen shouted, reaching for the wheel. "We've got to get away from her! She's a ghost ship, I tell ye! Cursed! And she'll drag us into the curse with her!"

"No! Don't you see?" Nicholas pled. "The only way we can break the curse is to close with her!"

"I don't think we have to, Professor," Adrian said, pointing across the bow. "Look! She's closing with us."

The long-lost merchant vessel was turning in the storm, her rounded bow swinging toward them, rushing through the tempest.

"All hands! Ready about!" Johansen bellowed into the

storm as he pulled Vestia from the wheel, tossing her down on the water-slick deck.

"What are you doing?" Vestia cried.

"Tack ship!" Johansen roared against the gale. With a great heave he spun the wheel of the ship. The *Revenge* groaned, heeling over as it tried to turn against the wind. Johansen slipped on the suddenly slanted deck, sliding away from the wheel. The ship was turning slowly to larboard, but the *Mary Ann* had the broad reach and was rushing in their direction. The crew on the deck below were scrambling to regain their footing, desperate to shift the yardarms for the turn.

Suddenly, the waves began to spin. The ocean storm opened into the whirling vortex, dragging the *Mary Ann* downward into its gaping maw. The *Revenge* continued its turn, balanced at the edge of the maelstrom, the following wind beginning to fill its sails.

Then Adrian Wright stood and gripped the ship's wheel. He spun back to starboard, and the *Revenge* plunged down the throat of the maelstrom and into the depths of the sea.

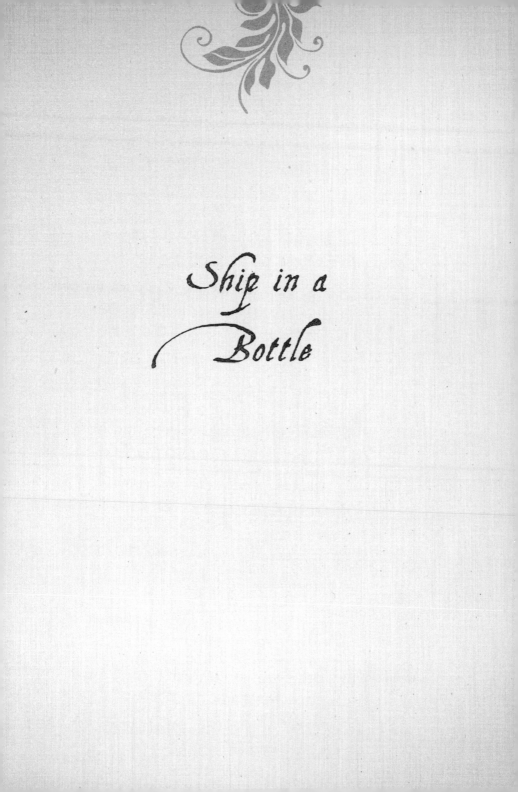

Ship in a Bottle

CHAPTER 17

Boarding Party

The wind howled over Vestia's head. The deck canted madly toward the bow. She tried to stand up, frantic to grab the ship's wheel, but a wave washed over the side and instead she lost her footing and slid toward the forward rail of the afterdeck. She caught a glimpse in the lightning flash of the swirling vortex of water dragging the ship down toward its maw. The bowsprit plunged into the whirlpool of the maelstrom, the water smashing down onto the deck of the ship with crushing force. Vestia caught her breath against the inevitable . . .

Then she realized that the world around her had quite suddenly changed.

Vestia thought it was like waking from a dream. She stood on a nearly motionless deck, her arms folded casually across her chest. A thick, chill fog blanketed the ship, muffling the common creaking of the planks underfoot and the rigging around her. It was difficult for her to tell the time of day, for the sun was indistinguishable in the gray gloom. She could see figures moving listlessly around the deck beyond the railing and even the shadowy forecastle and bowsprit. After the rage and thunder of the storm, the quiet was unnerving.

"Vestia!"

She startled visibly at the sound of her name.

"What happened?" Percival asked. He was standing on the quarterdeck next to Vestia. His head was wrapped in a pirate scarf, a bloody stain on one side. "Why have we stopped?"

"We . . . we haven't stopped," Vestia answered, struggling to find her voice. "I thought we were about to die and . . . what are you doing up here?"

"I don't know," Percival said as though surprised at the answer himself. "I was down on the gun deck on my way up here."

"Up here?" Vestia looked at him askance. "You've barely left your cabin for days."

"I've haven't been able to stop . . . well, I've been feeling in poor health," Percival answered. "I mean, *usually* the rocking of the ship does not bother me at all, you understand, but this particular vessel has a certain cadence in its gallop that leaves me—"

"You were seasick," Vestia interrupted. She peered forward,

straining to see through the mists. She could make out the water moving past the hull beyond the gunwale. The sails were carrying them forward on a slight breeze. She fixed her gaze forward, straining to see anything through the fog along their course. "There's no point in pretending, Percival. We all knew it."

"But I feel fine now," Percival shrugged, his face brightening. "Maybe I finally got my sea legs!"

Vestia straightened, unfolding your arms. "Or maybe you're just dead."

"Well, I'll admit there were a few moments there when I *wished* I were dead," Percival replied casually.

"Well, you may have gotten your wish," Vestia said, pointing slightly to starboard of the bow. "Look!"

A dark shape was emerging from the gray murkiness just to the right of their course. Nearly as tall as the *Revenge,* though somewhat shorter along the keel, it was another ship sitting still in the placid waters. Those few sails that were still deployed were in tatters and improperly set. They luffed softly in the slight breeze.

"Is that the same ship that we saw in the storm?" Vestia asked in hushed tones.

"A three-masted carrack," Adrian said behind her. "Aye, that's the ship, all right."

Vestia turned toward the shipwright, intense fire in her eyes. Adrian remained at the ship's wheel, both hands grasping its handles in separate quadrants. Next to him stood the bewildered Mister Johansen/Captain Swash. The Dragon's Bard was nowhere to be seen, which in itself was surprising to Vestia, since he always seemed to be around when least expected or, for that matter, desired. However, his scribe was still lashed to the after railing where she remembered him being before the ship dove into the maelstrom. Even Tuppence Magrathia-Paddock had inexplicably appeared from below deck and was now standing at the aft rail resplendent in an overly elaborate dress, her miniature version of a dog shivering in her arms.

"Where are we, Adrian?" Vestia demanded.

"I don't know," Adrian answered.

"What mean ye that ye don't know?" Mister Johansen demanded at once. "Ye be the one what steered this course and brought us here!"

"I mean that I don't know where *here* is," Adrian answered sharply. "I followed that ship and it brought us to this place—wherever or whatever this place is."

"But you already know what ship that is, don't you, Adrian?" Vestia's voice was accusing.

"She's badly weathered and listing a bit to port, but there's no doubt about her name. She's—"

"It's the *Mary Ann!* It's the *Mary Ann!*" Professor Balderknack was charging aft along the middeck, his arms gesturing wildly as ran. He stumbled in his haste coming up the ladder onto the quarterdeck. "You've done it, Percival! You've found her!"

"The *Mary Ann?*" Vestia gaped.

"Er, Captain," Mr. Johansen said quickly to Percival. "Whoever she is, we need to lose some headway. We're closing with her a bit fast."

"Huh?"

"We need to stop before we run into her," Johansen said under his breath.

"Right you are, Mister Johansen!" Percival said in a voice louder than necessary. "Avast, all hands! Prepare to stop!"

"Mister Volnak! Prepare to stop the ship," called out Mister Johansen across the deck. "Get the watch aloft and furl the sails."

"But we're not there yet!" Professor Balderknack said.

"Think ye that we'll just lay up alongside the hull and step from one deck to the next?" Mister Johansen replied. "We'd foul our rigging with his before you ever got close enough to cross without getting wet. The *Revenge* were just put back together, and I'll not be scratching her paint trying to come alongside that barnacled wreck! Mister Morkie, prepare the longboat, if you please."

"You mean to board her, Captain?" asked the minotaur from the well deck below.

"I do—I mean, he does," Johansen replied. "We've lost our

bearings and we're off the charts, mate. If anyone knows what course we need to steer, they'll be on that wreck."

"Rodrigan, my dashing beloved," Tuppence chirped, stroking the long fur of her guard dog.

"Oh, uh . . . yes, darling," Percival cooed, stepping quickly up to where the young woman stood in her formal gown and wide-brimmed hat.

Vestia considered her with a mixture of amusement and frustration. The woman had somehow managed not only to bring such a monstrously useless thing as an ornate dress onto the ship but to appear in it as though the occasion required formal attire. Her hair was perfectly coiffed and she appeared absolutely serene in the midst of their peril. Vestia could not determine if the woman was insane, brave, naïve, or just too dim-witted to understand the danger they were facing.

"Why is that horrid, portly man giving all the orders?" Tuppence pouted.

Mister Johansen grimaced through his gapped teeth.

"Him? Oh, he's Mister Johansen," Percival stammered for a moment before his face brightened. "He's my apprentice captain. He's training to take over my position after I give up the sea."

"And you would do that for me, wouldn't you?" Tuppence sighed, batting her eyes at the young man.

"This life of adventure is all I have ever known," Percival

asserted, assuming what he believed was his best Rodrigan pose. "But I would give it all up for the right woman."

Adrian cast a baleful glance toward Vestia as he spoke.

Vestia set her jaw and stepped around the wheel, pushing the shipwright aside. "I'll take the helm. I think you've managed to steer us into enough trouble for one day."

She could feel the ship slowing beneath her. The masts were shrouded in the mists, but she could see the crewmen standing on the lines and lashing the sails to the yard arms overhead. The *Mary Ann* remained a shadow in the fog, but they were closer now and could make out her elevated forecastle and quarterdeck.

"Why is she listing?" Vestia wondered aloud.

"Could be her ballast is off or she's taken on water in the storm," Adrian answered, his own eyes examining the carrack. "What I don't understand is why there is no one on deck."

"What do you mean?" Professor Balderknack asked.

"There is no movement in the rigging or at the rails," Adrian observed. "The quarterdeck looks deserted as well."

"A ghost ship?" Mister Johansen's eyes went wide. "You followed a ghost ship into a storm!"

"Nonsense!" Professor Balderknack said.

The steering was becoming sluggish as the *Revenge* slowed. Below, on the well deck, Morkie the minotaur and several more of the crew had released the longboat from its securing cables and rigged a quick hoist over the side. The longboat was already being lowered toward the impossibly still waters over the larboard side. Forgotten, Abel managed to untie himself from the railing without the notice or assistance of the otherwise engaged group on the quarterdeck.

The *Mary Ann* drifted barely a hundred yards away, her decks clearly devoid of life, her helm abandoned.

"Well, Mister Johansen?" Adrian asked pointedly.

"There be no need for haste," the portly man responded, licking his lips. "Perhaps if we were to consider . . ."

Adrian glanced at Vestia and then, turning, jumped down the forward ladder to the well deck.

"And just where are you going?" Vestia shouted.

Adrian reached the larboard side and climbed over the rail. His boot stumbled over a pile of canvas as he moved toward the bow.

"Percival! Take the wheel!" Vestia commanded. She pushed past Professor Balderknack and rushed down the ladder to the well deck, calling out toward Adrian as her booted footfalls pounded against the deck planks. "Adrian Wright, you got us into this and you're just going to have to get us out!"

"Vestia!" Adrian was adamant. "This is of no concern of yours and I'd thank you to stay out of it!"

"No concern of mine?" Vestia squawked. "You said you came along to protect me and now you're abandoning me?"

"Who's abandoning whom?" Adrian shot back, setting the oars across the benches of the longboat. "You've got your

Percival, just the way you wanted him—not that I think he's that much for the getting." Adrian turned to the minotaur holding the forward tackle lines that kept the longboat suspended over the water. "Morkie! Lower away!"

"Belay that, Morkie!" Vestia ordered in a voice that was not to be questioned.

The minotaur shifted his dark eyes from one to the other.

"I said lower away!" Adrian shouted.

"And I said to belay that!" Vestia yelled back. She reached the side rail and jumped into the longboat. The small craft swayed precariously over the water with her impact. She lost her footing and fell backward into the back of the small craft.

"Get out of my boat!" Adrian demanded.

"You can't tell me what to do, Adrian Wright," Vestia said, struggling to sit up, both her hands on the gunwales of the longboat. "And it isn't your boat—it's *mine*. I own it!"

"Excuse me," came a voice from just above them.

Both looked up.

Professor Balderknack was climbing down into the boat as well. He quickly took a place on the forward bench.

"Professor!" Adrian was exasperated. "You can't . . ."

"No, Adrian, I've waited a long time for this," the Professor answered with a quiet voice but a gleam in his eye. "You cannot deny me now. Mister Morkie, you may lower away now, if you please."

The minotaur raised his long face in a glance toward the

quarterdeck. With Mister Johansen's nod, Morkie began feeding the cable through the tackle securing both ends of the longboat. The keel slapped against the still water beneath it, soon bearing its own weight on the placid, dark water.

Adrian moved toward the stern to release the cable hook, but Vestia waved him away. "I've got it."

Adrian huffed and then moved toward the bow, tripping again over the canvas. This time a distinct "umph" came from under the rumpled cover. Adrian pulled back the canvas.

"Good morrow, good friends," the Dragon's Bard said through a yawn as he sat up, stretching. "My apologies, but I was carried away in the arms of blissful slumber. Did I miss anything of importance?"

Adrian reached forward, pushed the cable hook out of the bow cleat, and then gave a shove against the hull of the *Revenge* to push their boat clear. "Yes, Bard, I'd say you missed a thing or two."

"Well, I shall have to be sure to have my scribe fill me in on the details," the Bard observed. His face fell as he watched Adrian step past him to the center bench and begin fitting the oars in the oarlocks. "Oh, it seems we are going on an excursion?"

The oars made the quietest of splashing sounds as they entered the water. Adrian pulled hard against them. The longboat surged forward, cutting through the dark water.

"An excursion? Absolutely," Adrian said in dark tones. "We are the boarding party."

"Boarding party!" the Dragon's Bard said with a sudden, brightening smile. "So we're going aboard another ship, eh? Marvelous! They will have such a store of tales to tell. We shall storm the decks with my wit and conquer them with my songs! Do you think I'll be requested to entertain the crew? I am, as you undoubtedly are aware, among the most sought-after performers of both epic poetry and bard songs to be found in any of King Reinard's shires or protected lands. Of course, my performance fees are at a premium, and given the short notice of the engagement . . ."

"I doubt it will be that kind of party, Bard," Vestia said dryly, her hands still gripping the gunwales of the boat. She turned around, looking back. The familiar lines of the *Revenge* were growing soft as it fell behind them into the fog. Vestia could see Percival standing at the helm, his right hand gripping a handle of the ship's wheel and his left hand gripping the waist of Tuppence Magrathia-Paddock next to him.

"Why do you care what that whelp does?" Adrian asked as he slipped the oars out of the water, swinging his arms forward.

"I thought I cared," Vestia said, turning back around as much to face the shipwright as to not have to face the fading Percival. "I'm beginning to think that I cared more about what everyone else thought I was supposed to care about, if that makes any sense. Things look a lot different away from shore."

"That, at least, is true," Adrian said with a sad chuckle. "I've built ships, repaired ships, and set ships across the sea most of my life, but I've never sailed a ship outside of Blackshore Bay. But out here . . . you see farther. And, I think, you find beauty where you never would have found it on land."

Vestia looked into Adrian's deep-set eyes, trying to fathom the pain behind them. She wondered what it was he had lost that he needed to find.

He looked away from her as he spoke. "He's not worthy of you, Vestia. I've seen you do remarkable things—maybe for the wrong reasons, but that doesn't make them any less remarkable. He would diminish you, and that would be wrong—no matter how many people in your village see it otherwise."

The creaking bulk of the *Mary Ann* grew larger with every pull of Adrian's powerful arms.

"What about you, Adrian? What diminishes you?"

Adrian only stared back at her.

The dark hull of the *Mary Ann* towered above them. The wood was black and waterlogged. Adrian pulled them around to the larboard side where the gunwale of the silent ship was closer to the water. It made for a shorter climb up to the deck but left the bulk of the *Mary Ann* between them and the *Revenge*.

Adrian secured a line to the front cleat of the longboat and then climbed up the rungs fitted to the side of the ship's hull, the other end of the line in his hand. He vanished for a moment from Vestia's sight, but then, having secured the line to a deck cleat so that the longboat would not drift away, he reappeared, helping Vestia to clamber up onto the deck.

The ship was leaning to one side and the wood of the fittings was badly weathered. Even so, everything on the deck appeared to be in order, although even to Vestia's untrained eye the rigging looked strange. There were block and tackle sets with cabling running back from the yardarms toward the quarterdeck in an almost dizzying array.

"What is all this?" Vestia whispered.

"I've never seen the like," Adrian answered in hushed tones as he helped the Bard onto the deck.

"Where is everyone?" asked the Bard.

Adrian just shook his head. He then helped the Professor clear the larboard rail. Just as Balderknack set foot on the deck, the doorway at the back of the well deck creaked ominously. The sound galvanized everyone's attention. Vestia took a step back. The door fell open, accelerated by the slanting deck, and banged hard against the bulkhead.

Something moved in the darkness of the open doorway.

"What are you?" came the raspy voice from the blackest of shadows. "Whatever you are . . . get off my ship!"

Adrian pulled Vestia back behind him.

"Come out, my friend," the Professor said quietly. "We are lost . . . just like you, Captain Merryweather."

The figure shambled from the doorway into the lighter

gray of the foggy deck. He had a thin, haggard face with a long white beard and still wore the greatcoat of his rank though its color was faded and the cloth worn thin. "Merryweather? How do you know me, sir?"

"He's done it!" Professor Balderknack's face was rapturous, his eyes darting around the ship. "That Percival said he could bring us here and he's done it!"

"I'm sorry, Professor," Adrian said, his eyes cast down on the slanting, rough deck. "Percival didn't bring you here."

"But . . . but he said he knew the way!" The Professor shook his head. "He was the son of Captain Merryweather and he said he knew the way!"

"No, Nicholas," the shipwright said, looking the Professor in the eye. "He didn't bring you here . . . I did."

CHAPTER 18

Ghost Ship

Get back, all of ye!" Captain Edmund Merryweather said. He raised his strong right hand up, gripping a heavy belaying pin as a threat. "Ye come from that ghost ship yonder and I'll have none of your evil aboard my ship!"

"You are tragically mistaken, sir," Edvard sighed, shaking his head in sympathy. "We are standing upon the ghost ship now."

"The *Mary Ann* may be troubled as ever a ship was," Merryweather argued, "but it were your ship what came out of the storm to haunt us and crush our hopes of home! Ye be the ghosts of yon lost ship come to plague us!"

"Ghosts!" shouted the suddenly indignant Dragon's Bard. "*We're* not the ghosts—if anyone around here is a ghost, it's *you!*"

"We're honest seamen aboard the *Mary Ann,*" the Captain rejoined. "We'll have nothing to do with sea-devil spirits!"

"And yet you sail the oceans without a crew!" Edvard said

in what he considered to be a triumph of logic. "Only ghosts could sail such a ship without a crew!"

"You mad spirit!" Captain Merryweather sneered. "My crew is all below decks, secure from your keening wails! I've got a crew!"

"A dead one!" Edvard taunted.

"More alive than you!"

"This from a man who does not even know that he is dead!" Edvard sniffed. "If only we can find a way to convince you that you have died at sea, then perhaps that will remove your curse and your spirits will be free to return to—well, whatever it is that you sea-ghosts worship."

"I'll not be talked at in such a manner on my own ship!" Captain Merryweather bellowed. "Especially by some vaporous apparition!"

Edvard's face flushed. "And just who are you calling 'vaporous,' you—"

"Gentlemen, please," Professor Balderknack said, stepping between the two. "While you both make most interesting points regarding this issue, perhaps we could delay a determination of who between you is a ghost."

A tall figure stepped from the doorway behind the captain. He was a broad-shouldered man, slightly taller than Captain Merryweather. His face was clean-shaven and he looked for all the world to be a younger version of the captain. He wore a broad-brimmed tarpaulin hat and a faded blue jacket over his frayed shirt. His overall look was faded, but there was no mistaking the brightness of the cutlass blade he held in front of him.

"Don't trust 'em, Father," the young man said. "They're only here for the treasure!"

"Nonsense!" sputtered the Professor. "We've come because . . . wait! I *know* you!"

Captain Merryweather glanced sideways at the crewman. "Do you know this ghost, Ransom?"

"Ransom?" The Professor stepped forward. "Ransom Merryweather?"

The crewman took a hesitant step backward.

"Aye," Captain Merryweather said, a question implied in his tone. "This be my son, Ransom. How is it ye know him, spirit?"

"Captain Merryweather," the Professor continued, wetting his lips. "Some years ago, do you remember picking up a man adrift in a storm—a storm like the one you saw today? It would have been on the voyage just before your last return to Blackshore."

The captain lowered the belaying pin slightly, rubbing the long whiskers on his chin thoughtfully with his left hand. "Aye. Right strange it was, too. It were the same man we lost in a storm the year before. He were . . ."

The captain's eyes went wide as he stared at the Professor. He drew the belaying pin up again, his hand shaking. "By the depths of the Abyssal! It were *you!* You're the cursed spirit whose ghost is returned to haunt us again!"

"No, Captain," the Professor said in earnest. "I may have been cursed, but not in the way you think. I've come looking for someone—someone very dear to me—someone whom you might have encountered in this strange, terrible place . . ."

"Nicholas!"

Everyone turned toward the voice coming from the deck of the forecastle.

Professor Balderknack drew in a sharp breath.

The smooth, olive-colored skin of her oval face was flawless. Her full lips were fixed in a pout and her large, almond-shaped eyes flashed with the emotions playing on her lovely features. She still wore the immaculate high-collared silken blouse with the diaphanous sleeves. Her luxuriously long black hair was braided and hung down the length of her back, extending below her waist.

The beautiful woman folded her arms across her chest, her chin rising as she spoke. "Why didn't you come back to me?"

Professor Nick-Knack's jaw dropped, tears welling up in his eyes. "Djara!"

"You didn't come back!" Djara stated again. There was anger flashing in her eyes, but her lower lip quivered as she spoke. "Instead this ship came falling into my bottle. I thought perhaps you had found a way to bring the ship with you as a gift but you were nowhere to be found aboard! Why didn't you come?"

"I tried," the Professor stammered. "I've tried everything and everywhere I could. I've been everywhere you ever took me, searching across the face of the world for you ever since."

"But I've ever only been right here," Djara said. She stepped down the ladder to the main weather deck, her bare feet treading lightly on the sodden planks. "Where else could I possibly be but in my bottle? I only know of one way in or out—that's the ring that I gave you. Then this ship came, and I thought maybe there was another way. Maybe this ship knew the way out of the bottle and I could come and find you instead. Every year the bottle opened, and every year we tried to leave, but you were outside with the ring and—"

"But I don't have the ring," the Professor blurted out.

"Of course you have the ring," Djara said, shaking her head. "How else could the bottle be opened?"

"The ring's gone missing," Nicholas responded as he stepped up to stand in front of her, his hands spread open and empty. "It was taken from me the day before I was supposed to set sail, the day before the *Mary Ann* left the harbor . . ."

The Professor turned suddenly, pointing his finger at Ransom Merryweather. "The same day you visited me."

Everyone on the deck turned toward the young master seaman.

"Rans," Captain Merryweather breathed, dropping the

belaying pin onto the deck at his feet. "What have you done, boy?"

Ransom's eyes shifted between his father's face and those suddenly staring at him. He swallowed hard, sweat breaking out on his forehead, but the tip of his cutlass remained raised. "Nothing . . . I just wanted . . ."

The captain took a step toward his son. "Tell me what you've done, boy."

"Treasure, that's what I've done! The greatest treasure that the world has ever seen . . . and I got it for us, Father!" Ransom said in a rush of words. "Finding the same man we lost in the same storm a year apart and in the same place? That couldn't be chance, Father, it had to be *fate*. So I talked to a few people, learned a few things in Blackshore about the great Professor Nick-Knack and his marvelous adventures and uncounted treasures. There was this young witch in the town who told me about the man, and somehow she knew about this fabulous ring of his. I found his house and—I don't know—the ring was there among his treasures under a glass bell jar just as the young witch said. I didn't have to hurt anybody, just take the ring—which, the witch said, didn't really belong to him anyway, and she would make sure that no one followed us out of the harbor. All I had to do was promise her a share of the treasure when we returned . . ."

"But we never *did* return, did we, son?" Edmund Merryweather sighed.

Ransom gestured with the point of the cutlass toward the cargo hatch in the deck. "But the treasure . . ."

"Our hold is overflowing with treasures, wealth from a hundred different ports, from every shore we have ever heard of and several that were beyond the edges of the charts as well. We've so much of the stuff that our ballast is off and the ship's listing badly to starboard," Merryweather said, shaking his hoary head sadly. "What good has it done us, son? What good is it to us if we never bring it to port? What good is treasure if we never see home?"

"But Father," Ransom pleaded, "we could buy mansions . . . castles . . . kingdoms . . ."

"But we *don't,* son," the Captain said. "We just sail around with it, talking about it and dreaming about it. Now I'm thinking that we've been sailing the same waters for the last fifteen years, seein' everything and never going anywhere. I tell you right now: I'd sink the lot of it beneath my feet if I could just see your mother standing in our garden back in Eventide one more time. She's treasure enough for me, son."

Ransom lowered his cutlass. He looked down at the deck and then reached into his pocket, pulling out a silver braided ring. He held it out toward the Professor. "I'm sorry, Mr. Balderknack."

The Professor took the ring with a sad smile as Djara stepped to his side. "That's why the bottle opened every year—because the ring was here all along and you really didn't know how to use it."

"Use it you must, and soon," Djara said. "The bottle is still open . . . if you hurry . . ."

"Open?" Vestia asked. "But the storm . . ."

"The storm is still out there," Djara affirmed. "The bottle remains open, but not for much longer. You must move quickly if you are to escape the bottle and return to the world!"

"How much time do you think we have?" Merryweather asked at once.

"Perhaps an hour," Djara said.

"Captain," Adrian said, stepping up to Merryweather. "The *Mary Ann* is too heavy, too slow, and too weak to weather the storm again. The *Revenge* is strong and fast and unburdened by cargo, but she's undermanned and will need a full muster aloft to escape this place. We all stand a better chance together than we do separately."

Captain Merryweather nodded, then called out, "All hands on deck! Prepare to abandon ship!"

The hatchways flew open and the haggard crew of the *Mary Ann* began pouring out onto the deck.

"But Father!" Ransom squawked. "The treasure!"

"Carry only what you can, boys!" the captain bellowed. "If you can't float with it, leave it behind!"

"Captain," Adrian asked pointedly, "is there anyone aboard who requires . . . special care to move to the other ship?"

Merryweather looked astonished. "Indeed, there is, Master Wright! How be it that you should know such a thing?"

"A woman who requires fresh water?" Adrian pressed on.

"Aye! Who told ye?"

"Where is she?" Adrian demanded.

"When she's aboard, she keeps quarters in a right enormous barrel down in the hold," Merryweather said.

But the shipwright was already rushing down the ladder.

"Where are you going?" Vestia demanded. She grimaced and then dashed down the ladder after Adrian.

The hold had few lanterns lit, but their feeble light glinted off the surfaces of gold, silver, and faceted gems. There had been some pretext to store the wealth in casks, trunks, crates, and barrels but these had in turn been buried by an avalanche of gleaming statues, necklaces, amulets, platters, urns, and coins that lay in mounds, straining at the ship's hull.

Adrian plunged down the ladder feet first, his boots sinking slightly among the coins on the floor. There, secured to the forward bulkhead with thick ropes, stood an enormous barrel surrounded by treasure.

"Adrian," Vestia called to him as she followed down the ladder, "what are you doing? We've got to leave!"

"Go back to the *Revenge*," Adrian said. He looked around

the compartment and then saw what he was looking for near the aft bulkhead. He stepped quickly back and pulled a hammer and pair of chisels from the box of tools there. "I've got something I have to do."

"Then do it and let's get out of this dreadful place," Vestia snapped as she leaped down the last rungs of the ladder, landing heavily among the coins.

"Go or stay," Adrian said, "it's up to you."

"I'm staying!"

"Fine!" Adrian pushed his way back toward the enormous barrel through the mounds of wealth threatening to fall on him from either side. "If you're staying then be of some use— grab that bucket and bring it over here."

Vestia picked up the bucket with her free hand. "So you brought us here? I don't suppose you could tell me how you managed *that* particular feat of magic?"

"Not magic," Adrian said. He set one of the chisels to the uppermost hoop of the barrel and began hammering at it. "I've been looking for someone for quite some time. She was lost for quite a while, until a year ago I got word that she was aboard the *Gloriana*."

"She?" Vestia asked in a dull tone.

"Yes." The chisel pinged against the metal, cutting a slit into the band that was beginning to widen. "The *Gloriana* was due in Blackshore. I met the boat, but this individual was not aboard. I heard of a story being told by a crewman from the

Gloriana. A few drinks at the Mistrel's Mistress bought me the entire tale from MIster Alphose Griffin himself"

The metal band suddenly broke with a ringing sound. The staves of the barrel creaked.

"Alphose told of a strange storm they had encountered. He was on the forecastle of the *Gloriana,* trying to haul in the staysails on the bowsprit. He said that there, in a flash of lightning, he clearly saw the *Mary Ann*—the ghost ship—close aboard and off the bow." Adrian began hammering the chisel against the lower hoop, the groove widening in the metal. "Next thing he knew, there was a woman standing next to him at the rail, staring across through the tempest toward the ghost ship. They had been more than a month at sea by then, and Alphose Griffin knew there could have been no women aboard. The captain thought them bad luck."

Adrian stepped back just as the hoop gave way. The metal sprang outward, sweeping into the treasure and flinging coins in its path. The staves of the barrel shifted, water rushing out between the slats.

"Fill that bucket with some of this water," Adrian demanded.

Vestia pushed the bucket under one of the spouts of water gushing from between the staves. "So who was this woman?"

"Alphose said she had long, pale hair and eyes the color of a storm. He begged the woman to get below, but all she asked was whether his ship were bound for Blackshore." Adrian stepped forward again, water spraying around him as he raised his chisel to the final, middle hoop of the enormous barrel. "He told her yes, Blackshore was their next port of call, but before he could plead with her again, she leaped overboard. He frantically tried to alert the captain on the quarterdeck, but none of the crew believed him—there were simply no women on the *Gloriana* in the first place. The last he saw of her, she was swimming toward the *Mary Ann* through the driving rain. Now, get back with that bucket!"

Adrian grabbed Vestia's arm, pulling her farther back with him this time, as the final hoop gave way with a loud bang and a cracking sound. The staves of the colossal barrel fell beneath a cascade of rushing fresh water that sifted out among the treasures packed in the hold.

A lithe woman lay in the pool amidst the wreckage of the barrel. Waist-long, pale-green hair splayed down the back of her filmy, wet gown, which seemed to dissipate into the water at her hips along with the rest of her. She pushed herself up slowly with her long-fingered hands, her jade green eyes flashing as they fixed on Adrian. Her pouting lips shifted into a smile above her narrow chin.

"Adrian!" the naiad whispered. "You've come for me! You've come to rescue me from this terrible, boring bottle! I knew you would come. Please help me! Please . . ."

Adrian took the bucket from Vestia's hand and pushed through the inundated treasure to the pool of water at the bottom of the shattered barrel. He set down the bucket in the water as Nyadine struggled over the lip of it. At last her waist managed to slip into the bucket.

Adrian reached down for the bucket. Nyadine curled her exquisite arms up around the shipwright's neck. He stood up with the bucket, the naiad nestling her wet form against his body. He started back toward the ladder leading up from the cargo hold. "Come on, Vestia, let's get back to the ship."

"So *this* is why you came?" Vestia said, her chin quivering as she spoke. "You came to get *her* back?"

"No, Vestia, I did not come to get her back," Adrian said, his deep-set eyes liquid as he passed her and started up the ladder. "I came to be rid of her once and for all."

CHAPTER 19

Mutiny

Captain, look!" exclaimed the minotaur. He was leaning against the main deck railing of the *Revenge,* pointing toward the *Mary Ann* floating in the fog less than a hundred yards off their port side.

"What it is, Morkie?" Swash asked, crossing the middle deck in a few quick steps.

"The ghosts!" The minotaur's excited words sounded more like a trumpeting than speech. "They be coming for us!"

"Ghosts?" puzzled Captain Swash. He raised his spyglass to his eye, swinging it toward the other ship. "By all the depths, you're *right,* Morkie!"

"Captain, what are they?" Silent Sasha said as he rushed up to the rail next to the Captain.

"*Who* are they, more as like," Swash replied. "It be the crew of the *Mary Ann*, no longer content, it seems, with haunting their old ship but now they seem to be wanting to haunt mine."

"Do you see any of our crew?" Silent Sasha piped up. "That Bard, the Professor, and the shipwright went over with that Vestia woman."

"Hanged if I care about them," Captain Swash bellowed. "It's being boarded that I'm worrying about!"

"If they come aboard, Captain," said Mad Morkie, shaking his enormous, horned head, "we might not be able to take the ship back from them."

"Then best we do it now," Swash declared. "Sasha, sound the word! Cutlasses and daggers, boys. Just get me the off-watch lads and put the rest to the rigging. We'll take the quarterdeck back from that strutting Percival peacock while you get us under way. Is that clear?'

"Aye, Captain," Sasha answered.

"Quickly, now! We've no time!"

Sasha pushed away from the railing, dashing between the other men on the deck before disappearing down a hatch. Captain Swash could feel the crew moving beneath his feet, his own rats suddenly scampering through the ship, bringing it to life. In moments, Silent Sasha appeared again with the Captain's cutlass and the enormous broadsword favored by Morkie. The goblin Cutthroat Karka appeared next to Swash, as did Butcher Bill with his war axe and Wooden-Leg Smith with his own cutlass.

"What's the play, Captain?' Karka snarled.

"We're going to mutiny," Sasha answered behind her.

"Quiet!" Morkie grumbled.

"It ain't mutiny if we're taking back our own ship," Captain Swash insisted. "And Percival is the only one standing in our way if we hurry."

"Do we have to kill him, Captain?" Karka asked with uncertainty in her voice.

"Kill him?" the Captain seethed. "Since when have we ever killed *anybody?*"

"To be fair," said Morkie in his rumbling, deep voice, "we've never really had the chance. We only ever run when someone fights back."

"Because robbing ships that fight back is a good way to get *yourself* killed," Captain Swash insisted. "Look, I thought we were all in agreement on this whole killing business. Kill people and you get hanged for it. We're just going to do what we've always done: charge up the ladders to the quarterdeck screaming like madmen—pardon me, Karka, mad-*persons*—while brandishing our weapons in a most threatening manner, and let him surrender. Right?"

The group around him nodded.

"Right, then," Captain Swash said, the sound of his blade sliding from its scabbard ringing in the still air. "Make it loud and make it scary, mates, and no one has to get hurt!"

Captain Rodrigan stood on the quarterdeck, his keen eyes watching as longboats from the Mary Ann *made their way across the glasslike surface of the mysterious waters. Tuppence stood at his side, clasping closed the tear at the shoulder of her dress, her long, ebony hair wild and flying about her face in the wind. She stood near him for protection. He had steered this course into the cursed sea for the sake of his beloved Tuppence, but now, though his placid face showed no fear, he wondered if his good fortune had, at last, failed him in his most desperate hour of*—Abel's head jerked up from his writing at the sudden cries erupting from the middle deck below. Startled, he unwittingly dragged the tip of his pencil across the parchment, marring its now irreparable surface. He had been sitting on the deck with his back against the gunwales, but now he hurriedly stood and pulled out another parchment, determined to write down as much of the conflict as his breath and blood would allow.

As in his narrative, Tuppence was actually standing next to Percival—or Rodrigan—at the ship's wheel. There was no tear in her dress, nor was there any wind to disturb a single strand of her perfectly coiffed hair.

But the danger was very real—for Captain Swash and his cutthroat pirates were armed and charging up the ladders on both the port and starboard sides leading to the quarterdeck. Their cutlasses flashed in the dull light of the fog. Cries of death and havoc rang out across the deck as the pirates charged toward Percival at the ship's wheel. Tuppence drew close to Percival, crying out in fear, the lithe fingers of her smooth, right hand pressed to her hip while Triton yapped fiercely from the crook of her left arm.

The enormous bulk of Mad Morkie vaulted over the forward railing, coming down with a terrible boom on the quarterdeck planks. Captain Swash charged with his cutlass held high. Cutthroat Karka, Wooden-Leg Smith, Silent Sasha, and more poured onto the quarterdeck, armed and threatening. Beyond them, Abel could see the rest of the crew scampering up the ratlines and into the rigging.

In that moment, something in Percival changed. Perhaps it had been coming for some time, or perhaps something just broke inside of him under the strain. Perhaps it was the pressure of the pirates pressing toward him or of Tuppence pressing against him. Perhaps it was the blow to his pride. Perhaps it was the blow to his head. Whatever the cause, Percival somehow decided to become more than just pretend.

Percival released the ship's wheel. He pushed Tuppence protectively behind him with his left hand as he reached across his body with his right and drew his cutlass from the scabbard at his side. He planted his feet in a fighting stance, the tip of his blade held unwavering in the air.

"You shall not have her!" Percival cried out.

Captain Swash held up his left hand, his own cutlass in his

right. The pirate band on the quarterdeck obediently slowed, forming a crescent around Percival, Tuppence, Triton, and Abel as the scribe furiously scrawled what he believed would be the last events of his life. *Farewell, Melodi Morgan, if only I had found the words . . .*

"I do not want *her,*" grinned Captain Swash. "But I will be taking the *Revenge* back a bit earlier than bargained."

"I would have expected nothing less from a pirate!" Percival responded. The tip of his blade did not waver. "You . . . you short-sighted, thrill-seeking adventurers of the sea! Emboldened by your hot-blooded temperament, you care nothing for your own futures or fates! You would throw your lives away for the thrill of the open ocean, living the life of hard labor and drudgery just for a few moments' taste of danger and death."

Cutthroat Karka glanced at Swash. "Captain?"

"Surrender!" shouted Captain Swash with all the enthusiasm of an actor who is suddenly uncertain of his next line.

"Never!" cried out Percival. "I would rather die at the hands of hunted men—men who will each hang by a gibbet from the entrance to Blackshore Harbor—than let you foul, filthy monsters touch a hair on this perfect head!"

"Hey!" Morkie moaned in hurt disappointment as he lowered his broadsword. "I washed just yesterday!"

"Don't listen to him, lads!" Captain Swash shouted. "He's just trying it on! Surrender, Percival! Join us or face death and worse!"

"Argh!" shouted the pirates with renewed confidence as they pressed closer.

"I will *never* join your outlaw band!" Percival said, standing his ground. The wound on his head was beginning to bleed again. "Why would I wish to join with a group so foolish as to leave a perfectly good and comfortable life for an existence of pain and fear?"

"What is he talkin' about, Captain?" grumbled Wooden-Leg Smith.

"You must be desperate to get back to the life of a buccaneer at sea," Percival acknowledged. "There is no reasoning with the passion of piracy! To think that you would give up being land pirates and plundering those who come with your false maps and tales of buried treasure. All of King Reinard's fleet chasing you to the ends of the world when you could have kept your comfortable shop and thriving business!"

"I'd have to give up my shop?" Captain Swash stammered.

"You don't think the Governor would allow you to keep it after you abducted his daughter and took over the ship, do you?"

"Well, now, I hadn't rightly thought of that," Swash replied, gnawing at his bottom lip.

"A terrible shame, too," Percival nodded as he looked down the length of his blade at the Captain. "It was such a fine location."

The tip of Captain Swash's cutlass wavered in the air.

"And what with the tourist season coming next month and all," Percival whispered.

Captain Swash drew in a deep breath, then released the grip on his cutlass.

The blade fell clanging to the deck.

The remaining pirate crew dropped their weapons as well.

"Accept my surrender and my apologies, Captain Rodrigan," the pirate captain sighed. "It were a moment of weakness, us trying to take back the ship. Just an old, bad habit, you might say."

Percival stood tall on the quarterdeck, sheathing his sword once more. "We shall not speak of it again, Captain Swash."

"You may call me Mister Johansen, if you please," bowed the former Captain. "I believe I'd prefer to be giving up me old title permanently."

"Thank you, Mister Johansen," Percival said, stepping confidently to the ship's wheel and taking its handles in hand. "I see that we are prepared to get under way—that's the correct phrase, isn't it?"

"Aye, Captain," Mister Johansen chuckled through a gap-toothed grin.

"Then would you please see to it that the people coming from the *Mary Ann* are brought aboard safely before we go anywhere?" Percival said in a surprisingly commanding tone.

"Aye, sire," Mister Johansen sighed.

"And please see that these weapons are cleaned up," Percival ordered. "I wouldn't want someone to trip over them and hurt themselves."

Mister Johansen nodded, then turned to the formerly mutinous crew. "You heard the Captain! Clear this deck and prepare to bring those people aboard."

Morkie shrugged his enormous shoulders, but there was something of relief in the minotaur's dark eyes. Cutthroat Karka giggled to herself as she picked up her axe and retreated back down the ladder. Dead-Eye Darrel managed to wink at Percival, and Hook-Hand Horvath almost saluted but stopped himself before any real damage was done to his own face. Within moments, the quarterdeck was once again left to Percival and his companions.

Fortunately, Abel was still scratching his pencil across his parchment, or he might have missed what happened next.

Percival had his cutlass and his pirate boat. He certainly had his pirate flag and had already followed a pirate map to an entirely unexpected treasure. He had a crew complete with shovels and cutlasses of their own. Now it seemed he had not only abducted Tuppence but had saved her and the ship as well. Abel realized that Percival's list was complete after all.

Tuppence Magrathia-Paddock moved up behind Percival. She set Triton down—who gave every appearance of being glad to scamper about the deck on his own—and wrapped her arms around the young man from Eventide. She held him tight, pressing the side of her perfect face between his shoulder blades.

"Captain Rodrigan!" she murmured to him. "My hero!"

"At your service, Lady Tuppence," Percival blushed—and smiled. "But you may call me Captain Taylor—Captain Percival Taylor, if you please."

CHAPTER 20

Lost at Sea

The two longboats bumped up softly against the sides of the *Revenge*. Both small craft had their gunnels nearly to the waterline with the weight of the crew from the *Mary Ann* packed into them, along with the few small treasures they had managed to bring with them. The mists were swirling and the water was developing a definite chop.

The storm was looking for them.

Adrian stood precariously at the tiller, steadying the badly overloaded craft with both his hands against the hull sides of the *Revenge*, trying at once to keep the boat close to the ship while not so close as to slam against it. The increasing waves were fighting him. He could see the crew of the *Revenge* poking their heads over the rail. A rope ladder clattered down over the side, splashing into the water between the ship's hull and the small boat.

"Everyone aboard!" called out Adrian, reaching over the side and pulling the ladder into the crowded boat. "Lively, lads! There's no time to waste!"

The seamen responded at once, climbing the ladder quickly toward the deck above them. Adrian glanced aft. Captain Merryweather had pulled his own longboat against the ship behind Adrian's. The crew of the *Revenge* threw several lines over the side there as well as a second ladder. In moments, the haggard crew of the *Mary Ann* was clambering up the side of the pirate ship from the second boat.

"Morkie!" Adrian called up toward the minotaur gazing down over the railing from the deck above. "Lower a rope! I need you to pull us toward the bow!"

The minotaur nodded and disappeared from sight.

Adrian turned to look down the length of the longboat. The last of the crew from the *Mary Ann* were making their way onto the ladder. Adrian noted that the Dragon's Bard remained seated near the bow of the boat next to the naiad, engaged in low and apparently animated conversation. Vestia, standing on the bow and trying to steady the boat against the hull as Adrian was doing, managed to glance occasionally at the naiad with a look that left no doubt as to her disdain for the creature.

"Quickly, Djara!" the Professor said, rising to his feet and reaching for the ladder as the last of the *Mary Ann* crew members scrambled up onto the deck of the *Revenge*. "It's time to go."

"But, my beloved," Djara said, her large eyes tearing up. "You know I cannot—"

"I have not searched the world for you only to leave you behind!" the Professor insisted, taking her hand and pulling her to her feet. "There has to be a way that we can be together, and we are going to find it!"

Djara hesitated and then nodded, quickly climbing the ladder with the Professor following closely behind. As Adrian watched them, Mad Morkie appeared once more, lowering the end of a rope over the side.

A wave caught the side of the small boat, rocking it wildly. Standing was becoming a precarious matter. Adrian snatched the end of the rope and then quickly made his way over the thwarts toward the bow.

"Belay that!" Adrian knew the voice of Captain Swash calling down toward him from the deck above. "There be no time to haul the boats aboard! Just come aboard and we'll cut them loose!"

Adrian ignored the Captain, quickly looping the rope around the bow cleat back and forth into a cleat knot.

"Didn't you hear Swash?" Vestia said, still trying to steady the increasingly violent rocking of the boat with both her arms against the hull. "We're to get aboard and not worry about the boats!"

"I heard him," Adrian answered. "You and the Bard should get aboard now."

"An excellent suggestion," Edvard agreed, making his way toward the ladder. "Perhaps if you could assist the charming young naiad in joining us on the deck of our ship, she could finish her most enchanting tale of the Rogue of Zarbandi and the Wizard's Daughter . . ."

"The naiad has other accommodations," Adrian said, standing up and shoving the Bard toward the side of the boat. Edvard stumbled slightly, catching himself on the rung of the rope ladder before he fell.

"Well then, perhaps another time," the Bard stammered. He quickly doffed his large hat toward the naiad and then began carefully to climb the ladder.

"Oh, Adrian!" Nyadine giggled, flashing her large, jade-green eyes at him. "You always provide me with such delight! That Bard was wickedly ridiculous!"

Adrian ignored her and turned to Vestia, gesturing toward the ladder. "Now you. Go."

"No." Vestia was adamant as she nodded toward the naiad who had extended herself from the water-filled bucket to sit on the front of the longboat. "I'm not leaving you here with that . . . that *thing*."

Nyadine granted Vestia a smile that reminded Adrian of a razor.

"I'd argue with you if I thought it would do any good," Adrian said, shaking his head. He looked up and called, "Morkie! Pull us toward the bow."

The minotaur nodded again and quickly pulled the rope taut. Adrian moved to the side of the longboat next to Vestia, putting his hands back on the hull of the *Revenge* and using them to walk the boat forward.

"So this was all about you and rescuing your precious naiad," Vestia seethed, her hands also against the *Revenge*. "I thought you said you had come here to be rid of her?"

"Oh, he wouldn't do that," Nyadine purred, playing with her long, pale-green braid and batting her large eyes. "My Adrian is always so good to me. He always gives me the things I need."

"And I suppose you give him the things *he* needs?" Vestia snarled.

"No," Adrian said with a sigh. "Not once. She has never given me anything at all. Just help me get her to the figurehead on the bow and we'll be finished."

"Can't she just swim to her precious figurehead from here?" Vestia seethed.

"Oh, but the salt water burns me so!" Nyadine complained. "Please, Adrian . . . just this one thing. You can do this one last thing for me."

Adrian drew in a deep breath. "Yes, Nyadine, I can do this one last thing for you."

Whitecaps were beginning to appear on the waves about them. It was taking everything they had to keep the boat steady in the heavy seas. The bowsprit cables were swinging up and down with the motion of the ship. The dolphin striker hanging down from the bowsprit looked particularly menacing, plunging downward like a harpoon into the angry waters.

The ship's figurehead lurched above them.

"Well, you certainly captured the likeness." Adrian could hear the bitterness in Vestia's words as she gazed up at the carved figure. "Beautiful and heartless."

"That's close enough," Adrian said.

Nyadine flashed a brilliant smile. "You made it especially for me, Adrian?"

"Yes," Adrian said. "I made it for you. There's a channel from the cavity inside down into a freshwater hold. You'll be fine there."

"I knew you would never disappoint me." Nyadine burst out with a sparkling laugh. She reached up toward the figurehead as it plunged downward. As she touched it, her arms merged with the figure that looked so much like her. In a moment they became one and the same, her body flowing down into the ship and her torso, arms, and head above the water. "Adrian, it is almost perfect! You do love me, don't you?"

Adrian was already pushing the boat back along the hull.

Vestia's eyes echoed the question, demanding an answer as she and Adrian fought their way back to the rope ladder and the anxious faces peering over the rail.

Adrian kept his silence.

"We're going to make it!" Professor Nick-Knack shouted into the tempest raging around them.

Percival clung desperately to the wheel of the *Revenge*. His clothes were soaked through by the fury of the storm. He was secured to the frame of the wheel by a safety line, fighting to keep his feet beneath him. The wheel itself shook as he strained to keep it steady on the course through the mountainous vortex of waves capping and cresting nearly as high as the gunwales of the ship. This was nothing compared to the terror of the greater maelstrom in which they struggled, for they were sailing along the inner edge of a mile-wide whirlpool, slowly making their way up the steep slope toward the dark crest of the funnel high above them. The waters to starboard rose like a terrible wall cascading down in their direction, but the larboard side was much worse: a precipice of darkness plunging back toward the djinni's bottle from which they were so desperate to escape. Safety lines had been rigged along both the larboard and starboard rails fore and aft for the crew, and the need for them was readily apparent even to such an inexperienced seaman as Captain Percival Taylor. The waves would often break against the sides of the ship, cascading downward in waterfalls over the deck and threatening to sweep the crew overboard.

Percival shivered in the driving rain. He had watched as

the crews of both the *Revenge* and the *Mary Ann* had battened down every opening in the hull and then, despite the rising horrors on the deck, had set their hands to the ship. Many of them even gone aloft in the rigging so that the ship might take them home again. Some part of their courage took fire in his heart, and he knew he could not leave them to their fate while he waited idly by; he had to be with them. He knew he was clueless and completely useless when it came to the sails and rigging. Aloft on the yard arms, he would be more of a menace to everyone else than a help. He might have manned the pumps, but even there he knew that Mad Morkie would be far more effective than he would ever be. The one thing he knew—the only thing he had really learned—was how to handle the ship's wheel. So that was where he insisted on staying. Now he held the wheel hard over to starboard, desperately trying to keep the ship on a course that climbed with achingly slow measure upward against the maelstrom's sloping funnel toward the surface of the sea above.

Professor Balderknack had secured himself and Djara to the navigation binnacle just in front of the ship's wheel. Abel, the Bard's scribe, remained lashed to the aft railing and was deeply regretting it, while Adrian, Vestia, Captain Merryweather, and Captain Swash were all at the forward railing of the quarterdeck raging at each other as much as the storm.

SHIP IN A BOTTLE

"The rigging can't take the strain!" yelled Swash. "Listen to them backstays!"

"They'll hold!" Adrian yelled back at him.

"Lay on the sail, sir!" argued Captain Merryweather. "The wind's at our back and we can see the top now!"

"If we lose the mainmast we're done for!" Swash yelled back.

"We've no choice!" yelled Vestia. "If we don't get out now, we never will!"

"Let us handle this, Vestia," Adrian bellowed. "Get below where it's safe!"

"It's *my* ship!" Vestia yelled. "I will not just let you 'handle' this!"

"We're going to make it!" the Professor shouted again. "Look, Djara! We're almost there!"

Percival looked as well. The crest of the whirlpool was getting closer. Though his arms ached from the strain, now he could see that they were slowly inching their way to the upper edge of the maelstrom. If they could only hold this course against the wall of the vortex funnel, they could—

"NO!" screamed Djara, her beautiful face contorted with fear and despair as she looked up into the storm raging above them.

Percival followed her gaze, his jaw dropping in shocked disbelief.

Above the funnel of the vortex, the dark, swirling storm

clouds had formed into the shape of an enormous face. It featured prominent cheekbones and a narrow, pointed jaw. The featureless eyes flashed with shrouded lightning as they gazed down directly on the *Revenge.* Then great leathery wings that spanned the horizon took shape from the darkened clouds. Shoulders a mile wide formed beneath the face; tendrils of whirling cyclones reached outward in both directions to form muscular arms and hands with long-nailed fingers. Bolts of lightning flashed from the fingertips, crashing down about the upper edge of the maelstrom.

"What . . . what is THAT!" shrieked Vestia.

"It is Hitam," Djara said. "He is the ifrit—a type of our djinn blessed with cunning and strength. He is the master of my bottle—my punisher."

The Professor grabbed the terrified Djara by her shoulders, searching her eyes. "I've searched the world over for you, Djara. I know of the ifrit and the djinn—they all honor the balance of magic above all else. What was your crime? What did you do to deserve punishment?"

Djara gazed back into the Professor's eyes. "I used my magic wrongly, Nicholas. I defied the laws of our craft."

"What did you do?" Professor Balderknack urged as lightning blazed once more behind him.

"I . . . I subverted the will of man," Djara answered. "My mistress was a princess but had few graces. She demanded that I force a prince to fall in love with her. But the magic has its own balance, Nicholas. Ifrit honor the bonds of marriage above all, and I had mocked it. In the end, the prince so loved my mistress that he went to war for the sake of her honor. There he died in battle, my mistress fell into unending mourning and regret, and I was brought to this bottle to repent of my arrogant betrayal of magic."

"We're going to make it, Djara!" the Professor said, though his conviction was somewhat dampened at the grimacing countenance looming over them in the storm. "We've got to make it! We just have to . . ."

The Professor stammered and fell silent.

The titanlike djinn in the storm above reached down with his arm, beckoning with lightning into the depths of the maelstrom.

A dark shape answered, rushing up from the deep behind the *Revenge*.

It was the *Mary Ann*—but now in horrifying form. The dilapidated carrack was now truly a ghost ship, commanded and served by no living crew but by the bones of the lost from the bottom of the ocean. Magic had called them back into use—the form of life without its essence. The ship still leaned heavily over on one side from the treasures weighing her down in her hold. Her sails were rags flying in the wind, and yet she rushed through the waters of the maelstrom wall.

"She's closing with us!" yelled Captain Swash. "I think they mean to board us!"

"Board us?" Captain Merryweather asked. "What could we have that they would possibly want?"

"Me," answered Djara. She gazed up at Professor Balderknack, her tears lost in the driving rain. "They want me."

"No, Djara. I can't lose you again." The Professor stared down at her. Then, quite unexpectedly, he grinned. "Djara—will you marry me?"

Djara blinked. "I would with all my heart, beloved, but—"

Balderknack reached out for Captain Merryweather, grabbing him by the soaked lapel of his greatcoat. "Captain! Marry us."

Captain Merryweather stared at the Professor. "Sir! We be in the midst of a crisis! This is no time for —"

"This is *exactly* the time for it!" Balderknack demanded, pulling Djara up next to him. "There won't be any other time. Can you do it?"

"Of course I can," Merryweather sputtered, "but the ceremony alone takes so long that . . ."

Balderknack glanced back at the rapidly closing outline of the *Mary Ann*. "Just the essentials, and right *now*, if you please!"

"I'm not sure that I can recall—"

"Now, sir!" the Professor roared. "Before we're all dead!"

"But we need witnesses!" Merryweather protested.

"I'll witness," Vestia said, gripping the binnacle so that she might stand near Djara on the canting deck. "And Adrian will too."

"I will?" Adrian asked.

"Yes, you will!" Vestia commanded. "Get over here!"

Adrian obeyed, gripping the binnacle as well.

Merryweather looked over at the djinni. "Djara . . . do you have a last name?"

"It's rather long and difficult to say," Djara apologized.

"Never mind, then," Merryweather bellowed. "Djara! Do you claim this man as your husband?"

"Yes!" Djara said, the thunder shaking the rigging as she spoke.

"And you . . . uh, who are you?" Merryweather asked.

"Nicholas Balderknack," the Professor responded proudly.

"Nicholas Balderknack?" Merryweather said the name with some amusement. "Do you claim this . . . well, this Djara as your wife?"

"Yes!" Balderknack answered.

"They're nearly on us!" Captain Swash urged.

Captain Merryweather's words started coming in a rush. "Then, by my authority as Captain, I seal this union . . . wait! Do you have rings to exchange?"

"I do!" Balderknack declared. He pulled from his finger the ring that Djara had given him to open her bottle. He took her hand and slipped the ring onto her finger.

"Close enough! Wedding's over!" shouted Captain Swash

as he strode across the slanting deck to where Percival gripped the wheel. "You keep us on course or we're all for the fishes, you understand?"

Percival nodded, swallowing hard.

"Gunnery mages to the gun deck!" Captain Swash bellowed into the howling gale. "Open the ports and run 'em up! Keep it up as long as you can, and then it's cutlasses and blood, lads!"

The *Mary Ann* swung up the maelstrom wall starboard of the *Revenge*. The skeletons worked the rigging, slacking their headway. The animated bones on the deck lined the railings, their own rusty cutlasses at the ready. The *Mary Ann* slowed, swinging down the maelstrom wall toward the *Revenge*.

A fusillade of light and thunder exploded from the starboard side of the *Revenge*. The wand-cannons discharged in a ragged order, the bluish light and silver flecks slamming against the side of the carrack's hull. Wood splinters and smoke erupted from the merchant ship, scattering the bones of a dozen ghostly crew members and savaging the main deck railing and hull amidships. The main mast canted slightly but remained upright.

"Hit 'em again, lads!" Swash screamed into the hurricane around them. "Run 'em up again!"

The *Mary Ann* suddenly swung toward the *Revenge*.

"Brace yourselves!" shouted Adrian.

The carrack's hull slammed against the hull of the *Revenge*, smashing closed her gun ports. The ship rolled abruptly from the impact. Percival felt the wheel slip from his grasp as his feet slid out from under him. He fell painfully to the deck but his lifeline held. The young man scrambled to his feet, arresting the wheel and pulling it back to starboard with all his strength.

It was not working. The bulk of the treasure-heavy *Mary Ann* continued to press against their starboard side, driving them back toward the center of the maelstrom. Percival watched helplessly as the bow of the *Revenge* swung slowly toward the larboard side.

Percival looked about, frantic for help, when something caught his eye. He could see across the starboard railing to the quarterdeck of the *Mary Ann*.

There was no one at the ship's wheel.

He knew what he had to do. He had to save Tuppence. He had to save Vestia. He had to save everyone . . .

. . . Everyone except him.

Professor Balderknack was pulling Djara to her feet nearby. Percival called out, "Professor! Take the wheel!"

Balderknack shook his head as though he could not hear.

"The wheel!" Percival shouted. "Come and take the wheel!"

The Professor turned to look at the opposing quarterdeck, his eyes widening in understanding. He gripped Djara by the hand and ran toward the starboard railing.

"No!" Percival shouted into the raging storm. The bow

continued its slow shift toward the doom beckoning them on the larboard side, but Percival knew that if he let go of the wheel their plunge would be swift and final. "Come back!"

But Professor Balderknack did not hesitate. The quarterdeck of the *Mary Ann* was jammed hard against the side of the *Revenge* so closely that their rails nearly touched. Illuminated by the lightning rending the sky above them, Professor Nick-Knack and Djara stepped up onto the railing and leaped over the narrow gap onto the quarterdeck of the *Mary Ann*. Balderknack fell hard onto the weathered decking next to Djara. He struggled to his feet, pulling himself upright by the spokes on the ship's wheel, then reached down and hauled Djara up by his side.

The Professor turned to look at Percival, the two men standing at the wheels of their respective ships. Percival could see the Professor smiling through the driving rain. Balderknack nodded his thanks toward Percival—and, perhaps, his farewell.

Professor Nick-Knack spun the wheel of the *Mary Ann* to starboard. The damaged and heavily laden merchant ship twisted in the maelstrom, sheering away from the *Revenge*. Percival felt the ship beneath his feet suddenly free of its burden, the bow responding and moving back to starboard, rising further from the depths. Adrian, Vestia, and Captain Swash all rushed to the aft railing, staring as the *Mary Ann* fell astern and then plunged down the maelstrom wall toward the center of the vortex.

The ring on Djara's hand flashed like a star deep in the darkness below them. In that moment, the spiral of the maelstrom vortex slowed, the ocean waters rushing upward from below to fill the sudden void. The terrible face and menacing presence vanished into lighter clouds. The *Revenge* spun about once in the remaining eddies of the whirlpool before steadying in a gentle rain and calming sea.

The sudden calm was nearly more terrible than the storm.

"What happened?" Vestia asked as even the soft rain subsided. She still stood gripping the aft rail, her eyes searching the eddies swirling behind the *Revenge*. "Where did they go?"

"The ship is back in its bottle," Adrian said, standing next to her.

"But what about the Professor and his Djara?" Vestia asked.

"I believe the *Mary Ann* now sails in her bottle over distant seas to exotic lands," Adrian replied wistfully. "Her crew is comprised no longer of skeletal horrors but of hopes and dreams of a certain Professor who has found his real treasure at last and intends to keep it."

"But will he be able to stay with her this time?"

Adrian smiled. "The djinn and the ifrit both honor the seal of marriage. Old Nick-Knack knew that."

Vestia nodded. "Do you think that was his plan all along?"

"No, I don't think so," Adrian said. "I think he intended to bring her out of the bottle if he could. It's just that in the end he found a better way for everyone. Sometimes," Adrian said, looking back at her, "it's hard to let an old dream go to embrace a better one when it comes along."

Vestia turned to Adrian, her eyes searching his face. "Sometimes?"

"Sometimes," Adrian smiled back at her.

Arf!

Triton came bounding onto the quarterdeck in a staccato of tiny feet. His eyes might have shown fierce determination had anyone been able to see them beneath his fur, for his pink bows had become tragically dislodged during the recent conflict.

Tuppence Magrathia-Paddock climbed the ladder from the lower decks and promptly opened her parasol. She was, as always, impeccably coiffed. Her ensemble was new and crisp though her slippers were unfortunately stained from the water on the deck, which also threatened the hem of her gown.

"Oh, dear," she said, genuinely perplexed. "Did I miss something?"

"Mister Johansen!"

Everyone on the quarterdeck turned toward the commanding voice coming from the direction of the helm.

Percival Taylor stood with his legs planted wide on the deck, both his hands firmly gripping the handles of the ship's wheel. His puff-sleeved shirt sagged from the water and his soaked boots squeaked slightly as he shifted his weight. "Mister

Johansen, get the crew back to work and clear away any wreckage. As soon as you can, rig the ship and let's get under way. We'll set course back for Blackshore. I think perhaps we would all like to see port again, don't you agree?"

The broad-faced pirate flashed a gap-toothed grin. "Aye, Captain Taylor! By your word, sir!"

CHAPTER 21

Charting an Unexpected Course

Hang them!" bellowed the Governor. "Hang them all!"

"Papa!" Tuppence protested, stamping her foot against the deck.

"No, my Little Daffodil, of course I didn't mean *you*," huffed Governor Paddock. "I mean to hang all the *rest* of them!"

Percival stood miserably on the main weather deck of the *Revenge* along with the rest of the ship's complement surrounded by the Blackshore militia. Despite Tuppence being at his side resolutely gripping his arm in support, he was certain that this would be the worst day of his life—if he lived that long.

The Governor, the spear-carrying militia, and, it seemed, the entire town of Blackshore had been waiting for them on the docks and up and down the quay long before the *Revenge* passed Tobin's Lighthouse to enter the harbor. The mermen who came out to pilot the ship in through the difficult channel waited until they were nearly at the dock before informing them that the frantic Governor Paddock had enlisted the aid of their King Klestan and all available merfolk to search for the ship in the waters of Mistral Sound. By that time any thought of flight was impossible. Percival and the crew could only watch as they drew nearer to doom with every moment. The ship's moorings were still being secured when the Governor himself—an enormous man whose frame was roughly along the lines of a six-foot-tall bear—threw a gangplank over the railing and charged aboard. The militia, pikes at the ready, followed in a flood, quickly rounding up everyone on the ship and herding them around the base of the main mast.

"Tuppence, you be a good lass now and come out from among these pirates," the Governor coaxed. "This is no place for a young and delicate lady. Come here and tell your Papa who's the cause of all this trouble, eh?"

"No, Papa," Tuppence sniffed. "I certainly will do no such thing!"

"BLAST!" The Governor's face turned a terrible purple and crimson color. The ends of his long, thick mustache quivered. "I'll have his head at once! Who's the captain?"

Percival gulped and raised his hand.

His was the second hand up.

"Two?" the Governor shouted, glancing back and forth between both hands in the air. "There can't be *two* captains!"

"I am a captain, sir!" A white-bearded sailor spoke loudly. "I am Captain Merryweather, lately of the *Mary Ann*."

The Governor's eyes squinted suspiciously. "The *Mary Ann,* you say?"

"Yes, sir."

"Not possible," the Governor laughed as though he had caught the Captain in a lie. "The *Mary Ann* is a ghost ship. Her crew died at sea years ago!"

"An excellent point, my lord Governor!" Edvard pushed his way forward through the crowd of prisoners on the deck, dragging his scribe behind him even as Abel was trying to keep up with the last words of the condemned men on deck. "As I can personally attest, this *is* indeed Captain Merryweather of the *Mary Ann* as well as his crew—lately rescued from death."

"Rescued from death?" the Governor blinked.

"Yes, my lord," the Bard continued. "Not only are this man and his son—that tall young man over there in the back—most assuredly *not* pirates, but, having been declared dead by yourself and by the court of King Reinard, they are not subject to hanging."

"Why not?" the Governor bellowed.

"Because the King has already declared them to be dead," Edvard pushed on, flashing a brilliant smile. "It would be unseemly to hang men who were already dead."

The Governor opened his mouth as though to reply but stopped and changed his tack before continuing. "Well, we certainly won't hang the dead crew, but we *will* hang the pirates who abducted my daughter! Who's in charge here?"

Percival raised his hand again but this time two more hands sprang into the air beside his own.

Governor Paddock growled in frustration. "You! Who are you?"

"I'm just a humble shopkeeper, your lordship. Mr. Claire Johansen by name," said Captain Swash, holding his broad-brimmed hat with all the deference he could muster in both hands before him and bowing slightly. He affected a most credible impression of a sad-eyed hound. "I own a shop here in town. These here lads and that wee lass over there are under my employ. Our residence is just yonder, your lordship, on the quay. We be no pirates, sir, and have done nothing to deserve the drop."

"If that is so, Mr. Johansen," the Governor said, gazing suspiciously at the gap-toothed man, "then how is it you're aboard this pirate vessel?"

"Well, now, sir, it's like this . . ."

"Well, now, sir, it's like this . . ." the Bard echoed hastily. Abel, having noticed Melodi Morgan on the dock, was whispering to the Bard a version of their recent history that might be better than true. "A sad tale, Governor! This . . . ah . . . innocent local merchant was surprised by the . . . the pirates of the *Revenge*, who woke his shop . . . I mean, *broke into* his shop to take back a fabled measured nap . . . *treasure* map of their elusive Captain Swash. But Mister Johansen discovered the theft and attempted to take back their rightful property with the aid of his employees. Their bold plan failed and they were caught aboard the ship as it set sail."

"All right then, now we're getting somewhere," the Governor said, rubbing his forehead. "All the dead crew from the *Mary Ann* shift toward the bow! All employees of Mister Johansen, shift aft!"

The militia backed along the main deck to make room, their pikes still lowered and pointing at their prisoners. The group at the center separated themselves to the left and right of the Governor as directed.

Six people remained standing near the base of the mast.

"You're telling me that *THIS* is the pirate band?" The Governor shook with rage.

"Ah, technically, no," the Dragon's Bard continued. "I am but a singer of songs and a teller of tales, journeying through the world with this, my humble if somewhat limited scribe, Abel. You see, I am the Dragon's Bard!"

The Governor groaned. "Not *another* one!"

"I beg your pardon, sir!" Edvard affected considerable effrontery.

"There must be a dozen of you if there's one," the Governor snarled. "Chasing across the face of creation and gathering

307

stories for that dragon. And all for what? I don't know and I don't care . . . NOW all I have are four pirates—no, I mean THREE pirates because my daughter most certainly is not one of them!"

"Well, I'm not a pirate either!" Vestia said, planting her fists on her hips.

"Then who are you?" the Governor demanded.

"I am the owner of this ship," the woman replied.

"Then you ARE a pirate!" the Governor snapped.

"I most certainly am not," Vestia shot back.

"And why not?" the Governor demanded.

"Ah, because, your lordship," the Dragon's Bard intervened, "the same pirates who abducted your daughter also abducted the ship . . ."

"Which she purchased from me," Adrian affirmed.

"And who in blazes are you!" The Governor's voice was rising by the moment.

"I am Adrian Wright," he replied. "My construction yards are there across the bay. I am the town shipwright."

"Then I suppose *you* are not a pirate either?" the Governor sneered.

"No, your lordship," Adrian replied with a slight bow.

"Miss Walters came aboard to reclaim her ship from the infamous Captain Swash," the Dragon's Bard said quickly. "The shipwright accompanied her to assist in reacquiring her property."

"And her property acquired them both, I suppose," the Governor scowled.

Edvard beamed. "Well said, your lordship!"

"Where, then, is this desperate and elusive pirate band that abducted my daughter!" the Governor demanded.

"Overpowered by our gallant crew of the *Mary Ann* as well as Mister Johansen's staff," Edvard offered with a broad smile. "It was a glorious battle at sea for the ship, but in the end they were driven from the deck. The pirates were last seen cursing us as they sailed off in what wreckage remained of the *Mary Ann*."

"Well, that accounts for just about everybody," the Governor said in ominous tones. He strode across the deck toward the mast, towering over Percival. "All, that is, except you."

"Papa! You cannot think that—"

"Stay out of this, Tuppy," the Governor said, his bulk casting a shadow that completely engulfed Percival. He glowered down at the young man. "And just what do you have to do with all of this?"

"I have heard that he was on a voyage of the heart, my lord," the Bard said behind him.

"What?" The Governor's voice was flat and menacing.

"Well, the story I heard was that Percival was the fiancé of Vestia Walters—this same Vestia who is the owner of the *Revenge*," the Bard said through a winning smile. He walked over toward Percival as he spoke. "I heard that he came aboard the ship seeking to rescue this same woman from the clutches of the pirate band so that he could marry her. Then, having stolen aboard the vessel before it sailed, he confronted the pirates, took the ship, cast them adrift, and rescued his true love."

The Bard turned to look pointedly at Percival as he continued. "Of course, that was only a story that I heard. It may well be that this Percival is actually the rogue leader of this pirate band who would now say anything—*do* anything—to save his own neck from your most efficient gallows in Hangman's Square. But I believe there is someone here who can clear up the matter for you once and for all, my lord."

The Bard stepped quickly over to the golden-haired woman wearing breeches and a man's shirt near the starboard rail. "Tell us, Vestia, what do you know of this?"

Vestia glanced sharply at the Dragon's Bard.

Percival swallowed.

Edvard leaned in slightly and whispered to the woman. "All the world turns now on the point of a story. It's up to you to choose which tale is told."

Vestia turned to look at Adrian.

The shipwright returned her gaze.

"My Lord Governor," Vestia said. "The story the Bard tells is not entirely true."

The Governor grimaced at Percival.

Percival wondered if the Governor would hang him on the spot.

"It is true that Percival was on a voyage of the heart," Vestia continued. "But it was not my heart that concerned him. His heart belongs to your daughter. He saw that she had been abducted by these pirate fiends, and it was for her sake that he stowed away aboard my ship. His only thought was to rescue her from the clutches of these foul buccaneers."

"And . . . and this lad drew swords against Captain Swash himself!" blurted Mister Johansen. "Defended her honor on the quarterdeck at the peril of his own life, he did!"

"You're asking me to believe that this stick of a boy defeated the notorious Captain Swash at swordplay on his own ship?" the Governor asked as his eyes narrowed.

"Well, 'defeated' is perhaps too strong a word . . . but 'tis true, your lordship!" blurted Mister Johansen. "I saw it with me own eyes!"

"And I was there, Papa!" Tuppence added fervently. "I stood on that back part of the boat up there while he faced the dread pirate captain with only his single blade to protect my honor."

Percival gazed up into the glowering face of the Governor.

"Do you expect me to believe this story, boy?" the Governor said.

"It's true, sir," Percival only managed to whisper the words.

"And you defeated the pirate captain single-handedly?"

Percival swallowed. "Yes, sir."

"Well done, my boy!" The Governor reached out with both

his enormous arms, wrapping them around Percival. The young man found it difficult to breathe as he disappeared inside the overwhelming embrace. The strength of the Governor crushed the air from his lungs. "I absolutely insist that you stay close to me, son. VERY close, so that we can discuss your future."

"Yes, sir," Percival barely managed to squeak out.

The Governor leaned a little closer, speaking with a forced whisper. "And you'll want to discuss the plans for your wedding in the morning to my little Tuppy."

Percival looked up, catching the Governor's wink.

"What's your name, son?" the Governor asked.

"Percival Taylor." Stars were starting to swirl in his vision.

"Dismiss the militia and let these people go," the voice of the Governor boomed. "Come, Tuppy! We're bringing your hero home with us! Three cheers for Percival Taylor—the Scourge of the Mistral Pirates!"

The Governor dragged Percival off of the deck and down the gangplank to the dock below as Tuppence, bearing the loyal and fierce Triton in the crook of her arm, followed them with a brilliant smile. The entire town of Blackshore cheered for Percival as he was hauled down the dock.

As for the young man who had tried so hard to be forced into service and failed at every attempt, Percival now knew what it actually felt like to be press-ganged.

Vestia stepped down the plank of the *Revenge* and back onto the dock. The solid timbers felt strange under her feet. She had gotten used to the motion of the ship beneath her, and now it seemed that she continued to sway while the land held still.

"I'm so glad you're back, Vestia!" Melodi Morgan had waited for her there, and Abel had been emboldened enough by his recent voyage to chat with Melodi as she waited. "Your aunt would have come but she said she had the store to tend and the children to watch. She insisted that I come. I think she said that if I was to be your lady's companion I should spend more of my time next to you."

"It's all right, Melodi," Vestia sighed. "I don't think things are going to be working out exactly as either my mother or my aunt had hoped."

"It's still surprising to see you wearing that pirate outfit," Melodi commented. "I am certain you will be relieved to don your womanly clothes again. Those men's breeches seem improper, somehow."

"Actually, I rather like them, but I'm sure I'll be back in my corset soon enough." Vestia looked down the dock. The hull of the *Revenge* rose out of the water next to her with the masts, yards, and rigging towering into the blue sky above. She was a beautiful thing, Vestia thought—unexpected and beautiful. Her eyes followed the curve of the hull forward and then fixed on Adrian Wright, who was standing on the dock and staring up at the bow.

"Will you excuse me a moment?" Vestia asked.

Her booted footfalls sounded against the dock planks but not so loudly as to cover an annoying voice as she drew closer.

"Adrian, you are such a dear!" Nyadine cooed from the figurehead of the *Revenge*. "I'll visit you in our cove tonight, my Adrian! How I've longed to see you again in that charming home you built for us. I just need one little thing. It isn't much; just one last thing . . ."

"No," Adrian said, crossing his arms over his wide chest.

The naiad infused into the figurehead blinked, a storm flashing across her eyes. "What did you say?"

"I said no, Nyadine," Adrian replied. "I am done with you."

"But you came to rescue me," the figurehead said, shaking her beautiful head.

"No, Nyadine." Adrian stepped closer to the edge of the dock, looking up into the face of the figurehead he had seen so long awake and in his dreams. "I came to reclaim my heart. You took it with you, and as long as you were gone, I was left with doubt as to how you felt about me. But then someone showed me that you had taken my soul as well. I had to find you, face you, and know that you had never, ever loved me in return. Only then could I reclaim my soul and my heart. Only then could I truly be rid of you."

"Oh, you cannot mean that!" the naiad purred. "You still love me!"

"No, Nyadine, I don't love you," Adrian said, shaking his head sadly. "I thought I did. I used to think that love was all about giving. I gave and I gave until there was nothing left of me. But someone taught me that love isn't about giving—it's about sharing."

"I have no idea what you mean," the naiad sniffed.

"No, you don't," Adrian agreed. "You can't and you never will."

"And might I suggest," Vestia said, "that you vacate my ship at once. You are not welcome here."

Adrian and the figurehead both looked over in surprise.

"Adrian!" Nyadine whined. "Tell her she cannot do that!"

Adrian smiled. "I don't think I'll be *telling* her any such thing. This is not your ship, Nyadine, it is Vestia's. She told you to leave, and you will go. You have all morning; I'll be refitting this ship with a new figurehead this very afternoon—one that has no place for you in it. So go away, Nyadine. Anywhere . . . anywhere but here."

"Let's talk about this, Adrian," Nyadine pleaded, tears forming in her watery eyes. "I'll come to you in my pool and—"

"You will not come to the cove or to my home, not ever," Adrian said flatly. "I will be paving over the pool, filling in the channel from Naiad Cove, and reshaping every figurehead I've ever carved of you."

"But why?" wailed Nyadine.

315

"Because Vestia would want it that way," Adrian replied.

Vestia smiled at Adrian and nodded. Together, the shipwright and the owner of the *Revenge* turned and strolled down the dock side by side back toward Blackshore.

"I suppose your engagement to Percival is off," Adrian said casually.

"Yes, seeing as he will be married to the Governor's daughter tomorrow morning—willing or not," Vestia agreed. "I suspect my mother will be none too pleased with the outcome."

"Well, you got a fine ship out of the bargain," Adrian shrugged. "That must count for something."

The crowds from the town had dispersed back to their shops, work, and lives. Only a few of the centaur stevedores continued their labor on the waterfront, unloading a small merchant boat that had docked farther down and closer to shore. Vestia stopped and turned on the dock. Adrian turned with her. They both gazed back at the *Revenge*.

"It's my dowry, you know," Vestia said, shaking her head. "My mother sent the money to me, hoping it would help get Percival to propose to me. Now all I have is a ship."

"It's a good ship," Adrian observed. "Not a bad dowry for the right man. What do you plan to do with it?"

Vestia thought for a moment. "I used to think I knew what I wanted out of life. But then something better came along."

"This ship?"

"And other things."

"Well, perhaps you might consider a future in trade?"

"Yes," Vestia smiled. "Trade sounds good to me. Did you know that my father was a cooper?"

"I remember," Adrian laughed. "Why?"

"Well, he makes watertight barrels," Vestia said, her step feeling lighter than it had for some time. "You make essentially the same thing, only a good deal bigger."

"Trade would be difficult to establish at first. You could use a partner to help bear the load," Adrian suggested with a tilt of his head.

"Perhaps I could," Vestia agreed with a smile. "It would be so much better if I could share the journey with someone."

"And I think we should rename the ship," Adrian observed. "*Revenge* hardly seems appropriate any longer."

"I quite agree," Vestia replied with a laugh like sunshine. "Do you have a suggestion?"

"I do," Adrian affirmed. "I believe we should name it after something that remains strong at sea, determined to stay her course and weather any storms that come."

"And that would be?"

The shipwright reached over, enfolded the owner of the *Revenge* in his arms, and whispered softly in her ear.

"I believe she ought to be called *Vestia*."

CHAPTER 22

Home Port

The old man and his son paused on the Blackshore Road where it crested a small rise just south of the town. There they stopped for a moment to take in the sight of the small village that had for so long beckoned to them in their dreams, stayed alive in their memories, and given them a vision of home that they barely hoped to ever see again.

It was achingly the same and yet somehow more vivid. The south fork of the Wanderwine glistened before them in the setting sun just beyond the fields. Above the treetops, the pair could see the tower of the Pantheon Church and the shorter roofs of the homes and businesses gathered around it on the banks of the river. Thin wisps of smoke curled upward into the deepening evening light.

"You follow the road there to the left over the South Bridge," the old man said to his companion as he pointed.

"That will take you across Boar's Island and on over North Bridge. Stay on that course until you reach Hammer Court. Bear hard a-larboard down King's Road. That will take you to Charter Square. There be the Griffon's Tale Inn. Wait there in the common room, son."

"Are you sure, Father?" the young man asked. "Shouldn't I—"

"'Tis for the best, lad," the old salt replied, placing his hand on the younger man's shoulder. "Best not to lay on too much canvas in a gale."

"I'll wait for you there," the young man chuckled. "I even think I remember the way."

The young man shouldered his canvas bag once more and walked with confident strides down the left fork in the road. The older man tarried a moment, running his hand over his long white beard. He and his son had left Blackshore in such a hurry that now he doubted that decision. Would it have been better to have taken the time to trim his beard and make himself more presentable? At least, perhaps, more like his old self.

He took off his cap and ran his fingers through his tangled hair. There was not as much of it as there had been when he had left the town by this same road years before. Would it matter now?

He placed his cap back on his head, shouldered his own sea bag, and, longing overcoming fear, he turned onto Cobblestone

Street and marched resolutely toward the row of townhouses around Chestnut Court.

The Widow Merryweather stood at the gate of her picket fence listening halfheartedly to Ariela Soliandrus, the Gossip Fairy, recounting the latest news of their neighbors. She still wore her work apron from the gardening she had been doing late in the day and was anxious to get back to trimming her rosebushes. Her wide-brimmed straw hat had been a necessity while the sun was still above the rooftops but, in the course of Ariela's long discourse, had become completely superfluous. Nevertheless, it remained on her head, her shears still in her hand and a number of old blooms remaining to be pruned.

" . . . And now it seems that Taylor boy has been wed to the Governor's daughter in Blackshore. Winifred and Joaquim barely were given time enough to catch a coach to Blackshore let alone pack properly for the occasion . . ."

Marchant Merryweather nodded in perfunctory agreement. She had given up trying to excuse herself from the constant breeze of Ariela's news and could only hope to weather the storm. Her eyes wandered down Cobblestone Street. It was suppertime for most of the families along the paved street. She could see the warm light glowing in the window as night began to fall over the town. Her neighbors may venture out later in the evening, but for now the street was deserted . . .

. . . except for a tall, bearded man walking up the lane. He wore the greatcoat and cap of a man of the sea, and the gait of his stride told her he had not been on land long. Whenever she saw such men passing through Eventide on their way from Blackshore to the towns farther inland, she always knew them and looked on them with kindness.

" . . . with Livinia beside herself!" Ariela prattled on, her tiny wings beating excitedly as she hovered just above the fence. "Not only did Vestia pursue that Taylor boy all the way to Blackshore, but now that he is married, it seems she has professed an interest in shipping! Alicia Charon told me that Livinia told her that Vestia now owns a fleet of ships and . . ."

The sailor was coming directly toward her. He had removed his cap from his balding head as he approached. His face was gaunt and weathered, his bushy eyebrows knitted together as his lips behind his white beard struggled to form words.

"Excuse me, Ariela," the Widow Merryweather said to the Gossip Fairy, and then she faced the man who stood slightly stooped before her. "Good evening, sir. May I help you?"

"Perhaps you may," the old salt said with a one-sided smile.

Marchant Merryweather felt a chill run down her spine, but she had spent so many nights looking down Cobblestone Street that she did not trust what she felt. "Well, I . . . I've always tried to help the good men who brave the sea when they come to my door."

"I've been searching all the world for treasure," the sailor replied, his eyes downcast, but then he looked up at her. "Now I think I've found it."

The Widow drew in a sudden breath. The face was thinner than she remembered and more lined. The beard was longer and white.

But the eyes she knew and loved still burned brightly for her alone.

Tears welled up in the Widow's eyes. Her voice quivered as she spoke. "Did you find it, Neddie?" she asked.

The old sailor's face softened into a gentle smile. "Yes, Mary-mine . . . it's right here. It's you."

Edmund Merryweather swept his wife up into his arms. It was a fortunate move, for Marchant Merryweather had nearly fainted in her joy. They wept alone together in the deepening twilight for some time.

The Gossip Fairy had departed, of course. She had a great deal of work to do.

By the time Edmund Merryweather had brought his wife to the Griffon's Tale Inn to be reunited with her son, Ransom, the entire village had been informed of the Captain's return. The resulting spontaneous celebrations kept the Griffon's Tale open throughout the night and into the next day. Ransom was glad to support these festivities, but Edmund and Marchant left early in the evening, retiring to their home on Cobblestone Street in perfect contentment.

Ransom stayed a month with his parents before returning to Blackshore. Vestia Walters had offered him a lucrative position as captain aboard the *Vestia* and a share of the profits from their venture. Adrian had convinced her that Ransom had sailed to the best exotic ports while inside the djinni's bottle and therefore already knew how to reach them outside the bottle as well.

The night Ransom departed—as Ariela later discovered from Marchant Merryweather herself—the Captain presented his wife with the single treasure he had salvaged from the *Mary Ann:* a brooch with diamonds set around a large, light-blue sapphire. Its value was incalculable and could quite likely have purchased all of Eventide and its possessions.

"Whatever shall we do with such riches?" Marchant exclaimed.

"You shall wear it every day when we work in our garden," Edmund replied.

"In the garden?" she asked dubiously.

"Yes, in the garden," the Captain told her, "so that I may look upon you and remember that right here is all the treasure I will ever want to see again."